Louis Beauregard Pendleton

The Sons of Ham

A Tale of the New South

Louis Beauregard Pendleton

The Sons of Ham
A Tale of the New South

ISBN/EAN: 9783337001094

Printed in Europe, USA, Canada, Australia, Japan

Cover: Foto ©Andreas Hilbeck / pixelio.de

More available books at **www.hansebooks.com**

THE SONS OF HAM.

THE SONS OF HAM.

A Tale of the New South.

BY

LOUIS PENDLETON,

AUTHOR OF "IN THE WIRE-GRASS," "THE WEDDING GARMENT,"
"KING TOM AND THE RUNAWAYS," ETC.

BOSTON:
ROBERTS BROTHERS.
1895.

University Press:

John Wilson and Son, Cambridge, U. S. A.

To

THE AFRICAN COLONIZATION SOCIETIES
OF THE FUTURE

THIS BOOK IS HOPEFULLY INSCRIBED.

THE SONS OF HAM.

I.

THE time was early fall, morning, of the year 188–; the place, an upstairs office in a small Southern town. The room was large for an office, but contained little furniture beyond a desk and two or three chairs. The walls were not so bare, there being a plentiful array of lawbooks on shelves, and not less than four small portraits, a glance revealing that these were intended to represent Washington, Bismarck, Gladstone, and Grover Cleveland. Their owner was wont to point them out with a look of pride, while remarking that he had always liked to surround himself with " big men ;" and even now, as he sat alone, his feet mounted upon the desk, threatening the stability of an inkstand on the right and two bottles of beer on the left, he stared vacantly at the first-named, which hung directly in his front.

This lover of fine company, Samuel Thomas by name, and lawyer by profession, was a young man of twenty-five, full in face and body, fair, florid, and rather good-looking in an external way, in spite of his air of self-satisfaction. Markedly different in appearance was the person whose step was now heard on the stairway outside, and who presently entered the office, the door being open. The visitor, also a young man, was dark, thin, and sallow, and at the first glance nothing about him seemed attractive but his eyes, which were of a peculiar dark gray color and distinguished by a strange, haunting beauty. But for these, the firm jaw and serious face would have combined in an expression of unmistakable sternness.

"Hello, Morton! come in," said Thomas, cheerfully, without moving. "Have a seat. Care for a glass of beer this early in the morning?"

"No, thank you."

"Is it business?" was then asked, the visitor being seated.

"Well, yes — in a way," was the cold response. "I'd like to get at the truth of those reports about Miss Black."

"What reports about Miss Black?"

"Those stories about her in connection with you; about her allowing you to take liberties — to kiss her."

"Who said so?"

"It's all over town."

Thomas slowly removed his feet from the desk, looking steadily at his visitor. "I'm surprised that *you* should want to know," he said, after a pause.

" I have good reason for wanting to know."

" Well, then, if you are serious, there's nothing in it. She has a free, breezy way, different from our Southern girls, but it means nothing; it means simply that she's jolly. I never kissed her. I knew right away that I could n't."

" But they say you boasted publicly that you *did.*"

" Oh, that was all a joke," replied the young lawyer, flippantly. " I just wanted something to crow over the boys about. They ought to have known it was nothing but a joke."

" And what about the young lady's reputation? " A stern expression was creeping into Morton's peculiar eyes. " One would think that would have occurred to you before you amused yourself with such a ' joke; ' and also that she was far away from her home and without protection."

Thomas uttered a mild oath and inquired uneasily what was the " earthly use " of being so serious about a mere trifle. How could Miss Black possibly be harmed by a few jesting remarks such as he had uttered? She was a stranger in the town and did not expect to stay permanently; the local photographer had engaged her to assist him during the fall and winter months only. Besides, she had not as yet been taken up by " society," and probably would not be; therefore, what could it matter to her?

" I have heard you make a better argument,"

commented the visitor, as the lawyer paused. " It could be, and *is*, a serious matter to her. I happen to know that one person, at least, who was very friendly toward her, has been affected by — "

" Oh, pshaw ! "

" You have set every gossip in this town to talking about an innocent woman," insisted the sallow young man, icily.

"Well, it 's not my fault if they do. You know how people will talk. I intended nothing of the sort. But look here, Morton, you must be interested in that quarter," laughed the young lawyer, attempting to throw his interrogator on the defensive.

" I am not even acquainted with her," was the haughty retort. " I have merely seen her come and go and heard people speak of her and quote you. But I *am* interested in a way; I don't like to see a defenceless woman suffer for — for — Let me have a pen and a piece of paper, will you ? "

Morton rose as he uttered the last words. A slight flush appeared on his sallow cheek, improving his appearance; but the lawyer did not like the stern, determined expression of his eye, and was quick to vacate the desk and put pen and paper in place. Morton sat down and wrote deliberately, pausing frequently to choose his words : —

" I hereby solemnly affirm that I have either been unaccountably misunderstood or maliciously misquoted in

regard to Miss Black, a lady for whom I feel only the most
profound respect. I deeply regret that her name should
have been coupled with mine in any way annoying to herself, and earnestly beg her pardon for any word or deed
on my part which may have led thereto."

"'I solemnly affirm that I *lied*' would be more
appropriate," was Morton's thought as he rose,
"but he will like it better in this shape. I'd rather
avoid a quarrel if I can," he said aloud, looking
squarely into the lawyer's eye, "but I must ask
you to sign this paper. I am determined on seeing that young lady vindicated, and I want this
paper — after you have signed it — to show to
those people who are talking about her, so as to
stop their mouths."

"I won't sign any paper," said Thomas, with
suppressed anger and slightly changed color, refusing what was handed to him ; "but I'll tell you what
I will do, although it is no business of yours : I'll
go around and tell the boys that I didn't mean it,
— that it was all a joke. And I'll do it for Miss
Francie's sake ; not because you — you — "

"If I could be sure that you would, and that
they'd — shut up, I'd be glad enough to drop it
at that ; but no, it won't do. The matter has gone
too far. Just read what I have written, will you?
To sign this can't put you in a much worse light
than to do what you propose."

Thomas reluctantly took the paper, read it, and

dashed it excitedly down on the desk,— amazement, alarm, anger, pictured vividly on his face.

"Will you sign it?"

"No, I won't. You must be crazy, Bob Morton, if you — "

"Then you will have to fight me. Understand that. I am going to make you sign that paper if — if — no matter what it costs."

There was a good deal of the tiger in the eyes of each as they stood glaring at each other, although Thomas's manner was rather that of threatening bluster, compared with the unconquerable determination written in every line of Morton's face. It was not long before the eyes of the one quailed before the eyes of the other. The lawyer was convinced that his visitor was a brave man, while, as to his own courage, he suffered from grave doubts. All at once he collapsed into the chair before the desk and bent his head to look again at the paper.

"After all," he said, in a shaken voice, between quick breaths, "it is no more than I would freely say to anybody. I — I never meant to do her any harm, and if— I'll sign it," he concluded, "for Miss Francie's sake, and [he took up a pen and wrote his name] and then I'll *fight you!*"

"I hope you will think better of that," said Morton, more mildly, after possessing himself of the document. "But if you insist on it, you'll know where to find me." He then turned and walked deliberately out of the room and down the stairs.

"And now he'll go showin' it to everybody,"
sighed Mr. Samuel Thomas, casting a fretful, angry
glance toward Bismarck, and another toward Gladstone, as if to accuse these patron saints of having
failed in their duty of protection. Receiving no
expression of regret or sympathy from those quarters, the young man's troubled eyes travelled back
to his desk and rested on the two bottles of beer.
A moment later he poured out a brimming glass,
swallowed it at a draught, then thrusting his hands
deep into his pockets and resting his chin on his
breast, he ruminated.

Suddenly the sound of a loud, continuous laugh
— a laugh of the "horse" variety — reverberated
up the stairway which led from the hall just outside
of his door to the street. Roused instantly from
his troubled reflections, Thomas got swiftly upon
his feet, glaring about him. He knew that laugh
and leaped to a conclusion.

"He's showin' it already," he growled. "He's
showin' it to Bud Mitchell." The unhappy man
listened intently, his face drawn up in a frown and
his eyes full of rage, as the echoes of more than one
laughing voice rolled up the stairway and subsided.
"I'll get even with Bob Morton," he burst out
furiously, "if I — if I have to ruin myself!"

It was indeed as he supposed; Morton was
"showin' it already," and he was determined
to continue showing it until the whole town had
the news. Beginning with the stentorian-lunged

"Bud" Mitchell and a few others who quickly gathered round and joined in the laughter and expressions of astonishment instantly provoked by "Sam Thomas's proclamation," — so it was facetiously termed by one of the group, — he passed down the street, stopping here and there to invite some acquaintance to inspect the interesting document.

The street was in the centre of the business quarter, but there was little noise or stir; although September was at hand and cotton was " coming in," — a half-dozen wagons with a bale or two each were in sight, — the business season had hardly opened. Here and there a salesman was seen idling at the door of the long low brick stores, and in some cases the merchants themselves sat outside, their chairs tilted against the brick wall, conversing for the most part about commercial matters ; here and there a white loafer or negro vagrant was seen shuffling aimlessly along, and from the general aspect of affairs, a stranger would have guessed far below the volume of business done in the town within a year. Morton walked down the quiet street in the shade of the ubiquitous China trees, choosing to commune with such persons as he judged would the most quickly spread the story he had to tell. Two men standing with their shoulders against the same tree and nervously whittling small bits of white pine as they talked, were among the first who were thus favored. A little farther on,

another, who was very tall and thin and stood
statue-like with his hands in his pockets and one
foot in a chair, suggesting a sleeping stork or crane,
was roused from a revery and asked to read the
paper thrust beneath his nose. Still farther on,
the determined young man stepped into the sandy
street and craved a word with one of two merchants who were standing about a bale of cotton
exposed in a cart for sale, digging deep into it for a
genuine sample. A few minutes later several
young men in a drug store were communed with
in turn. In every case the favored individual examined the paper eagerly as soon as its nature was
understood, expressing great amusement and surprise, some being moved to swear mildly and declare that in all their days they had never seen the
like, and that it was certainly " a good one on Sam
Thomas."

" He 'll never hear the last of his ' proclamation,' " said one, chuckling. " The whole town will
be laughing at him by night."

Turning the corner on the way to his office,
Morton almost ran into a grizzled veteran, com-
manding in build and fine of feature, who bade him
good-day with pronounced cordiality.

" I think you would like to see this, Colonel Sanford," said the young man, offering the paper for
perhaps the twentieth time.

" What! " ejaculated the veteran, as he absorbed
its import. " I knew it. I liked that girl from

the first. I — but — of course — I could n't be
sure. How did Sam Thomas happen to sign such
a paper?"

" I — I got him to do it — after — after he confessed that he — that those reports were not true."

"You *made* him do it! I see."

Morton dropped his eyes before his friend's
look of undisguised admiration and hurried on, as-
cending to his office; for he, too, was a lawyer,
although as yet only upon the threshold of his
profession. The room was even more sparsely furnished than the office just visited, but contained
twice as many books, these not being confined to
the law alone. Locking the " proclamation " in a
drawer and pocketing the key, he sat down before
his desk and fell into revery.

" He will be twitted about this until he is furious," was the young man's thought, " and he may
screw his courage up to the point of demanding a
fight, — he may challenge me. Well, let him. My
chances are as good as his, and right will be on my
side. But I hope it won't come when a chill threatens. I wonder if I shall ever get rid of these
wretched chills. This the day for one, by the way."

Suddenly he wheeled round and took a book
from the shelves. It was a well-worn volume of
" Blackstone," and as he opened it, his eye fell on
the words, " A gift against the innocent he accepted not," written in faded ink on the fly-leaf.

" My father meant it when he wrote that quotation," was Morton's instant reflection. "*He* never accepted a reward at the expense of the innocent. That is the kind of a lawyer he was, and I hope always to be like him. Sam Thomas will take any sort of business he can lay his hands on, but I will starve before I will do it."

Miss Francie Black was a native of Boston, but had been a resident of Barcelona, Ga., now about two months. Her father being only a sub-book-keeper with an increasing family, at eighteen she had felt it necessary to exert herself and for five years had served for a moderate return in a photo-grapher's establishment. A slight cough and an advantageous offer had brought her South, and she had not as yet regretted the change. She was good-looking, intelligent, and capable, what is usu-ally termed "a nice girl." She was much too young, and too lonely in her new situation, not to be pleased with the attentions of as agreeable a young man as Sam Thomas, whose office was next door, and it is possible that she allowed their acquain-tance to progress a little too rapidly. She had made one or two other friends, among them Colonel Sanford, a leading man of the town, whom she greatly admired and who appeared to have a com-mensurate fancy for herself, to judge from his atti-tude, he having stopped at the photographer's to chat with her a number of times, and his daughters being the only ladies who had as yet called on her. But within the past week or ten days she had observed an unaccountable change in these few friends. Colonel Sanford, for instance, whose smile had been so pleasing, now passed her on the street with a distant nod and came no more into the photographer's, although his law office was but two doors distant.

On the afternoon of the day Morton went about showing that curious paper, however, the colonel again appeared at the photographer's, and with more than his former cordiality announced to the surprised young lady that he was commissioned by his wife to bring her home to supper the following evening. Miss Black mentally remarked that she heartily disliked people who were cordial by fits and starts, but admitted that it was impossible to resist Colonel Sanford, and she accepted the invitation with every evidence of pleasure. When her friend had retired and she went on with her work, the brief history of her life in Barcelona was reviewed, and she tried to account for the strange, apparently capricious behavior of her few new-found friends, wondering if she had done anything to offend, or if such caprice were merely characteristic of these folk of the far South. Realizing that she had cherished many illusions with regard to them, some of which had promptly been dispelled, she wisely decided not to be in too great a hurry to form conclusions.

She came South expecting to find the most intense heat, a landscape composed almost entirely

of immense steaming cotton-fields, a people who,
for the most part, lay around in a state of semi-
coma and were active only in the use of their fans.
The activity in Barcelona was one of her greatest
surprises; she found that farmers, carpenters, etc.,
worked from sun to sun, and that merchants or
their employees were in harness from twelve to fifteen hours a day. She mentioned the matter to
Colonel Sanford, who as usual laughed, reminding
her that Georgia was in the temperate zone, and that
greed of gain inspired people to overwork there
just as it did everywhere else in the world. The
colonel added that, after all, the facts did not justify the current notion that a hot climate is a foe to
progress. All our earliest recorded civilizations
belonged to regions which, if not tropical, almost
equal the tropics in intensity of heat. The enforced
inertness during the noontide glare in such localities may indeed be an evidence of enervation, but
there is a compensating energy during the cooler
parts of the twenty-four hours.

As she grew up Miss Black had heard and read
much about the down-trodden negro, and had supposed that the spectacle, to put it figuratively, of
a white foot on a black neck was to be seen every
day. But on arriving in Barcelona, although she
was quickly made aware that a most intense race
antipathy really existed, she saw the blacks coming
and going, idling or working, in perfect freedom,
with no sign of molestation whatever, and, what

was still more surprising, a great many of them
were fairly prosperous.   During the first week or
two, her interest in these people led her to
visit them in their little houses, and, when the place
was not too dirty, to sit down and talk with them.
But she soon gave up this practice, not because she
realized that she did violence to local prejudice, —
such a motive would have involved, she thought, an
abject surrender of her independence and ideals;
but simply because the negro at close quarters and
in gross reality failed to engage her sympathy and
imagination as he had done at a distance.   Strange
as it may seem, her interest in him fast weakened
and was finally lost.

   She was wondering if it could be this, her interest in the negro, which had temporarily displeased
her Barcelona friends, when her employer entered
and handed her a letter.   The information that it
contained was, in brief, that her aunt, a Mrs. Blossom of Philadelphia, intended wintering in Florida
and the West Indies, and that sometime in October,
while on her way, she contemplated stopping for a
day or so in Barcelona.   The halt would, of course,
be made for the sole reason of seeing her niece,
there being nothing to interest her in a small interior Georgia town.   The writer mentioned that
she would be accompanied by one Paul Shepherd,
her husband's nephew, a young man unknown to
her niece.   Miss Black felt pleased, but somewhat
troubled.   She had never seen her aunt, who was

very wealthy and never visited or kept up cordial
relations with her less fortunate sister in Boston; it
seemed odd that such a person should give herself
the trouble to visit a relative whom she had hitherto made no effort to see, and who was, from her
standpoint, only a poor working girl.

Late in the afternoon, when going to the neighboring post-office in order to mail her response,
which expressed gratification at the prospect of
the visit, Miss Black met Morton, who lifted his
hat but did not look directly at her. In Barcelona
no gentleman ever passed even a strange lady
without acknowledging her presence in some such
fashion. Although not an acquaintance, Miss Black
had long since learned the young man's name;
something about him attracted her and she amused
herself a good deal with speculations concerning
him. Her quick eye now told her that his shoulders drooped forward, that he seemed to shiver, and
just as he passed her she heard his teeth chatter.
The chill had come and he was now on his way
home.

Returning a few minutes later, she exchanged a
smile and a bow with Sam Thomas, who passed
rapidly in a hack bound for a railway station in a
distant part of the town. She saw that he had a
travelling bag and supposed that he was off for a
stay of several days; she wondered that she had
not seen him during the day, he who usually came
and went on the street at all hours, and was far

from guessing why he had secluded himself. Upon
mature reflection this cautious young man had concluded not to seek an encounter with Morton, but
to "fight" him as occasion offered in a way that
would prove more effective, make no noise, and in-
volve no personal danger. He also decided, as he
himself would have stated it, not to "face the music,"—the fire of irritating jest and raillery which
his "proclamation" would inevitably provoke in
certain quarters,—but to pack his bag and devote
two or three weeks to looking after his interests in
a neighboring county.

II.

ITs history was by no means as brief as that of countless mushroom communities in the West which spring up and attain to a giddy prosperity within a year, but Barcelona was relatively a new town. It had been settled during the war by refugees from the exposed coast cities and plantations, and had grown from their children and accessions from the homespun provincials of the surrounding interior. After the lapse of twenty-five years the difference between the cracker and the more gentle refugee was almost as marked as at the beginning, although the native, more readily adapting himself to the changed conditions of a new era, had gradually become prosperous and was beginning to take the lead in public affairs, — the other more unfortunate element for the most part losing ground in corresponding ratio. However, except where the more intimate concerns of life were involved, as those of marrying and giving in marriage, there was no lack of friendship, or indeed of hearty good-fellowship, between these two elements. The presence of a common danger, whether real or fancied, impelled them to stand together and expose an unbroken front to the view of that absolutely distinct and extraneous body composed of freed slaves who lacked but a little of equalling the combined forces of their white neighbors. But, although regarded *en bloc* as a growing menace to the well-being and safety of the town and country, the black man as an individual was for the most part neither regarded nor treated as an enemy; indeed, in so far as he was industrious and did not seek public office, he was often esteemed as a useful member of society. Temporarily at least, the two races were mutually dependent on each other, and the situation was and is full of inconsistencies and curious complications.

In this much-mixed community, among the smart new houses and blooming gardens of the more prosperous Barcelonans, here and there was still to be seen a dilapidated home where shabby respectability lurked behind closed doors, linking the past era of profound depression with the more agreeable present. One of these, which stood on the outskirts of the town, a wide, low house with almost as many piazzas as rooms, stretching them out like wings, and seeming to spread itself lazily on its brick legs like a squatting fowl on a summer's day, had doubtless been in need of fresh paint for fifteen years. It faced a quiet street, along which stood oak and China trees, and had a somewhat imposing front, a series of tall wooden columns, white now no more, mounted on brick pedestals and supporting the ornamented over-reaching roof of the piazza. The front yard, once a pretty flower garden, was now a troubled scene of untrimmed rose-bushes, cape jessamines, white and pink oleanders, and young cedar-trees. In the large back yard were a few equally neglected fig and orange trees and crêpe myrtles, besides the everywhere conspicuous China-tree to furnish shade. Beyond this was a separate inclosure intended for vegetables, and adjoining it, a field of two or three acres devoted to rice, which sloped downward to the low pine bottoms environing this portion of the town.

The only sign of life about the place as Sam Thomas drove by on his way to the station was a young girl who sat on the secluded back piazza engaged in sewing. Had she not been screened from observation, the most casual of observers would have noted that she worked with an anxious, hurried air and was not in a tranquil state of mind. After a careful scrutiny a physician would doubtless have guessed that she was not in the habit of receiving a proper share of nourishing food. Although unquestionably very young, her expression, as she now sat in troubled thought, was that of a mature woman; it was clear that she was thinner than she had once been, and there was a drawn look about her mouth curiously at variance with the strength and joyousness of youth.

Yet Reba Lawrence was distinguished by unusual beauty, — not so much the beauty of delicate outline and color, though that was not absent, as of an inner loveliness which seemed to shine forth through her large, dark eyes.

Her story was not a cheerful one. As was the case with so many other refugees, her father's broken fortunes had effectually prevented his return and resumption of former place and position, and he had begun life anew under sadly changed conditions in Barcelona. Soon after the war was over he invested his all in the meagre outfit of a small country newspaper, as editor and publisher of which he succeeded, however, in providing his wife and daughter with more comforts than were enjoyed by many of their neighbors in those days of widespread distress. He was able even to secure for his only remaining child (the two grown sons having fallen in battle) fair educational advantages while she grew up. When she was sixteen he died, and, at the advice of Colonel Sanford, the widow sold the paper and invested the proceeds in railroad stock. Owning their home and having now from this source an income of a little over $300 a year, the mother and daughter, by carefully filing down their expenses, had managed to live. But within less than two years Mrs. Lawrence broke down and became a confirmed invalid, her profound and continuing grief having complicated an old nervous affection. After that she scarcely ever

left her chamber and never left the house, the
management of the household and all business
affairs devolving upon Reba, who was less than
eighteen. All went well enough, however, for two
years longer, until the railroad went into the hands
of a receiver and the stockholders ceased to draw
their dividends.

Resolved to keep the news of this disaster from
her suffering mother as long as possible, Reba
went to consult Colonel Sanford, who assured her
there would be no opportunity to sell the stock for
a long while to come, and offered her a loan. This
she declined, telling him they had been able to
save some money, and omitting to mention that the
amount saved was not quite fifty dollars.

When little more than nineteen Reba Lawrence
was confronted with the problem of caring for an
invalid mother, not to speak of herself, for an
indefinite period on the sum of fifty dollars. She
had two devoted young cousins in the town,
Charles and Betty Walton, in whom she might
have confided with some expectation of assistance,
their step-father, one Adam Brown, being a very
prosperous man; but she felt that starvation alone
could drive her to appeal to him, everything considered. Resolving to battle for herself to the last
if possible, she immediately set about reducing the
expenses of the household, and considered how she
might earn something by means of labor done at
home. She promptly had a reckoning with and

dismissed the negro girl who came three times a day and cooked the three meals; she sent no more regular orders to the grocery store, and decided that she would hereafter go out less than ever and need not buy any more clothes; she engaged an old negro, a former slave of the family who was fond of her, to cultivate the vegetable garden and rice patch on shares; she made an arrangement with a twelve-year-old white boy who lived on a small farm just out of town, and whose parents were too poor to send him to school, by which he was to come twice a week and cut wood or do other small jobs, and she in return would give him an hour's instruction in reading or writing; and, finally she determined to solicit plain sewing. All this was done quietly, almost secretly, that the mother might not know, and that their friends might be kept in ignorance of their desperate need.

It was this consideration which led her to seek sewing among the blacks rather than the whites. Josephine Witherspoon, a good-natured young negress, who had been a slave in the family as a child, solicited the work for her and collected, or tried to collect, the money. Josephine had remained on friendly terms with the family, and for many years had made them a periodical visit, always going away well pleased with a gift of some sort, which for some time past had usually been a garment no longer of any use to the invalid Mrs.

Lawrence. This hopeful copartnership resulted in a heavy addition to Reba's other cares and but a trifling pecuniary return; for if she advanced her price for making a calico dress beyond seventy-five cents, she received no more orders, and, what was worse, as a rule Josephine was not able to collect more than one-half of what was due, and sometimes nothing at all.

During six months, by incessant effort, by the most careful economy, and by the help of the fifty dollars on hand, the girl was able to keep her mother barely comfortable, and herself from starving. But not until the last dollar of that hoarded sum had disappeared did the real pinch begin. Then it was that Mrs. Lawrence, a patient woman by nature, began to complain and demand the why and the wherefore of this and that, and poor Reba to make evasive excuses. Then it was, too, that the girl began to cook for her mother alone and to eat only what was left. Having now battled with this last extremity for many weeks, it is not wonderful that she had grown thin in spite of her youth and strength.

As she reflected upon the desperate situation now, scalding tears fell upon the garment she was making. But, although nearly always hungry, Reba was not always unhappy, having attained to a certain resignation and learned to feed on hope. Misfortune sours some dispositions, but softens others; it is thus that hardships bless us when they seem a curse.

Aroused by the sound of the side gate, the girl looked up and saw a portly, smiling negress advancing across the yard, carrying a bundle wrapped in a newspaper.

"How you come on, Miss Reba?" she inquired cheerily, as she lifted her great weight up the piazza steps with slow and stately dignity. "I brung you another dress to make," she announced, opening her bundle and exhibiting a piece of flowered calico.

"Thank you, Josephine. Whose is it?"

"Rosetta Hightower's. She say she want it tight in de wais'. She say she don't care ef hit do hurt her, she got to have it tight in de wais'."

"What a giddy thing she must be."

"*She* ain't got no sense," declared Josephine Witherspoon, emphatically. "Now me, I won't do dat. I don't care ef I is fat, I ain't gwine to choke myself in de wais' dat-a way."

The visitor had observed that the girl's eyes were tearful, and was now well pleased to see her laughing heartily. "Anyhow, I'll have to cut it by the pattern," said Reba.

"She had dat pattern cut too small a-purpose. Dese young gals ain't got no mo' sense 'n chillun. I seen Susan comin' 'long," Josephine continued, "and she tole me she want you to make her a dress, too."

"Which Susan?"

"Dat Susan wut cook for Mis' Whittin'ton, — Susan Brown."

"I made one for her last spring, and she has n't paid for that yet."

"I know it, and I tole her so, too," said Josephine, in great indignation. "I tole her ef she did n't git up dat money and pay it, I 'd everlas'nly beat her all over dis town."

"Let her keep it rather than do that. But I wish you would collect it if you possibly can."

"Oh, yuh's de money I cleckted from Sally John," said Josephine, producing a handkerchief and untying a knot in one end of it. "Fifty cents is all she gim me. I don't b'lieve she 'low to pay de other twenty-five cents. How yo' ma, Miss Reba?"

"About the same."

Reba now rose and disappeared through the back hall-door, returning presently with a bundle which she presented to the waiting black woman. "I went through a trunk yesterday and found several things I thought you could make use of," she said.

And so Josephine departed, well satisfied with this exchange of substantial courtesies. Left to herself, Reba began to gather up her work, concluding that it was too late to sew any longer; she must go in and see how her mother fared, and then prepare something for her supper. As she entered the long, wide hall which divided the house into two equal halves, she heard some one calling her from the front yard or the street. Going out, she found that her presence was desired by a slender, well-dressed young lady, hardly to be called handsome in the usual sense of the term, but about whose colorless, shapely face, and clear, intelligent blue eyes there was something which pleased at once and by and by strongly attracted.

"Come in, Betty," called Reba from the piazza, as the visitor remained standing at the gate.

"No, you come here. I have n't time to go in," replied Miss Betty Walton, positively. No one was now to be seen on the quiet street, and she had not hesitated to call out loudly. "I stopped a minute because I had something to tell you," she added.

"What is it?" asked Reba, drawing near.

"Well, in the first place, Charlie — he said he did n't care if I told you — he thinks he is going to win, and if he does, he wants to crown *you.*"

"Oh, Betty!"

"They 've been practising again to-day and he beat everybody."

Reba first flushed with pleasure, then looked doubtful and reflective. Betty hurried on: —

"I have one more piece of news to communicate, and then I must go." With this introduction she told a story which her step-father had brought home at noon and which her mother had repeated to her shortly afterward, — the story in which Miss Black, Robert Morton, and Samuel Thomas were the *dramatis personæ.*

"Oh, Betty, did *he* do that?" interrupted the listener, as soon as she had grasped the facts. An

unusual light shone in her eyes, which her cousin
did not fail to note. The emphasized pronoun of
course referred to Morton.

"Yes, he did, and I only wish he had
thrashed that disgusting Sam Thomas while he was
about it. I never could bear that man. I 'm going
to call on Miss Black sometime soon, and I want
you to go with me. Colonel Sanford asked me to
go two or three weeks ago."

" Does he — does he visit her? " asked Reba.

" Not that I know of," said Betty, understanding
perfectly that the pronoun did not refer to Colonel
Sanford. " I doubt if he knows her at all. He
was disinterested, I 'm sure. That 's his way."

Betty had recklessly announced that she would
stop only a minute, but half an hour or more had
elapsed when she finally cut short the conference
and hurried away.

In that chamber of Out-at-Elbow Castle — so
Reba with a sad smile sometimes called it — which
was the most favored as to sunshine, air, furnishing and commodiousness in general, a pale-faced
woman lay wearily abed. She had been reading,
but the light had failed some time since and she
now patiently awaited the appearance of her daughter. The hollows in her cheeks and the lines of
care about her mouth were not prominent in the
waning light, and the whiteness of her hair, combined with the perfect regularity of her features,
suggested a marble statue. She was scarcely fifty

and looked seventy. The room was neat and not uncomfortable; there were snowy white lace curtains, a few pictures, a faded lounge, a worn-out carpet, a fine old easy-chair with one arm gone, and a few other necessaries, all the worse for wear.

"Was that Betty calling you a little while ago?" asked the invalid in a low, gentle voice, as Reba entered.

"Yes, mamma. How do you feel? Are you comfortable?"

Receiving an affirmative answer, the girl proceeded to throw open the blinds of the nearest window, letting in more light. It could then be seen that the two women closely resembled each other, although a careful observer would have conjectured that the daughter, even with all her delicacy of color, the charm of her eyes, and her grace of movement, was distinguished by less external beauty than must have belonged to the mother in her youth.

"Betty says Charlie wants to crown me queen at the tournament ball, if he wins," announced Reba, returning from the window with a pensive smile.

"Would you like him to?"

"I — don't know. I have nothing to wear. It ought to be something new."

"There is an old ball dress of mine wrapped up in linen in one of the trunks," said Mrs. Lawrence, speculatively. "Perhaps you could make it over.

I could give you some help. Suppose you get it out and show it to Betty. There is some beautiful lace on it. How well I remember," she added with a sigh, " wearing it at a ball in London just before the war broke out."

Reba showed great interest in the suggestion, expressing a hope that the old gown had not changed color.

" Who is going to this ball, — anybody beside the young people?" Mrs. Lawrence then asked.

" Betty said Colonel and Mrs. Sanford were going."

" I am glad of that. I dislike seeing young girls go off to a public ball all alone. When I was a girl I was always matronized at a ball. Betty tells me that not one married woman was present at those dances at the hall last winter. It is positively shocking. How everything is changed. Cracker customs seem to prevail nowadays. I am sorry you had to be brought up in this part of the country."

" Some of the girls say," laughed Reba, " that there would be no chances to flirt if chaperons were always around."

" It might be well if some of them had their chances in that direction curtailed. That, however, is nonsense. I never felt that I was deprived of any freedom whatever."

Reba's thoughts returned to the story just told by Betty and she repeated it to her mother, whose eyes flashed as she listened. " How gallant!" she exclaimed. "They are of the right sort, those Mortons. I knew his father well in the old days, and he was one of the most honorable of men. They were refugees, you know. That girl will fall in love with him now."

Reba made no rejoinder to this speculation, and rose to leave the room. It was now growing dark. "I must go and get you something to eat, and make your tea," she said.

"Reba, you look overworked and thin," said her mother anxiously. "You are doing too much; you won't be able to stand the cooking."

"I have stood it nine months."

"You seem to be trying harder than we ever did to economize. We have always been able to afford a girl to do the heavier work about the kitchen. It costs very little. What made you turn Susan off anyhow?"

"She was so trifling and incompetent," was the evasive answer, though this was true enough. "And her ideas were too high. She called herself a kitchen-lady, and with some reason. She never came at all on rainy mornings, and toward the last she sometimes turned up as late as nine o'clock, and in a carriage to boot. We are too poor to afford a kitchen-lady."

"A carriage?"

"One of those ten-cent hacks driven by negro men."

"Truly, the bottom rail *is* on top, to quote Adam Brown," said Mrs. Lawrence, laughing.

III.

FOR the masses it was not as great an event as the circus, which usually shook Malvern County to its foundations, as well as its neighbor Richmond, collecting the people almost to a man from the whole region within the circumference described by a radius of twenty miles, and causing camp-fires to burn along every road on the night before the great day; but still the "tournament"—so the great riding contest was called—was no small sensation and drew a large crowd. And unquestionably it furnished entertainment not to be despised. True, it was scarcely a faint reminder of the genuine tourney of the middle age; there was no clash of arms to quicken the pulse and light the eye of the old soldier, no incidental bloodshed to cloy the taste of the savage-hearted; but yet there was a charm. The mere fact of a contest of any sort could rivet the attention of these spectators who had few diversions; and there was no little charm in the perfect horsemanship, in the plumed knights' gay attire, in the array of shapely horses that moved with such spirit and held their heads as proudly as even their masters could desire.

The scene of the contest was an extensive area in the suburbs of Barcelona, encircled by a rough board-fence, along which, amphitheatre fashion, were tiers of elevated seats of the same material. These seats extended less than one third of the way around the inclosure, but where they ended a long circling line of wagons and other vehicles began, all available space soon being taken up. By ten o'clock A. M., the time set for the opening of the contest, not only were these seats and vehicles filled to the overflow, but all the roofs in the immediate vicinage were occupied as well. Nearly half the spectators were black, and these for the most part flocked together, as a matter of course.

Reba was present in the company of her cousin Betty, and her aunt, Mrs. Brown. The latter, to the lasting regret of Mrs. Lawrence, had not been a refugee, which is almost equivalent to saying that she was uneducated. George Walton, a brother of Mrs. Lawrence, had shocked his family by marrying a pretty native cracker girl soon after the settling of the refugees in Barcelona; ten years later he died, and after a year or two of sincere mourning his widow, to the dismay of her sister-in-law, presented her two children, Charles and Elizabeth, with a second father in the person of one Adam Brown, an uneducated farmer, who afterwards became a prosperous and prominent citizen of Barcelona.

"Where's Charlie?" asked Mrs. Brown, eagerly scanning the arena the moment they were in their seats. "Does anybody see Charlie?" She had lost all her early bloom, but the gentle, motherly expression of her face rescued it from what might be termed the hopelessly commonplace.

Betty promptly pointed her brother out. "Don't you see him waiting over there with the other riders?" Yes, there he was, looking very handsome and knightly in his broad-brimmed black hat with its long, graceful white feather, in his dark velvet coat with its gold lace trimmings and crimson horseshoe embroidered just below his left shoulder, — the "Knight of the Horseshoe."

"I hope Mr. Straitlace won't say nothin'," remarked Mrs. Brown as she gazed fondly toward her son. "It's the ball he don't like, I reckon; for what can be the harm o' comin' here to see 'em dash round and take the rings, especially when Charlie's one o' the ringleaders and papa got something to do with it, too. Betty, do you see papa?"

"He's over there at the judge's stand."

Mrs. Brown heaved a sigh of relief and content. With "papa" at the judge's stand and her own Charlie one of the "ringleaders," why shouldn't she be there to look on? Where else should she be, all the reverend Straitlaces in the world to the contrary notwithstanding?

3

"There's Mr. Jones, Betty," said Reba, with a smile.

Her smile meant that the young man was the subject of jest between them. "Jim" Jones, universally so-called, was an uneducated young farmer of good character and rustic manners and speech; but, being prosperous, he was received into Barcelona's best circle, prosperity having now successfully displaced the old-fashioned "good-family" standard. He was really a shrewd and clever man on his own plane, but his expression was dull, his face as red as a lobster, and his hands hard and knotty from constant rough work. Charlie Walton was also a farmer, with hands hardened by manual labor, but the two men were totally different. Young Jones was often invited to his house by Adam Brown, a kindred spirit, and had recklessly fallen in love with Betty, despite her chilling reception of his advances.

"What's that on his coat?" continued Reba. "Isn't it a plough? I like that; it's quite original, — the 'Knight of the Plough.'"

"Not original with him, poor man," declared Betty. "Some one suggested it to him, I'm sure."

"It is so much better than something high sounding," said Reba.

"Yes; fancy Mr. Jones the Knight of the — the — Moonlight, for instance," laughed Betty. "Of course there's never been anything quite as ridicu-

lous as that, but Charlie did say a man from Richmond County once proposed to ride as the
'Knight of the Blue-Eyed Maiden,' but fortunately yielded to entreaty. And there was one
year a 'Don Quixote de la Mancha, Knight of the
Lions.'"

"Did he have a Sancho Panza?"

"Probably not. They haven't introduced squires,
except to the extent of one mounted darky who
is a sort of squire for all hands."

Sam Thomas, who had now returned to Barcelona, passed near them in going to his seat and
stopped to speak to them, addressing his remarks
chiefly to Reba; but he fancied that all three
ladies treated him coolly, particularly the one he
desired most to please, and he was not slow to
take himself off. A few minutes later Morton
appeared and also stopped to speak to them, his
dark, grave face relaxing in a tender smile and his
fine eyes kindling. Mrs. Brown literally beamed
on him, and Betty was as cordial as she had been
cool to his predecessor. Reba left the talking to
the others, but there was no lack of friendliness in
her glance.

"Why ain't you ridin'?" asked Mrs. Brown,
fondly. "Oh, yes, I forgot; I reckon you don't
feel able right now. I'm powerful sorry about
them chills-and-fever. You must take care of
yourself."

They were silent for a few moments after he

left them, each one thinking of him. Betty's reflection was that there was an indescribable expression in his peculiar, haunting eyes, as he looked
lingeringly at Reba. The latter's thoughts could
not easily be translated. Mrs. Brown, as usual,
expressed hers in words.

"If he *was* to ride," said she, enthusiastically,
"I'd be willin' for him to beat everybody, even
Charlie. A young man that will take up for a
unprotected woman like he done deserves to beat
'em all."

One other person stopped and spoke to them
before the contest began, a very young man who
smiled rapturously and almost blushed as he looked
at Betty. The girl was a year his senior and therefore regarded him almost as a "little boy," although
he was nearing twenty and was well grown. Her
lofty attitude, however, had not prevented him
from falling desperately in love with her, love at
that age being always desperate. His name was
Jack Sanford, and he was a son of Miss Black's
friend, the colonel. All three ladies greeted him
cordially, — Betty with some raillery; and Mrs.
Brown inquired why he, too, was not to take part
in the contest.

"I did so badly the last time we practised that
they ruled me out," he replied, with a blush and
an appealing look at Betty. "They could n't afford
to have any but the best riders; it would have
made too many."

It was now announced that the contest was to begin, and conversation ceased, or was resolved into exclamations of admiration, as the riders galloped round the area in single file, in order to accustom their horses to the crowd. The horsemen having resumed their former positions, a man with a white flag took his stand near the starting point and young Walton's spirited mare edged nervously toward the track. She had to be coaxed into position and seemed to tremble with excitement, but a few caressing pats on her neck accompanied by the encouraging voice of her master tended to calm her, and when the signal was given she started away nobly. The young man sat his slender, fleet-footed mare with admirable ease, and poised his wooden lance in a way to convey the impression that he could do nothing awkwardly.

The white flag drops, a shout goes up, away they go! The first post is near; the upheld lance is heard to strike the tiny suspended iron ring. Hurrah! he has it safe on his lance! On, on,— the second ring is taken, and the third, the fourth, the fifth. Bravo! what luck! what speed! what a calm, unerring eye! One more — will he get it ? — the sixth! There is the sound of contact; is it safe upon his lance? Too bad; there it flies off at a tangent. Nevertheless a great shout goes up; he has done well.

"Oh, what a pity he did n't get that 'n, too," sighed Mrs. Brown, a mother's fond pride showing

on her face as she looked around on the shouting
people.

Next appeared a rider with the slightly ambigu-
ous title of " Knight of the Fair " who made a
disastrous run, his horse proving unruly; and after
him the Knight of Putnam, who lost only two rings.
Then came the turn of Mr. Jones, the Knight of the
Plough, and the interest was intense as he dashed
around the track in awkward and apparently reckless style, and came out at the finish, amid enthusiastic shouts, with every ring on his lance.

" This is terrible," said Betty, with a wry face.
" If that man wins, he will write me a note as sure
as — I feel it coming now! No tournament ball
for me, then. I refuse to make myself conspicuous along with that big, lumbering — "

" You Betty! " remonstrated Mrs. Brown. " You
ought not to talk so; he 's a good young man."

" He 's good enough, but — dear me, he is
absolutely hopeless. I wish Jack had asked me to
go with him. He wanted to, but generously left
it open to one of the victors to invite me."

There was now leisure to forecast the probable
results and make bets while the remaining
" knights," no one of which particularly distinguished himself, took their several terms. Judging
from his first brilliant run, it was confidently
expected that the winner would be none other than
the awkward Knight of the Plough; but his second
and third runs proved less successful, while young

Walton took every ring in both his second and third rounds, and when the contest closed the four leading names on the score were: —

"Knight of the Horseshoe, 17 ; Knight of the Plough, 15 ; Knight of Putnam, 14 ; Knight of Red Bank, 12."

Much shouting had already been indulged in by the spectators, but nothing like what was heard when Charlie Walton, the victorious " Horseshoe," rode forward a little in advance of his comrades, a wreath of flowers upon his lance, and taking off his plumed hat, bowed in acknowledgment. Mrs. Brown's cup was full — and her eyes. As they descended from their seats, unnoticed in the crowd she suddenly embraced and kissed her niece with a meaning look, which plainly said: " He wants you, and if you'd only have him now, that would be all I'd ask for." And Reba thought: " My first cousin? — never! "

Before they were quite clear of the crowd they passed near and bowed to Miss Black who was in the company of a strange lady and gentleman. These had the air of the men and women of the world and looked about them with critical scrutiny, but were evidently no little entertained. Both had attractive faces, and Miss Black seemed to be on good terms with them.

" I like that man's looks," announced Betty, promptly.

"Who are they?"

"Those Northerners Miss Black told us she was expecting, I suppose."

Poor Betty's fears of trouble to come were not groundless. Early in the afternoon the following missive reached her at her home: —

> BARCELONA, Oct. 16, 188–.
>
> MISS BETTY, — Complements of J. L. Jones to Miss Betty Walton and would be pleased to have the plesure of her comepany to the turnnament ball tonight to crown her the first made of Honor if agreeable.
>
> Yours in Friendship,
> J. L. JONES.

"This is too much!" cried Betty, exasperated. "I think he *might* have got somebody to write it for him, or to correct his mistakes. Well, *I* stay at home," and, deaf to her mother's entreaties, she wrote a polite refusal and gave up the ball. "If Jack had only asked me this morning," she sighed.

It was quite a great ball for Barcelona, attracting visitors from among the inhabitants of several neighboring towns as well as being an event of all-absorbing interest at home. A temporary stage had been erected at one end of the large hall, and at the appointed hour the curtain went up, disclosing a pretty imitation of a woodland scene,— the "Queen of Beauty" seated in the centre, her victorious cavalier standing at her side, in the act of placing a crown upon her head. In the back-

ground were also seated the three ladies-in-waiting
or maids of honor, each attended by her own
knight, who was placing a coronet upon her head.
The tableau was an exceedingly pretty one and
the source of unbounded pleasure to the spectators
who for the most part knew little of the theatre.

The curtain was not down again five minutes before the crowned young ladies appeared on the
arms of their cavaliers, and the ball was opened.
Immediately the "royal set" was danced under the
admiring eyes of the wall-flowers and the somewhat envious side glances of those participating in
the several other cotillons. The young queen,
who, after much anxious planning, had been very
successfully costumed, was now radiant, and every
eye was riveted upon her and her handsome knight.
Refused by Betty, who pined at home, young Jones
had solicited in another quarter with more success,
and the first "made" of honor whom he now led
through the cotillon was undeniably pretty and
graceful. So much could not be said for the young
man himself, who, having received his early terpsi-
chorean education at backwoods balls, failed to
exhibit that even balance of grace and dignity dis-
tinguishing the good dancer, his feet, as is sometimes said of orators, being determinedly boisterous
and inclined to gesticulate too violently and too
much.

Miss Black watched the tableau and the dance in
company with Colonel and Mrs. Sanford and her

two visitors from Philadelphia, whom she had introduced as Mrs. Blossom and Mr. Shepherd.

" Very, very pretty," the last-named remarked, as the curtain went down, " but quite a surprise. I was expecting to see the ladies crown the knights with wreaths of laurel, or something of that kind."

" Oh, were you? " murmured Mrs. Sanford.

" Is it something in imitation of the tournaments of the middle ages? " asked Mrs. Blossom.

" I think," said Colonel Sanford, " the idea is taken from representations of the mediæval tournament given in England in the earlier part of this century. I remember hearing of one, when I was a young man, given at Eglinton castle about the year 1840. Lady Seymour was the Queen of Beauty."

At the last moment Mrs. Brown had decided to go to the ball with her husband in spite of the reverend Straitlace, who, to judge from her frequent reference to him, always loomed threateningly in her background. She had watched the tableau and the dance with emotions which, but for the recollection of Betty's obstinacy, would have approximated indescribable bliss; and later, at the first opportunity, she congratulated Reba and Charlie after her own indiscreet but well-meant fashion.

" Oh, you two did look so sweet! " she murmured, beaming on them. " But go on now, and promenade, and have a nice long talk."

Reba gave her aunt an affectionate glance in return, but Charlie frowned, not relishing this friendly espionage. His mother's crude compliment almost made him blush, and her significant parting suggestion was worse still; he was by no means averse to the long chat, but preferred to do his own courting. However, there was scant opportunity, for Sam Thomas soon approached and importuned Reba for a waltz, and presently she went off on Morton's arm.

By this time Miss Black was dancing with Jack Sanford, Mrs. Sanford and Mrs. Blossom were looking about them and lightly commenting, and the colonel was engaged in a very serious conversation with young Shepherd.

" The presence of the black man as a slave," he was saying, " was the curse of the old South; his presence as a freeman is equally the curse of the new. As regards material prosperity, he was and is a curse, because on his account the thrifty foreign immigrants pouring into this country during the past fifty years have steadily avoided the fair lands of the South, and settled always in the North and West, helping largely to make those sections populous, rich, and great. This is the true explanation of the slow development of our resources. The material side of the question, however, is not the most important. The main point is that the negro is a foreign body and we cannot assimilate him; we can only look forward to an indefinite extension of the inevitable struggle between two opposing factors, two hostile races, in one country."

"It might be urged, and perhaps without injustice," said Mr. Shepherd, "that the Southern people brought all this on themselves."

"We are much to blame," said the colonel, readily, "but by no means wholly so. The entire union of States was responsible. We fought to perpetuate slavery after it involved the preservation of an enormous property, and after we had come to regard it as a necessity, but in the first instance you or your ancestors were equally guilty. You must be aware that slavery, which existed in all the original thirteen States, was gradually abandoned in the North from reasons of interest rather than of sentiment, although it is unquestionable that a revolt against it began among your thinkers at an early day, as was also the case among us and among the English. The 'change of heart' with the latter was one of the most remarkable transitions of public sentiment on record, considering that they exported more than 600,000 slaves from Africa to Jamaica alone ; and as late as 1770 their king refused to take notice of the petition of the Virginia Assembly, which declared the importation of slaves 'a trade of great inhumanity, and dangerous to the very existence of his Majesty's American dominions.'

"But it is idle to talk of blame or responsibility now," the colonel added. "What we need to consider, to reflect seriously upon, is the situation before us. Surely it is one which no thoughtful person can fail to view with alarm, considering the intense race antipathy which exists and steadily increases."

"I was under the impression that it was ameliorating," said Mr. Shepherd, evidently much interested.

" It appears so because the negro has practically given up the struggle for political advantage. But wait until he is stronger."

"When you have forgotten that he was a slave the situation will perhaps soon adjust itself."

"It is not that, my friend, although that is undoubtedly one of the complications. If our slaves had been white serfs little prejudice could survive a generation. The freed white serf would need only to become prosperous and educate his children, and the fusion would begin. But the negro is black, a race totally distinct and hopelessly inferior, a race set apart in his own land and never intended to inhabit a common country with the whites. You know as well as I that he never would have been allowed to put foot in this country in the first place except as a slave. You who gradually drove the red man across this wide continent, staining every mile with his blood and your own, you who are determined to shut the Golden Gate against the yellow man, — how can you expect *us* to live in peace with, to assimilate, the black man, a third equally distinct and opposite race?"

"I must say I never thought of it in that light before," said Mr. Shepherd, thoughtfully.

" I have often wondered why Northern men show so little sympathy for us in our struggle with the negro. The bitterness following a bloody war was sufficient to explain your desire to humiliate us in making our slaves in many instances our governors, but — "

" Many people in the North," interrupted Shepherd, " doubted the wisdom of conferring the suffrage immediately upon the freed slave. In my opinion it was a mistake. It should have been done gradually."

" But," continued the colonel, " even that is insufficient to explain your attitude of criticism at this late date whenever there is an outbreak between the races. In the very nature of the situation these outbreaks are inevitable, and yet, whatever the circumstances may be, your sympathy is always with the black man as you look coldly on the struggle from a distance. One would think you would sometimes recollect that the whites of the North and South are men of one race, one instinct, one inheritance; while the blacks are totally of another, equally with the Chinee and the Indian. Deploring as you do the influence of the low white foreigner in the North, one would think you would be ready to extend your sympathy to us in our struggle with an ignorant, slavish, alien *race*."

" It does seem so," the younger man admitted, " and doubtless it would be so but for the question of partisan politics involved."

" That's the point. The North seems to believe
that the whole struggle is one of political parties.
My dear sir, it is a struggle of *race*. In reality the
' solid South' is literally torn with all sorts of political isms, and if the negro were out of the way, it
would fall apart to-morrow. We should have a
free-trade party, a protectionist party, and everything else under the sun; as it is, we have, and
will continue to have a ' solid South,' every other
interest fading into insignificance in comparison
with the one all-absorbing necessity of maintaining
white supremacy."

The colonel went on to ask a question which his
companion readily admitted as one not easily answered. It was this: Suppose the Chinese were
voters and had a narrow plurality, would the white
people of California allow them to capture the
State and municipal governments? "If this is not
a parallel case," declared Colonel Sanford, " it is because *our* situation has been and threatens again to
be worse than the Californians' would be under
those circumstances. Our white laboring men
make the same complaints of unequal competition
with the negro that are made by the same class in
California in respect to the rice-subsisting Chinee.
Both these alien races are able to support life on
much less than the more highly organized white
man, and therefore can work for less pay and thus
drive the competing white man to the wall. Your
working classes North who are so restive under the

system of importing white foreign laborers, know
little or nothing of what is involved in competition
with the negro, and I venture to say that if the
situation North and South could be reversed, if
well nigh one half of your population could suddenly be converted into blacks with the same characteristics of those among us here, there would
grow up among your wage earners within five
years an overwhelming sentiment favoring their
forcible expulsion from the country."

"It is difficult to conceive of such a situation,
but there would be trouble no doubt."

"This brings me to my point, my hobby, as some
of my friends call it, — namely, not the forcible
expulsion of the negro, but his gradual removal by
means of colonization. He was brought here forcibly and should not be forced to leave; but it be-
hooves the whites, primarily for their own sakes,
and secondarily for his, to do everything in their
power to encourage him to emigrate to Liberia,
the Congo Free State or elsewhere. That is the
only salvation for this Southern country, as I see it.
My friends who fear agriculture would be disor-
ganized — and it might be temporarily — may call
it my hobby if they please, but I could know no
greater happiness than to see such a scheme
accomplished."

"Your 'hobby' is surely not one to be ashamed
of," rejoined the younger man, admiringly.

The colonel launched forth again, but his wife

interrupted him. "You must not keep Mr. Shepherd talking there all the evening," she said. "This is a ball, you know. Take Mrs. Blossom around the room; she's tired of sitting, I know."

Colonel Sanford rose promptly and offered his arm.

"And," his wife continued, "if you will take me across the room, Mr. Shepherd, I'll introduce you to some young people. That is, if you like."

"I should like very much to be presented to the 'queen.'"

4

IV.

IT was three o'clock in the morning when the knight of the horseshoe left his queen at her own door. The sound of drizzling rain in the China-trees of the yard first arrested her attention upon awakening, and then, her mother's voice faintly calling. It must, then, be very late. The empty ball dress and sham crown now presented the aspect of reproachful phantoms, and Reba was conscious of something like remorse for having enjoyed herself so thoroughly. Hurrying into the adjoining room, she found that it was past ten o'clock, and that her mother was suffering from the effect of a sleepless night, besides being weak for want of nourishment.

"How careless of me to sleep so late," she said regretfully, kissing the invalid's pale face.

"You could n't help it, dearie. You needed the rest. And what did you think of the ball, eh?"

The girl began an enthusiastic description, but soon cut her words short and hurried to the kitchen. Her mind was so full of the lights and triumphs of the ball that she found it difficult to

concentrate her attention on the preparation of a
tiny omelet and a cup of coffee, and realized presently that she had neglected the first and most
necessary step involved, — the building of a fire.
And now a look of dismay overspread her face as
she recalled that the supply of wood was exhausted
and the wherewithal of a fire was not at hand. A
temporary blaze from the chips usually scattered
about the wood-pile was not impossible, but a load
of wood had been needed for several days and the
gleanings from this source had already been con-
sumed. Reba thought of the fable of the cricket
that danced and chirruped all summer, laying
nothing by, and when the winds of winter came
crept about hungry and shivering.

"If I can't find a board somewhere about, I'll
have to go down to the woods and get a lightwood
knot and chop it up," was her troubled reflection,
as she took down her work-day bonnet from a peg
on the piazza.

But for a fine mist, the rain had now ceased, and
Reba started across the little field a few minutes
later, with no worse prospect threatening than a
pair of wet feet. She hoped that no one passing
on the neighboring road would see her or suspect
the object of her errand, and pulled the old cloth
sun-bonnet far down over her face, trusting that in
any event she would not be recognized. The
secret of this desperate poverty must be kept.

Once beyond the open field and among the trees

of the pine woods, she felt less concerned and
centred her whole attention upon the search for a
suitable piece of wood. But, as was soon evident,
small lightwood knots were rare, and large ones,
too, the ground having been foraged full often
already. Her glance being confined to the immediately surrounding area of wire-grass as she moved
forward in her anxious search, the girl strayed
further than she intended and unknowingly stood
within a few feet of the road before discovering a
piece of wood which she thought she would be
able to carry. While struggling with it and feeling
very forlorn and wretched, poor Reba's attention was
suddenly arrested by the sound of approaching
wheels. Dropping her find and casting a frightened
glance over her shoulder, she saw that the occu-
pant of the vehicle was young Morton, that he had
drawn rein, had almost stopped, and was looking
at her with wonder-struck eyes.

The girl knew that her limp bonnet very successfully concealed her face; she thought it possible
and earnestly hoped that, although the distance was
so short, he had not recognized her. In any event
she was determined not to allow him to carry her
burden, an intention which seemed to be indicated
in his manner, or the fact that he had drawn rein;
and a moment later she was stooping and plucking
a wild flower within a foot of the lightwood knot,
just as if this has been the object of her struggles
in the first place. Then, apparently unconscious

of his presence, she walked away, stooping presently to gather another flower, and farther on still another. The observer, who had not quite stopped, now drove on, wondering at what he had seen. He was not quite sure, but strongly suspected that it was Reba, and was at a loss to explain the situation. He had distinctly seen her struggling with a piece of wood, as if she intended to lift and carry it, and it certainly seemed improbable that she would go into the wet woods at that hour of a rainy morning in order to gather wild flowers.

Five minutes later Reba was crossing the little rice field, dragging her prize after her and congratulating herself upon having escaped detection. She did not know that even at that moment two negro men who had halted on the road were observing her and commenting. It was an hour when other men were at work, but these two had been strolling aimlessly along, with the air of persons with nothing in the world to do.

"Jes' look at dat young white 'oman," said one. "She must be mighty po' if she have to go out and git her own wood dat-a way." The speaker was celebrated for his name, which was no less an absurdity than Mamie-Lou John, his mother having felt moved to adopt and bestow upon him in infancy the compound Christian name of a pretty little white girl. John was his father's surname.

"Dat's Reba Law'nce," said the other, who was known as Cicero Witherspoon and was the husband of Josephine. "You mighty right, she po'; she have to make clothes for Rosetta and dem other gals and Josephine she cleck de money for her. (I made Josephine gim me some of it one time.) She wut you call po' buckra sho-nuf."

When Reba finally carried in her mother's breakfast she was met by the first real complaint she could remember to have heard from her. Mrs. Lawrence was a patient woman; she had suffered much and had schooled herself to endure in silence ; but she was not wholly free from the notorious selfishness of the average invalid. And this morning she had been sorely tried; she had waited until she was faint and her patience was gone.

"What made you so *long?*" she asked, irritably. "I am astonished."

"I could n't help it," Reba answered, her eyes filling. She sat down in a corner, feeling hurt, and waited until her mother had eaten. At last she said : "There was no wood, and I had to go down into the woods and get a piece before I could build a fire."

"What!" exclaimed Mrs. Lawrence, deeply shocked. "Why, what does this mean? Why is there no wood? Did you forget to order it?"

"A load passed here yesterday, but I could n't stop it because I did n't have the money," answered Reba, absently.

"You did n't have the money to pay for a load of wood!" said Mrs. Lawrence, her eyes expanding. "What has gone with it all, then? We can at least buy wood, I hope."

The implied reproach was too much for Reba to endure in her present mood; she felt that she could bear the burden of responsibility no longer. Bursting into tears, she told the whole pitiable story, — the loss of their income nine months before, the melting away of their little hoarded sum, the sewing for the negroes, and all her painfully careful little economies. After a few exclamations of amazement, Mrs. Lawrence listened in silence to the end. Then she rose in her bed to a sitting posture, clasped her daughter in her arms, and wept as Reba had never seen her weep.

"Don't cry so, mamma," begged the girl at last. "We have been able to manage for nine months and we can still go on."

"To think that I could have been so thoughtless and selfish when my poor, brave child was going through such a struggle," sobbed the unnerved invalid. "I can never forgive myself, Reba. I thought you were mismanaging and wasting our little income foolishly. Why — why did n't you tell me everything?"

"If you had been strong I should have, but I wanted to spare you; and now — now that you know all about it, something must be done. You are not getting proper food. I 'll speak to Aunt Matilda, and it may be Mr. Brown will advance us some money until —"

"No!"

Mrs. Lawrence's tears ceased to flow at this suggestion, and leaning back among her pillows, she calmly discussed the situation, although weak from unwonted excitement. No, they would do no such thing. For the present they would go on as Reba had begun. They would continue to solicit sewing and would do the work together; hereafter Reba should not work so hard, — the mother would do the larger part of the sewing, propped up in bed when she could not sit up. She believed it would be better for her anyhow than so much reading. She was handy with the needle, fortunately; she had taken to fine needlework when quite a child, — had once, she recollected, pleased her father very much by embroidering the family arms in colors. There were many things about the house of no real use to them which Josephine would be glad to own; they would encourage her by more frequent gifts to procure more work than heretofore, and perhaps she could be induced to try harder to collect the money. How strange it seemed to be reduced to such depth of poverty, — to a pittance gained by sewing for one's former slaves, — after what the family had once been!

"My father took me all over Europe before I was married," said Mrs. Lawrence, sadly, "and a few years afterwards my husband took me again. The money spent during those two years abroad would make us rich now. I never dreamed what real want was before. Even after the war your father managed to keep us comfortable."

But she soon shut her mind to this painful contrast and again bravely faced the present, going over the particulars of the proposed plan. Reba listened doubtfully yet hopefully, relieved to have another share with her the burden of responsibility. When at last she lifted the tray and left the room, however, the enthusiasm in her mother's face slowly died out.

"I understand now why Reba looks so thin," she told herself, in great pain. "I suspect that for a long while she has been cooking only for me and eating scarcely anything herself. I will see to that in future."

And she saw to it. From that day on Reba observed with grave solicitude, but without suspicion, that her mother's appetite steadily failed. She complained that she could not eat, and left untouched full two-thirds of the scant meal that was set before her three times a day. This slow starvation was, however, not allowed to interfere with the labor which she had engaged to do. Whenever the work was in the house she could not be persuaded to let it alone, and sewed regularly and hard.

"We shall be able to manage," she would say, "until the railroad begins to pay again; or," she once added, "until you marry. You have had no offers as yet, Reba?"

"I could have had from Charlie and from Sam Thomas, but I always discourage them when — when —" The girl halted, as if disliking to continue. "Charlie is like a brother," she added, "and nothing on earth could induce me even to *think* of Sam Thomas."

"*I* like Robert Morton," said Mrs. Lawrence; and observing that her daughter adroitly avoided discussing this young man, she drew an inference which was far from displeasing to her. "I would rather see you in your grave," she added, "than to see you marry for anything but love."

It was on the afternoon of the same troublous day that Reba received a visit from an old negress who had been for many years a slave in the Morton family, and who was in most respects a slave still. That is to say, she was in no sense a part of the present with which her children and grandchildren were identified, but was one of the few fossil-like relics of the past. These antique survivals are now-a-days so rare that they stand out in bold relief, so to speak. "Maum Katie" — so she was called in the Morton family and by most people of her own race also — could not read and write, and was otherwise unlike the younger generation, taking little interest in its ambitions and struggles, and being little influenced by its suppressed hatred of the whites. She had lived fifty years as a slave in one family, in the household as maid and seamstress, and, being kindly dealt with, a genuine

affection for those with whom she was in constant
association did not fail to awaken in her and live.
Those fifty years, in fact, had been more satisfactory
as regards bodily comfort than the succeeding
twenty-five during which she had shifted for herself; and she remembered this slightly to the detri-
ment of the present. Maum Katie knew that there
was a present and was vaguely conscious that
there would be a future, but was herself essentially
of the past.

The family in which she would proudly say that
that she had been "raised" was now broken up
and scattered; some had fallen in the war, others
had died at home, others still had married and
moved to a distance. The only representative of
this family in Barcelona now was her young "Mas'
Robert" whose linen she washed. Maum Katie
also served the Lawrence household in the same
capacity; for washing was her trade, and she was
still an active woman, in spite of her white woolly
hair and her seventy-five years.

"I come to git de wash, Miss Reba, honey," she
said, cheerily. Reba had heard her step and gone
out on the back piazza to meet her.

"I can't give it to you any longer," said the girl,
sadly.

"Ain't I doin' it right? Don't it suit you?"
Maum Katie had a good face, and the anxiety now
written upon it clearly indicated a fear that she

had failed in her duty rather than concern for the loss of custom.

" It is n't that. You do it beautifully. I meant that I would have to do it myself hereafter."

Maum Katie looked inexpressibly shocked. "Wid all you got to do?" she ejaculated, after a moment. " You got to cook, and you got to sew,. and you got to wait on yo' ma; *you* can't do it. You ain't strong enough, nohow."

"We can't afford to pay for it any longer. I don't mind telling *you*, Maum Katie."

" Nem mind 'bout payin', Miss Reba, honey. You lem me do de washin', an' you kin des pay me when you git de money. Nem mind 'bout payin'."

Reba's eyes filled with tears as she listened to this speech, which was uttered with the sweetness and gentleness of an angel of mercy.

" Oh, Maum Katie, I could n't think of doing that. How could you afford it? You are very good."

Maum Katie protested that she could afford it; she was able to lay by a little money every month. Anyhow, she was going to do it; they could n't turn her off without warning in that way !

If she really thought she could, then, Reba confessed that it would really be a great relief to them; and they would pay her as soon as they could. In the mean time, they had " clothes and things " which she could make use of perhaps. "And Maum

Katie," the girl added, as the old woman, having determinedly possessed herself of the wash, was ready to start, "Josephine said you had a grandson who was a school-teacher; we could give him some books which he could make good use of, if you will tell him to stop here some day."

"I'll tell him and he'll sho' come," said Maum Katie, much pleased. "He love to git all de books he kin, Neil do."

She went down the steps laughing and saying good-by, but as soon as Reba re-entered the house, she put down her bundle and retraced her steps. Maum Katie knew that when a white woman of the higher class in Barcelona attempted to do her own washing it meant extreme poverty, and she determined on an investigation of the present case. Stealing across the latticed piazza, which separated the main body of the house from the dining-room, she cautiously opened the door of the latter and entered. After a hasty survey of kitchen and dining-room, and a minute examination of the contents of the pantry, which was not locked, she reappeared on the piazza, went softly down the steps, took up her bundle, and walked away shaking her head and muttering.

"Oh, people!" she ejaculated, "dem two po' women gwine to starve, you see 'em so. Dat won't do, dat won't do. Can't last long dat-a way. I aim to tell Mas' Robert de fust chance I git. I know Miss Reba de lady he want; I know it mighty

well from de way he ax me 'bout her dat day, an' if I
tell him dis he 'll hurry up an' ax her to have him.
Look yuh, Katie," she checked herself suddenly,
standing still in the street, " may be you better not
now ; ' t ain't none o' yo' business nohow. Yes I will,
too, bein' it 's Mas' Robert," she continued, walking
forward. " I know mighty well he ain't de kind o'
man to back out jes' 'cause she so po'."

Her grandson, whom she called Neil, but who
was known among his friends as Professor Brice,
appeared promptly on the following afternoon. He
came up the back steps, as she was wont to do, and
rapped on the hall door, taking off his hat when
Reba appeared. He was well dressed and distinguished by quite an intelligent expression of
countenance.

" I suppose you are the school-teacher," said
Reba, knowing he could be no other.

" Yes, ma'am."

The girl left him standing where he was and
returned presently with an armful of books.
" Maum Katie is so kind," she said, " I want to do
something to please her. I think you can make
use of all these."

" Thank you, ma'am," said the ' Professor.' with
gratitude, looking eagerly at the titles as he took
the books. " I 'm mighty glad to get 'em. I love
to read. I 's read a heap o' books in my time," he
added, with a species of childish vanity which
amused Reba. " If I can do anything for you any

time, ma'am, please call on me," he said finally, and departed.

"He might have cut me a little wood *now*," thought Reba, with a smile, as she saw him go ; "but I hardly liked to suggest his doing what he would doubtless consider beneath his dignity."

V.

ABOUT four o'clock in the afternoon of the day
after the ball, the visiting Philadelphians parted
with Miss Black at the photographer's door, and
went for a walk. They expected to take the south-
ward train early in the evening, and desired to employ the intervening time in seeing the town, or
such of its external features as might interest them.
Greatly to the satisfaction of Miss Black, whose
unconscious attitude was one of responsibility for
everything connected with Barcelona, they avowed
having been highly entertained at the ball, and regretted that they could not see more of some of
the people whose acquaintance they had made on
that occasion.

"Paul fell in love with Miss Lawrence," laughed
Mrs. Blossom, "and wants me to invite her to
Philadelphia."

"Don't you agree with me, Miss Black," the
young man had rejoined, "that a 'Queen of
Beauty' fresh from a semi-mediæval tournament
would be a pleasing novelty in the Quaker City?"

They first walked straight out a prominent street
into the suburbs, admiring a house here and there
built after an unusual pattern and with perhaps yellow jessamines or Madeira-vines clambering over the
trellised piazzas. A mocking-bird in the top of a
China-tree arrested their attention now and then,
and once they glimpsed the rare cardinal-bird as it
flamed through the dark green of the pecans.
Farther out they stopped to look at sugar-cane
growing, and recognized a few orange and banana
trees. But it was the people who most interested
them, particularly the blacks; and they soon returned to the business quarter, boldly invading the
contiguous haunts of busy and idle negroes, where
no native white woman was ever seen, stopping to
look and comment with the freedom of travellers
who had no reputation at stake.

The narrow, dirty back street which they had
entered was occupied chiefly by negro restaurants,
but there was here and there a cobbler's shop, a
fish market, or a drinking saloon. Near one of the
last-named they stopped to look at a large wire
cage containing four dogs, two raccoons, a goat, a
monkey, and a grinning, full-grown young negro.

" Darwin would have gone half-way round the
world to see this," laughed Shepherd, — "a case of
natural selection ready to his hand."

The monkey was unquestionably the handsomest
animal of the lot, and the most agile; when the
dogs barked and the goat jumped, this favored

5

beast would mount the side of the cage in a twinkling and save his fur, — a resource not open to the brother last named in the catalogue. The aim of this curious collection was to hold the interest of the passer-by till thirst reminded him that he stood at the door of a saloon. The two Northerners agreed that the caricatures of men who sell their backs to advertisers in New York and Philadelphia are relatively dignified characters, and must yield the palm to the last-named member of the Barcelona menagerie.

It was while halting here that they observed a young negro stop a passing reverend of the fair race, and ask what would be his charge for joining two dusky lovers in wedlock. On being informed that the price of such service would be one dollar, he promptly rejoined : —

"I kin git it done cheaper."

"Go ahead, then," was the disgusted retort. "I ought to have said five dollars. You'll be paying some lawyer fifteen for a divorce in less than six months."

The street came to an end in an open square where a merry-go-round attracted crowds. Anywhere in the world there is magic for the child in the monotonous round of those gayly painted chairs and horses, accompanied by the boisterous harmony of a young hand-organ or the distressing plaint of an aged one; but here was delight for any and all representatives of a semi-childlike race.

The dusky damosel and her swain, the middle-aged, and even old black men and women, were here seen to mount the fascinating wooden horses and ride them with all the glee of their grandchildren.

On retracing their steps through the same narrow dirty street described above, the tourists were genuinely surprised to find two representatives of this race, both women, who were attempting to ride a horse of a very different species, which noble animal was none other than Pegasus himself. They were said to establish themselves there every Saturday — on the porch of a negro restaurant — and sell hymns which they had themselves composed. These compositions were printed on slips of paper and offered to the public at five cents each. One of the dusky poets was blind, and was known as the Blind Lady; the other was a robust young creature with a heavy contralto voice, who attracted crowds [of blacks] by singing her own and the Blind Lady's productions, the music being unquestionably a native product also. It was intoning rather than singing, and was chiefly remarkable for monotonous repetition and the absence of any but the most rudimentary elements of harmony; but there was a certain rhythm of word and richness of tone that were not without charm.

A slip was purchased and examined by the travellers with great curiosity, desirous to form an estimate of the talents of these unexpected minstrels. At the top was printed in large letters, " Noah,

Hoist the Window, By Rachel Macky." Then
followed the hymn, epic poem, or whatsoever it
might be, which they had heard delivered in the
rich, chanting voice of its author: —

> " God commanded old Noah one day,
>   Told old Noah to build an ark.
>   In the woods old Noah did go,
>   And the first thing that old Noah done,
>   Noah cut his timber down.
>   Next thing that old Noah done,
>   Old Noah laid the foundation down.
>   The ark was made of gopher wood.
>   The next thing that old Noah done,
>   Old Noah commenced to frame his ark.
>   How long was Noah building the ark ?
>   Noah was a hundred and twenty years
>   Building on the ark of God.
>   A foolish man came riding by,
>   And pointed the finger of scorn at Noah,
>   And called Noah that foolish man —
>   Building his ark on this hard dry land.
>   And Noah replied to the foolish man:
>   ' Foolish man, you had better pray ;
>   I am looking for judgment every day.' "

And so on, at great length. At the end of each line
the following " chorus " was sung without fail: —

> " Hoist the window, let the dove come in."

Young Shepherd thought of blind Homer, with
a smile at the comparison. He thought the subject
chosen was alive with the elements of an epic, how-

ever, and that it might well be doubted if the bard
or rhapsode who struck his harp in the andronitis
of the Greek home and recited from Hesiod or
Homer was accorded more earnest attention than
was now given this robust young negress. He
thought it unlikely that the names of Rachel
Macky and the Blind Lady would ever be written
on " fame's eternal bead-roll," but there was every
indication that they would always remain a wonder
and delight to their friends.

" The landlord said we should go down into the
' Neck' if we wanted to see negroes," he remarked,
as they were returning to their hotel.

" They are so disgusting, but yet so interesting,"
said Mrs. Blossom. " Perhaps I 'll go there next
spring. I think I shall stop here on my return
from Jamaica. I want to see more of my niece, and
of that ' queen ' of yours, too."

The place called the " Neck" which they had
been recommended to visit was the negro section
of the town, in reality a teeming suburb containing
almost as many inhabitants as Barcelona proper.
Here were two churches, a public hall, two school-
houses, and many fairly comfortable little dwelling-
houses, containing from two to five rooms each,
and not a few cheerless hovels. In one of these
latter lived Josephine and Cicero Witherspoon.
They were not as prosperous as some of their neighbors, and found it necessary to live in an aged
shanty of two rooms, for which, including the

surrounding inclosure of half an acre, they paid a
rent of two dollars per month. It may seem
strange, but Josephine thought the amount excessive, and loudly abused the landlord for his shameless avarice whenever he sent her a dun for rent
overdue. This, it may be, was partly because she
did all the paying that was done herself, her
husband being a conscienceless vagabond who was
never known to pay anything. Fortunately, she
was a celebrated laundress, and did the washing of
a number of single men of the white race, each one
of whom paid her monthly a sum exceeding the
rent, and so she managed not to be turned out, and
contrived to clothe her children, feed her husband,
and indulge herself in a few vanities.

Josephine was a fat blooming matron of thirty
summers, strong, healthy, good-humored, willing
to work, satisfied with little, easily moved to
laughter, enamoured of song; her children never
went hungry, and she herself was always decently
clothed. ' Yet she was not happy. She was willing
to forgive Cicero for shirking all responsibility and
compelling her to support the family, but she
could not forgive him for being unfaithful. He
was a youth of eighteen when they married, and
she a widow of twenty-five, and there were now
three more children added to the five resulting
from her first very early marriage. Cicero was
a hunter, a fisherman, a loafer addicted to light
theft and lying, — anything, everything but what

he ought to have been. He condescended to hire
himself out just often enough to escape the vagrant
law, meanwhile working havoc in the fowl-houses,
melon-patches and potato-banks of the white man.
Josephine was of an easy conscience and accepted
the spoils without rancorous comment; but when
Cicero smiled too openly upon the comely dusky
maids of the Neck she did not spare him.

At the same hour that the Northern visitors
started on their tour of exploration near the business quarter in Barcelona, Josephine stood singing over her wash-tub at her home in the Neck.
There was a China-tree in the rear of her house
which provided a cool shade, but Josephine preferred to work in her front yard, whence she could
see those who came and went on the street, and
now stood there bare-headed in the hot October
sun. As she took the steaming garments from her
wash-pot, placing them in dripping wads on an
upright sawed round of a pine-tree, and belabored
them vigorously with a stout " battlin'-stick," every
blow precipitating a light shower upon all things
within a radius of ten feet, including her three
younger children playing near, Josephine sang
with that joyous forgetfulness which is the African
woman's solace. Now and then she stopped singing to order her children away from the fire, or to
soliloquize, the burden of her oral thought being
the recreant Cicero as a rule; and again she would
call to the woman seated on the porch of the

neighboring house and exchange with her a few friendly remarks. Anon, seeing a young woman passing on the street, she left her work, went and leaned on her gate, and gossiped with her for ten minutes. As the girl was about to move on, she detained her with the following : —

"Look yuh, Susan, Reba Law'nce want dat money for dat dress, you see her so. She say she got to have it."

"Let her come git it, den," said Susan, contemptuously.

"You been owin' it six months."

"Don't care if I is. I'll owe it six years if I want to. I aim to pay it when I git ready and not befo'."

Josephine laughed loud and long, as if greatly amused, and her look of appreciation seemed to recognize in Susan's pert remarks the very soul of wit. Josephine was one of your good-natured chameleons who always take their color from the nearest object.

"You better pay dat money," she said, still laughing. "Reba say she'll have you 'rested and put in jail." Clearly Josephine's memory could not be relied on, for not only had the unhappy young seamstress not threatened an arrest, but when the enthusiastic Josephine proposed to "beat" the stubborn Susan she had distinctly advised a less violent course, preferring even to relinquish her claim.

Susan received the threat with indifference, re-
torting scornfully as she moved away, " Dat po'
young buckra woman better not fool wid *me.*"

The next passer-by who distracted Josephine's
attention from her labors was a white woman, a
tall, gaunt, pale-faced creature who was far from
attractive outwardly. Her name was Simpson, and
she lived with her husband and children on a small
farm just outside of town. The Simpsons were
natives of a New Jersey village and had settled in
their present position soon after the war, having
come South for the benefit of a milder climate.
Simpson was a brick-layer, but ill-health prevented
him from following his trade closely and he had
never been prosperous, being now less so than
ever. He was too poor to send his children to
school, and it was one of his sons whom Reba was
teaching to read in return for his labor at odd
times. Simpson was a man of some intelligence,
and his voice was now and then heard in the political debates which could frequently be heard on the
main street of Barcelona. He lost no opportunity
to revile the State law which, in effect, provided a
free school for the blacks but not for the whites.
The school-fund was from a tax on property,
nine-tenths of which was owned by the whites, and
was distributed per capita, irrespective of color.
The fund was not adequate, and no educated
white man could be found to open a school without
further remuneration. On the other hand, fairly

competent negro men were glad to take the
chances and teach for the public money alone; and
so the black schools, being absolutely free, were
crowded, the pittance apportioned to each child
amounting to a considerable sum in the aggregate
and satisfying the teachers. But in the case of the
white schools, the public fund served only to re-
duce the regular price of tuition, and the very poor
were obliged to stay away.

On going back and forth from town, the Simpsons were obliged either to make a wearisome
détour or pass through the Neck. It is notorious
that the average Southern negro has no respect
for the poor white man or woman. This is only
the appearance; the reality is that, in such cases,
he dares to allow his suppressed hatred for the
race in general to appear openly. The rich or
otherwise powerful realize little of this; the Simpsons understood it thoroughly, being not infre-
quently the victim of it in their journeys through
the Neck. Josephine had never been personally
aggrieved by the gaunt Mrs. Simpson, and yet her
contempt for that woman knew no bounds; and
she one day purposely ran against her in the street,
loudly declaring that " po' buckra " should " give
her the road "! It was a fact patent to the dullest
comprehension that whatever collided with the
heavy Josephine would be rudely shaken, and Mrs.
Simpson had not failed to suffer from the shock.
Thereafter, on passing through the Neck, she

invariably provided herself with a short, sharp-
pointed stick or a similar weapon, which, one later
day when Josephine again attempted her playful
manœuvre, came into rude and painful contact
with the latter's fleshy person and caused her to
avoid such amusement in future.

All this is to explain why Josephine began to
laugh as soon as she observed the approach of the
unfortunate Mrs. Simpson, and to call out loudly
to her friend on the porch of the neighboring
house :—

" Ca'line ! O Ca'line ! you want to see a pond-
gannet ? " [1]

" Wher'bouts? " responded " Ca'line," looking
toward the swamp in the distance.

" Shoo !— don't have to go to de swamp to see
a pond-gannet dese days," shrieked Josephine,
almost overcome with laughter. " I see a lank,
white pond-gannet go walkin' by yuh 'most every
day."

Caroline now understood the situation and
laughed as loudly as her neighbor, meanwhile
staring straight at the passing white woman who
understood also and looked the other way in
labored unconcern.

" Ca'line, you sen' your chillun to school and I
sen' my chillun to school," continued Josephine,
in great glee, " but heap o' dese buckra so po' dey

---

[1] Locally, a tall white crane.

have to keep dey chillun home. If I was like some o' dese po' buckra I 'd go off and crawl in a hole and stay dere."

" And if I had my will," muttered the furious Mrs. Simpson, passing on, " I 'd have you and every other nigger drummed out of this country ! "

Josephine continued to indulge in these pointed remarks, punctuated by shrieks of laughter, until the " pond-gannet " was well out of hearing, then returned to her tubs. About half an hour later the schoolmaster known as Professor Brice, and another well-dressed and well-fed man, a good many years his senior, stopped at the gate. The latter was one of the many negro preachers of Barcelona and Malvern County, and was known as Parson Smith.

" Is Mr. Witherspoon home, Mis' Witherspoon ? " they asked.

Josephine said he was not, but she was expecting him every minute; would they not come in? She advanced toward them with a smile of rapture, reflecting upon the honor of having both the parson and the professor at her gate, and hoping the watchful neighbors were duly impressed.

" We ain't got time to stop now," the professor replied. " I wish you 'd tell Cicero we 'd like to meet him at the hall to-morrow night. We want to organize a debatin' club."

Josephine promised effusively to transmit the message, and the distinguished visitors passed on.

"Cicero is mighty triflin'," said the parson when they were out of hearing, "but he's smart, and I reckon he could make a pretty good speech. We ought to have Mamie-Lou John, too; he ain't no fool hisself."

Josephine accomplished little at her tubs that afternoon. The parson and the professor were hardly out of sight when her attention was again taken off her work. Two persons, a young man and a young woman, were now passing on the opposite side of the street, apparently much absorbed in each other. A low, delighted laugh from the latter reached Josephine's ears and she immediately made use of her eyes. Yes, it was she — Rosetta; and there beside her was Cicero deftly employing his flattering tongue.

"Chillun, keep out dat fire!" ordered Josephine, savagely, as she buttoned her loosened sleeve above the elbow, grasped the hickory clothes-stick firmly, and rushed forward as if to battle. Her husband, to all appearances, was merely taking the air in agreeable company, but when she saw him and his companion Josephine boiled over more impetuously than her wash-pot had ever done over the hottest fire. The fire of jealousy — ah! Flinging wide the gate, she flew across the street and bore down upon them, to the mute astonishment of Cicero and the terror of Rosetta. It was the same giddy Rosetta who had sent Reba urgent word to make her dress "tight in de wais'."

"Look yuh, Cis'ro!" cried Josephine, flourishing her battling-stick, "you better be in dat
g-yardin' plantin' turnips and holpin' me feed dem
chillun, stidder foolin' 'long yuh wid dis gal!"
Then to Rosetta: "Wut you doin' yuh, you triflin'
hussy! Cl'ar out from yuh right straight!"

"Wut in de name o' goodness I done to you?"
demanded Rosetta, with spirit. "I like to know is
it any yo' business if I walk 'long dis street? 'Tain't
none o' yo' street."

"Leave yuh!" cried Josephine, furiously.

"I won't do it till I git ready," the girl retorted.

"You sha'n't sass me dat-a way in front o' my
own yard, you triflin' —!" and losing the rest
of her words in the tempest of her rage, Josephine
suddenly collared her enemy and inflicted several
smart raps across her head with the battling-stick.

"Look yuh, woman, is you crazy?" remonstrated Cicero, endeavoring to interfere. "You
want 'em come and take you to jail yuh dis ebenin'? Better mind wut you —" But the stick just
then came in contact with his own head, and he
made haste to stand out of range.

Her attention thus divided, Josephine's grasp of
Rosetta's collar relaxed somewhat, and the frightened girl broke wildly away and ran; whereupon
the unsatisfied avenger entered upon an exciting
chase, but being soon outdistanced she retraced
her steps, puffing and blowing with great energy,
and bent upon a more satisfactory reckoning with

her recreant spouse. But sly, slippery Cicero, in the local idiom, had made himself scarce.

Does this sound like burlesque? No one will think so who has visited Barcelona and explored the Neck.

VI.

CICERO turned up in time to get his supper, however, and for two hours there was a war of words,
verging now and again perilously near a physical
scuffle. In some neighboring households the dispute would have been settled in short order by
means of a stick in the hands of the husband;
but Josephine was as strong as an ox and Cicero
was afraid of her. Therefore his weapon took the
shape of an olive-branch. He talked earnestly and
repentantly, being vividly impressed with the fact
that his course had imperilled his claim upon the
three meals a day which his wife provided; for
Josephine vowed that she would " quit " him, that,
in other words, she was done with him forever.

The pretended penitent solemnly promised not
only to smile upon Rosetta no more, but to reform
and go to work, and so there was a truce. But
Cicero's promises were no more to be relied on
than water in a sieve, — he who had been known to
engage his service to a half-dozen farmers for the

same Monday morning, only to leave them all in the lurch and go off for a day's fishing! Heedless of consequences, refusing to shoulder the responsibility of anything under the sun, — this was his character, as Josephine well knew, though none the less fond of him. Within two weeks, if there was any change at all, his behavior was worse than ever. He began to absent himself from home for days at a time, and finally ceased to make even the most insignificant contribution towards the household food supply, either from the despoiled hen-roosts and potato-banks of the white man or from more legitimate sources.

About this time Josephine fell sick, her children suffered for attention, and she longed for the recreant Cicero's presence in vain. During her illness an event occurred which shook the Neck to its foundations, an event of no less great importance than the arrival of the circus at Barcelona. The Neck turned out *en masse*, and Josephine's children begged to go with the rest of the world; but there was no money, and Cicero was out of reach. On the morning after all was over, their neighbor "Ca'line" appeared among them. She was full of the "show," and after expressing due sympathy and concern for the ailing Josephine, allowed her tongue full freedom of exercise upon the engaging topic.

"I would n' 'a miss it for five hundud dollahs," she declared. "Josephine, you des ought to been

6

dere. I never see de like o' de big gang o' people
struttin' dem street, and den dem poscessions
gwine thoo town wid mens all dress up in red
shiny clothes settin' up in dem big gold wagins
tootin' dey horn — oh-y! dat was putty! Me and
Doshy Bostick and a whole passel o' people
followed 'em round town tell we was plum' wo' out.
But all dat was n' nut'n to when we got inside
de show and seen all dem lions and taggers and
hoppypotymusses, and all dat cuttin' up and gwine
on in de show ring! Gentermens! I could n'
hardly b'lieve my eyes to see dem mens in dem
tight putty clothes, lookin' like dey was 'most
necked, swingin' so reckless up in dem swings 'way
up de top de tent. And den dat sassy clown talkin' he funny talk, and den when dey brung out de
ole elephant in de ring — oh, people! hit make me
putty nigh bust a-laughin' to see dat tremenjous
big ole creetur git up on he hind legs! Mighty
sorry you sick; you ought to been dere sho'."

"Did n' hab no money nohow," said Josephine,
with gloomy resignation.

Whereupon "Ca'line" looked inexpressibly
shocked, and asked why Cicero could not have sup-
plied it. Cicero was at the show and had money,
too; "Ca'line" had seen him with her "own eyes"
in the company of Rosetta Hightower and another
dusky damosel. He paid their way in,— she had
seen him "haul out de money;" furthermore, after
the performance she had seen him treat them to

parched peanuts and the seductive red lemonade. Why was he not spending all that money on these children? — that was what "Ca'line" would like to know.

Josephine made no rejoinder, but when her friend was departing she said: "Ef you see Cis'ro, I wish you'd tell him I want him. Tell him I sick, and dese chillun ain't got nuthin' to eat, and ef he don't make 'ase and come on yuh he better! Tell him I ses-so."

"Ca'line" promised to carry the message, but there was no sign of Cicero that day. On the following morning a small bag of meal arrived, but still no Cicero. Josephine was now better and left her bed, cooking some corn bread and giving it to her children with sugar-cane syrup from a jug which still survived the famine. Then she stirred up the remainder of the meal for an immense pone of bread; it has been asserted that she stirred "brick bats" into the mixture, but this was doubtless only an inference. At any rate, she baked it very brown and very hard, then got ready to go into town.

About an hour before sunset that afternoon, as the rascal Cicero sat on a goods-box in the rear of a shop in Barcelona, enjoying a chat and a stalk of sugar-cane with his chum Mamie-Lou John, he suddenly became aware that his wife was bearing down upon him with the speed and spirit of an avenger. Her gaze was fierce from afar, and, convinced that the bag of meal, instead of being received as a peace offering, had produced the effect of the last straw in the fable of the camel, Cicero trembled.

"H-yuh you is, is you?" cried the enraged woman, as she rushed upon the scene.

Cicero slid from off the goods-box and darted toward the back door of the shop, but Josephine was quick to cut off his retreat. Before he knew it he was hemmed in a corner or angle made by a pile of boxes and the house wall, facing his triumphant accuser, who stood glaring at him, one hand on her hip while the other hung hidden in the folds of her dress.

"Be ashame' o' yerself!" she said breathlessly.

"G' way from yuh, 'oman and lem-me 'lone!" cried Cicero, attempting to slip out of his prison.

"Git back, nigger!" shouted Josephine, more enraged. "Ef you don't stand up dere and listen at me," she continued, in the extravagant, wind-bag language characteristic of her kind, "I swear I'll fling you down and stomp you right yuh in de broad open day!"

At this fearful threat the culprit hesitated to move, and, steadily glaring at him, Josephine slowly lifted her left hand from the folds of her frock and brought to view the enormous pone of corn bread.

"*Dis* wut you send me to feed my chillun wid, eh?" she cried contemptuously, holding it up and breaking off a large piece. "Why n't you come home, go to work, and feed my chillun?—say! you low-down, triflin' scamp!" And she let fly the broken piece of bread and struck him in the face, to the intense amusement of the gathering crowd.

"Is you crazy, 'oman?" was Cicero's nervous ejaculation, while dodging the next piece. But she refused to desist, breaking up the pone and hurling fragment after fragment at him, sometimes striking him, but more often the house wall a foot or two to the right or the left.

"Now den," concluded Josephine, after pausing to catch her breath, "mind wut I tell you: I don't want nuthin' mo' to do wid you from dis on; and ef ever you come foolin' round my house I aim to bust you wide open, you year me! Des put yo' foot inside o' dat do' ef you dare!"

With that she raised aloft the knotty remnant of the pone of bread, and hurled it at him with all her strength. It struck the wall two feet above his head and fell upon him in a shower of fragments; after which fitting climax Josephine wheeled about with an assumption of extravagant haughtiness and contempt, and went her way homeward, angrily and audibly communing with herself all along the road. Left to himself, the humiliated Cicero lost no time in making his escape from the gibing spectators, who were loath to see the end of so unusual and so entertaining a "fight."

Meanwhile Rosetta Hightower was absorbed in her own passions, desires, and interests. She was only about eighteen, but already loved unlawfully and had entered into very close relations with the green-eyed monster. She was of the New South, had attended school during several years, and could read and write; but her passion for Cicero and her hatred of Josephine were made none the less violent thereby. After being attacked on the street she burned with a desire to revenge herself, and watched for an opportunity, meanwhile doing everything within her power to attract Cicero to herself, and keep him away from his nominal home.

Her father was a carpenter who made a fairly comfortable livelihood and occupied one of the more pretentious houses of the Neck, which he had built himself. It was thus unnecessary for Rosetta to go into service, and she employed herself in assisting her mother at home, in visiting her friends, and largely in strolling about the streets of Barcelona in the company of her admirers, and riding on the merry-go-round. She spent much of her own money and that of her admirers — the most favored among these being Cicero — on the latter.

A day or two after her encounter with Josephine, Rosetta heard some of her acquaintances speak fearfully of the powers of a certain Mammy Nanny, who enjoyed the dark reputation of being a trick-doctor or sorceress. It was claimed that this person, whose knowledge of the black art was reputed to be unlimited, had recently " put bad mouth on " (bewitched) a young black man who formerly was in robust health, but now seemed rapidly going into a decline. He had found one morning before his door the leg of a toad, two rusty nails, and a piece of brier-root, tied together with a strip of red flannel, and from that hour his health failed. An unknown enemy had procured this " bad mouth " concoction from the sorceress and placed it in the victim's path with the sinister result indicated.

Rosetta had often heard of Mammy Nanny's secret and unlawful doings, but never before had she listened with such absorbed interest and turbulent emotions. This was her opportunity; she wondered that it had not occurred to her before. Cost what it might, she determined to visit the old woman and obtain not only a love-philter which she would give to Cicero, but a sinister charm as well, with which to afflict her enemy, Josephine. The girl knew where Mammy Nanny lived, and lost no time in seeking an interview. On the same afternoon she slipped away stealthily, and penetrated the woods below the Neck, where the conjurer's hut was to be found, her courage and determination gradually failing her as she approached. The old, tumble-down house was inclosed by a zigzag rail-fence, and stood almost in the edge of a low

swamp which stretched gloomily away, all a tangle
of vines, bushes, trees, slimy moss, and stagnant
water, with here and there a towering cypress or
pine lifting itself above the average level.

A dead black-snake hung across the fence, its
blue-white belly upturned to the sky, in mute petition to the god of rain. This, at least, was Rosetta's
interpretation as she looked away with a shudder.
Climbing the "gap," the girl approached the
house, but suddenly drew back with a gasp of
terror as a small live snake ran across her path.
What if Mammy Nanny kept a house full of
snakes as pets! It might be she tamed them by
the score, and played with them, and then ate
them, thus to league herself with the devil and
acquire that unlawful power for which she was
noted. Rosetta became so unnerved, in the sway
of such thoughts, that when she reached the cabin
door, which was closed, she dared not knock.

"Mammy Nanny! Mammy Nanny!" she called
faintly at last, starting at the sound of her own
voice.

There was no answer, and the sudden, threatening cry of a hawk in the swamp so upset the girl
that she drew hastily away from the door and
started for the gap, ready to abandon her design.
But now the odor of cooking meat saluted her nos-
trils and stayed her feet. This was human, reasonable; after all, the situation might not be so full of
horrors. Rosetta concluded to steal around the

house and obtain a back view. Perhaps the rear
door would be open, and she would be able to
observe the old witch and her surroundings before
making her own presence known. Tiptoeing past
the angle of the house, the girl halted abruptly and
stood staring.

The rear inclosure was hardly to be called either
a yard or a garden, being overrun with wire-grass,
bushes, and trees in their native wild state. Near
the centre was an open space, screened on the one
hand by a thicket of blackjack, and on the other
by a Cherokee rose-vine which clambered in wild
luxuriance over everything within range, including
the tall stump of a pine. Nettles, fennels, and
jimpson-weed grew unchecked about the doorstep,
and through these for a distance of some forty feet
a path led out to the open space, in the centre of
which a fire was burning. Over the fire a large
pot swung from a tripod of three long sticks, and
near by on a corn-husk mat sat a white-haired old
black woman. Rosetta now comprehended that it
was a piece of meat stewing in this pot which had
agreeably affected her olfactories and restored her
courage. The sun shone hot upon everything and
the old woman sat baking in it, with nothing but a
cotton cloth protecting her head. Heat is the
typical negro's element.

Mammy Nanny sat with her back toward the
house, muttering darkly to herself, and Rosetta
dared not approach. However, she shifted her

position in order to obtain a better view, observing then that glowing coals had recently been raked out of the fire and that a blackened pan was heating upon them immediately at the trick-doctor's feet. She saw also that the old woman had a live dove in her hand, and wondered how she could have caught it. Hardly had she made these observations when Mammy Nanny ceased her mutterings, and, seizing the dove by the neck, deftly wrung off its head; then, without removing its feathers, she opened its quivering body with a knife and tore out its heart, and this, all covered with blood as it was, she put into the hot pan where it was soon scorched and blackened. When little was left but a tiny bit of charred flesh she took it up with her bare hand and dropped it into a small copper mortar at her feet. Having poured in a large spoonful of a grayish powder which may have been dark wheat-flour, she seized the pestle and pounded vigorously. It was while thus engaged that she was startled by the sound of a dog barking in the woods and looked searchingly about her with a pair of sharp, black, glittering eyes. These did not fail to discover Rosetta, who then felt compelled to walk forward. The girl was greatly frightened, but was the first to speak.

"How you come on, Mammy Nanny?" she asked, politely.

"Wud you doin' yuh? Wud you doin' yuh?" was the old woman's startled rejoinder, in a husky

voice, as she hastily covered the copper mortar
with a cloth lying at hand. "Who is you? Who
is you?"

"My name Rosetta Hightower. I come git you
to kunjer somebody for me."

"Who tole you I kunjer? Who tole you I
kunjer?" asked Mammy Nanny, suspiciously.
"You come to de wrong 'oman, de wrong 'oman,
and you kin des turn right round and leab yuh;
you kin leab yuh. I don't fool wid no such triflin'
young gal lak you, wut can't never keep 'er mouth
shut 'bout nut'n; I don't fool wid gal lak you."

"I won't tell nobody. I never tells nobody
nothin'. And I'll *pay* you," said Rosetta, craftily.

"Kunjun work ginse *you* ef you tell,—work ginse
you right straight," threatened the old hag.

Rosetta offered to hold up her right hand and
swear that she would never tell. She then seated
herself uninvited on the grass near the fire, staring
at the pan in which the dove's heart had been
scorched and looking curiously at the cloth which
covered the mortar.

"Wud you want wid me? Wud you up to?"
suddenly demanded Mammy Nanny.

"I want you make him love me,—love nobody
but me," faltered Rosetta, with averted eyes.

"Who dat?" asked the old woman, involuntarily
glancing toward the covered mortar. "Who dat
you want lub you?"

"Cicero — Cicero Witherspoon. I want you

make him quit dat ole fat Josephine and marry me."

Mammy Nanny's black restless eyes were riveted on the trembling girl, as if they pierced to her soul. "Dat all you want? Dat all you want?" she demanded.

"I w-want you put bad mouth on her — Josephine."

"Wud she done to you?"

"She — she — run out in de street t'other day and beat me. She pounced down on me and beat me."

"An' Cis'ro he was dere, eh?"

"He was jes' walkin' de street wid me."

Mammy Nanny reflected. "Come nex' week," she said at last. "Fotch me a chicken an' two dollahs an' I'll git it ready; I'll gie you bofe wut you want. A chicken an' two dollahs, ricollec'."

"Goodness me! — two dollars?" exclaimed Rosetta with an outraged look. "You mus' think I own a bank. Two dollars — shoo!"

Whereupon the old woman flew into a violent rage and ordered the girl off the place. "Leave yuh!" she shrieked, "an' don't you put yo' foot yuh agin; don't you put yo' foot yuh agin. An' if ever you tell anybody I'll gie you de devil, you yeh me? I'll gie you de very devil!"

Rosetta fled as if for her life, being thoroughly frightened by this outbreak. She almost made up her mind that her dark designs had better be abandoned, but only for the time. By the following day her fears were forgotten, and all her eagerness to carry out her plans returned. She begged her father to give her two dollars, but he refused; and then she went the round of her friends and attempted in vain to borrow the sum. Finally she determined to hire herself out and earn the money, and as she always did as she pleased, no objection was raised when she announced that she was going into service. She spent the greater part of a day going from house to house in Barcelona before she secured a situation. Many · housewives wanted help, but they looked askance at Rosetta, disliking her appearahce and manner of speech. During a whole morning, on mounting the steps of an ordinary or pretentious house and ringing the bell, the girl invariably made known her errand by means of the following formula: —

" Does the woman want to hire a nurse-lady? "

It is true enough that the girl of the Rosetta sort has no real desire or intention of doing her duty when in service, — true that she accomplishes as little as possible, and that little carelessly and unfaithfully, desiring only the reward; but it is equally true that the attitude of the average white housewife toward her is not encouraging. She recognizes the Rosetta type at a glance and gives her no quarter before she has been tried; without examination, she considers her, individually, as dirty, heedless, selfish, and untrustworthy as she is typically. The type of servant nearest to the self-effacing slave is what she likes, forgetting that self-effacement and humble service, except where the employer is rich and pays high, are now laid away among the fossils of another age.

Rosetta was not stupid, and it gradually dawned on her, from certain indications, that her formula was impolitic, and she reversed it, inquiring more meekly if the lady of the house wanted to hire a nurse-girl. After this she observed that her proposition received more consideration, and finally, at a house where sickness made the situation desperate, she was engaged. The girl disliked nursing heartily enough, but was determined to endure it until she obtained the desired sum of two dollars. She made little effort to please, however, and, but for her employer's extremity, would have been promptly discharged. Although not detected in it by those most nearly concerned, it was her common practice to handle the infant in her arms with rudeness until it cried itself to sleep; then, being free, she would steal away and spend an hour or so down town riding with Cicero on the merry-go-round or standing gossiping in the neighborhood of that object of perennial attraction.

At last she felt that she had stayed long enough to be entitled to an advance on her month's wages, asked for it and was not refused. She was always free to go home as soon as the baby was asleep, and on this evening departed early as usual, giving

no word of warning although fully determined not
to return. Descending the back steps, she stole
softly to the fowl-house, caught a hen by the feet
and neck all at once, thus forestalling an outcry,
and escaped to the street with her prize. With
two dollars in her pocket and a suffocating chicken
under her shawl, she walked through Barcelona
and into the Neck, lifted high with hope. To-
morrow she would again visit Mammy Nanny,
carrying the required offerings, and would no
doubt obtain the means of securing the two dearest
wishes of her heart.

She was not disappointed. The trick-doctor
promptly furnished her with a teaspoonful of a
gray powder wrapped in a fragment of an old
newspaper, instructing her to give it to Cicero in a
glass of water, after drinking a part of it herself.
Rosetta examined this powder curiously, remembering the mixture she had seen pounded in the
copper mortar, one ingredient of which she knew
to be the charred heart of a dove, and would have
liked to ask questions, but dared not. However,
there was nothing alarming in a mere powder, and
she felt reasonably tranquil until Mammy Nanny
presented her with a soiled pasteboard box about
four inches square, and instructed her to place the
contents on Josephine's doorstep before break of
day on the following morning. The painful misgivings thereby awakened were rendered the more
acute by the solemn injunction not upon any ac-

count to open the box before that hour or before she arrived at the place designated. What if a snake were in the box, and, when she opened it at that dark morning hour, what if the reptile should bite her and the curse thus fall upon her instead of her enemy! She earnestly begged that other conditions might be set, but Mammy Nanny was immovable and she was forced to submit.

During the afternoon of the same day Rosetta successfully contrived to have Cicero join her in drinking the tasteless love-philter without exciting his suspicion, but she unfortunately overslept next morning, and when she reached Josephine's gate day was breaking. Nevertheless she unhesitatingly opened the Pandora-box and emptied the evil contents upon the doorstep, afterwards making good her escape,—as she believed,—lifted high with hope that the charm would work in spite of the dawning light.

However that might be, the dawning light was unquestionably disastrous in another sense, betraying the personality of the evil-doer. A ten-year-old child of Josephine's happened to be up and out in time to see Rosetta's hurried retreat and recognize her face. Consequently by seven o'clock the Neck was in almost an uproar, Josephine going from house to house, with loud outcries, declaring that she was bewitched, that Rosetta had struck her the blow, and that she would have the culprit " up fo' de Mare," or die in the attempt.

VII.

THE mayor's court was unusually well attended next morning, the court-room, in fact, being quite full. Three cases were to come before him, two of which excited wide interest. The blacks crowded in to see what would be done with Rosetta for "bad-mouthing" Josephine; the whites gathered to witness the arraignment of a young rowdy of their own race who had distinguished himself, while slightly under the influence of drink, by shooting at some half-dozen men on the principal street and failing to hit even one. A desire to witness the spectacle of an ignorant and incompetent mayor struggling with troublesome cases, exclusive of the interest in the cases themselves, had attracted many.

The great war upheaval which brought down the leading class in so many communities, and placed the bottom rail on top, as men said, was instrumental in bringing to the front such spirits as Adam Brown, the mayor. As a small tradesman and farmer, young in years, and not a slaveholder, he had taken no interest in the war, voluntarily sacrificing nothing; during the period of profound financial prostration succeeding that struggle he had managed to hold his own, and later had forged ahead, in a material sense, of the great majority who were utterly ruined. He was of the Malvern County native homespun, without education or training of any sort to fit him for public office, but his continued prosperity, and perhaps also his marriage with the widow of George Walton, the educated refugee, had given him standing; and by posing as the friend of the uneducated white man and the negro, the vote of which latter he did not scruple to buy, he had beaten the opposing forces which represented the intelligence of the community.

This successful "man of the people" was now about fifty, iron-gray, determined, hard-fisted, but really not hard-looking; as long as he did not open his mouth he might pass for a respectable representative of a country town. The most hopeless ignorance is that which is self-satisfied. Adam Brown was the laughing-stock of Barcelona and did not know it. He knew nothing of the forms of procedure in a mayor's court, apparently considering it unnecessary that he should learn; and yet he was a sharp, shrewd man, by no means lacking in what he termed mother wit. On the present occasion he opened the examination of the cases brought before him by swearing the prisoners

as well as the witnesses, whereat the veriest tyro
of a law student was able to smile broadly.

The first case was that of four tramps who had
been surprised by the local police in a vacant house
in the suburbs, arrested and locked up. There
was absolutely nothing in the house for them to
steal, and the fact that they had built a fire and
were toasting the bread begged about town was
prima facie evidence that they had gone there
merely to enjoy their supper together and spend
the night. But a note-book had been found on one
of them, who was evidently of a literary turn, in
which there were reflections upon the sights seen
along the course of his travels, and here and there
a brief quotation from the original of Victor Hugo's
poems. This note-book had been carefully examined before the opening of court, and the foreign
lingo promptly excited grave suspicion. What if
it were a cipher containing a plot to rob the Barcelona banks! And so, after swearing each of the
four tramps, his honor eyed them very sternly and
demanded to be told their several histories.

"Gentlemen," said he, solemnly, "I expect you
to tell me the truth."

The tramping "gentlemen" very readily confessed that their starting-point had been New York
and that they were bound for Florida, that ill-health
compelled them to winter in a warmer clime, and
as they could not afford to ride, they had walked;
but when their more intimate concerns were in-

quired into, when they were taxed with the guilt of
laziness and were solemnly asked why they did not
go to work and behave like "gentlemen," two of
them said nothing and the other two laughed.
Finally, when the owner of the note-book was en-
joined to confess the intention of the dark and
mysterious sayings contained therein, and the man
endeavored to explain that he had merely quoted
from his favorite author, there were evidences of
suppressed laughter in various parts of the court-
room. The mayor was not satisfied and again examined the dark sayings, but they were as puzzling
as ever; and at length he sent the book to Robert
Morton who was in the hall, with the request that
he would examine it. Two minutes later the note-
book was returned with the message that there was
nothing therein to implicate the prisoners. After
this his honor was if possible more perplexed than
before, not knowing what to do with the accused
but unconvicted tramps.

"What would you do with 'em?" he asked in a
low voice of a lawyer seated near him.

"You might order them out of town."

"Gentlemen," said Adam Brown, promptly dis-
missing the case, "I give you twenty minutes to
leave this town." Whereupon the four "gentlemen" rose and tramped out of the court-room,
broadly smiling.

The shooting case was less embarrassing, but
still the mayor was troubled. The young law-

breaker belonged to that class of whites who were his own political and personal friends, and he feared that the imposition of a proper penalty would estrange the father and other relatives of the prisoner; on the other hand he knew that great indignation was expressed by the more intelligent element, who demanded that the offender be punished to the full extent of the law. His honor had finally concluded to please the latter by talk and the former by act. Assuming a sad and stern expression of countenance, he addressed the prisoner for fifteen minutes on the subject of his shortcomings in general and his recent crime in particular. His father was a good man, his grandfather was a good man, — the mayor declared that he knew the whole connection, — but he, the prisoner, alas, had developed into a rowdy of the worst type! It was sad, it was outrageous; this wicked young man would surely bring down his father's gray hairs in sorrow to the grave. Think of it! Nobody's life was safe if such crimes were allowed to go unpunished.

"If you had n' 'a been too drunk to shoot straight, you might 'a killed six men," concluded the mayor, solemnly. "For this most hy-c-nous crime, Gus Mitchell, I therefore fine you twenty dollars!"

The descent of a thunderbolt into the midst of the court-room would scarcely have occasioned a more complete surprise. Some of the spectators

laughed outright; others swore angrily beneath
their breath, and there was heard during several
minutes the sound of low excited comment.

The quarrel of Josephine and Rosetta was next
inquired into. The former was first questioned
and stated her complaint, indulging unchecked in
a wholesale attack on the latter's general character,
independently of the present offence. Meanwhile
the comely Rosetta looked daggers and threatened
to interrupt this tirade. The mayor listened till he
wearied of it, then bade the plaintiff sit down, and
turned to the defendant.

"What is your name?" he asked, with the first
semblance of formality as yet shown.

" Rosetta."

" Rosetta *what ?* "

" Rosetta Hightower."

Being now allowed to speak, the girl solemnly
denied the charge and returned Josephine's personal
attack with superior violence, detailing the history of
the assault made upon her in the street with pictur-
esque additions to and extravagant exaggerations
of the facts. Neither the accuser nor the accused
dared mention the name of Mammy Nanny, and
so the old sorceress herself had not been sub-
pœnaed to appear in court.

"Don't you b'lieve dat nigger," cried Josephine,
tearfully. "She gone and put bad mouth on me
des like I tell you."

"Well, how did she do it, then?"

A male friend of Josephine's (Cicero was not to be found) then reluctantly undid a package wrapped in a newspaper and the dreaded "kunjer" found on the doorstep was exhibited in court. The mayor ordered it to be placed on the table before him and examined it with some curiosity, but with signs of growing impatience.

"'T ain't nothin' but a lot of foolishness," he promptly exclaimed, and seemed to wonder that Josephine still gazed upon it with evidences of the liveliest terror.

The evil charm consisted of a large live toad with a strip of red flannel about twenty inches long securely fastened to its right hind foot, the other end of the flannel being attached to a small pine splinter. Knots were tied at intervals along the red strip, and here and there were fastened short pieces of white sewing-thread. Attached to the centre of the string was a small red-flannel bundle, in which were found several roots and sewing-needles.

"Look h-yer, Josephine, ain't you got no better sense than to think this pile o' trash can hurt you?" asked the mayor, contemptuously.

Poor Josephine shook her head sadly and wiped her overflowing eyes. "I feel it in my bones a'ready," she said, with solemn conviction.

The practice of or belief in witchcraft appears to be widespread among the blacks in the South. The negroes of the Virginia tobacco-farms, the rice plantations of Carolina and Georgia, the sugar-cane plantations of Louisiana, and elsewhere, have been found to have as firm a belief in the black art as the naked savages of the pathless African bush. Among them, therefore, the adept in the art, the wholly or semi-professional trick-doctor or con-jurer, is a person of great importance and an object of dread mingled with something of venera-tion. The chief business of the adept, whether man or woman, is the casting of spells upon speci-fied victims, or, on the other hand, the bringing to bear of counteracting influences against an evil charm already active from some other agency. At one time he is sought by negroes who believe themselves to have been bewitched by a rival pro-fessional, and again by such as may desire a spell to be cast upon those who have aroused their hatred. In the latter case the adept usually operates by causing a small bundle of apparently trivial articles to be placed either inside or near the house of the victim, who promptly recognizes the medium of the art, the material used varying little, and is at once the prey of great fear and distress of mind.

Once convinced that he has been bewitched, the negro sinks into the deepest despondency, and, unless persuaded that the baleful influence has been removed, his health declines steadily. The trick-doctor is thus a medium through which per-sonal enemies strike secretly at each other, and

his presence in a community necessarily tends to
keep alive the recollection of injuries and stimu-
lates the desire for revenge. The manner of con-
veying the curse varies somewhat in different
localities and at different times, but no "bad-
mouth" bugbear is apt to be found without one or
more of the following ingredients, — bits of red
flannel, pieces of brier-root, sewing-needles, toads
either alive or dismembered, some portion of a
snake, cotton thread, rusty nails, etc. Sometimes
a rude human effigy covered with blood or pierced
through the heart with a nail is used, suggesting
the burning of clay or waxen images in the middle
ages, which was supposed to cause the persons
named to be "melted or dried away by continual
sickness." [1]

Adam Brown was much perplexed and annoyed
over the case, and finally dismissed it without
either passing judgment or imposing a penalty.
The evidence against Rosetta depended wholly on
Josephine's ten-year-old, which could not therefore
be taken as conclusive; and even had she been
convicted, the mayor failed to see what punishment could be rightfully inflicted on a young
woman for merely throwing a "lot of trash" on a
neighbor's doorstep. Sorcery was a thing of past

---

[1] Compare with the ingredients of the "hell-broth" stewed
in a caldron by the three witches in Macbeth, and note the
striking similarities, as the live toad, the adder's fork, lizard's
leg, fillet of a fenny snake, etc.

ages, and the law did not recognize it, so far as the mayor could learn.

"Take this trash and throw it out of the window," he said to Josephine's friend, in great disgust. "And," he continued severely, "you two women can go, and don't you persume to come before me again with any more such foolishness. If you know what's good for you, you'll keep the peace after this. If I hear of you fightin' in the street again, I'll have you both put on the chain-gang." And, having duly impressed them with his determination to make good this fearful threat in case of a second offence, he announced that his court was adjourned.

"Look at him," said Morton, with a smile, as the mayor strode pompously out of the court-room. "He looks as if he imagined that he had won the applause of mankind. He'll be running for the legislature next. Then he'll want to go to Congress."

"What an exhibition of incompetence," said Colonel Sanford, in rejoinder to Morton. "Those very tramps were able to laugh at our mayor. Well, it is only another object lesson in the evils resulting from the disorderly association of two races in one State. If the negro and his bought vote were out of the way, it would be impossible for such a man as Adam Brown to ride into power. Of course he would have a following among his like, but he could not defy the banded intelligence of this or any other community."

Had Adam Brown overheard them he would doubtless have chuckled and repeated his favorite aphorism to the effect that now-a-days the bottom rail was on top. If questioned on the subject, he would have remarked in homely language that society in Barcelona was divided between those who had seen better days and those who had not. He "thanked his stars" that he belonged to the latter class, that his best days were now; and he would not have exchanged present prosperity for any amount of superior intelligence linked with by-gone success.

Rosetta walked triumphantly away, but the sad-faced Josephine lingered in the court-house square and received the condolences of a number of friends, the female portion of which were less absorbed even in sucking the snuff-sticks always in their mouths than in discussing the merits of this interesting case. The majority advised her not to give herself any further uneasiness, arguing that the discovery of her enemy and her prompt outcry and resistance of the evil, if not her appeal to the civil authorities, ought to break the spell. Some thought that the failure to deposit the charm at the door before break of day was in itself sufficient to break its force. The professor, indeed, went so far as to laugh at her fears, declaring that witch-craft was a superstition of the past, and that all she had to fear was her own weakness in allowing herself to be disturbed. The parson, however,

who was also present, reminded the professor that
magical arts were mentioned in Holy Writ, and
he thought it was still possible for men to league
themselves with the devil.

" The white folks don't b'lieve in it,— they don't
b'lieve in nothin' hardly," he said, " but all our
people b'lieves in it."

However, the consensus of opinion was that she
need have little or no fear, and Josephine was at
length in a measure reassured. Rosetta would
have been sorry to learn this, but now that her
venom had been indulged, she cared little whether
her victim suffered or not. All her hopes were
now centred on the success of the love-philter
which already seemed assured, for since drinking
it Cicero had devoted himself to her more assidu-
ously than ever before.

Sam Thomas had attended the mayor's court
and after its adjournment retired to his office.
Josephine had seen him go, and now, leaving her
friends, she followed him there. Entering his
office, she took note of three empty beer bottles
on the floor near the young lawyer's desk, and in
the same moment, without consciously connecting
the two facts, observed that he was growing rather
stout. The young man had been bowed over his
desk, pen in hand, laboriously copying and carefully imitating the characteristics of the letters in
the words of a manuscript document which lay
before him. The sound of the approaching step

caused him to start guiltily and hastily gather up the two sheets and crowd them into a drawer.

"Well, Josephine, what can I do for you?" he then asked in a friendly tone, leaning back in his chair and putting his feet up on the corner of his desk. He did not invite her to sit down, and she stood throughout the interview.

"What you gwine charge to git me a — what you call it? — a v-voce?"

"A divorce, eh? So you are going to quit Cicero?"

"Done quit him a'ready," said Josephine, with heavy dignity, "and I want to git a divoce 'cordin' to law. Some dem women in de Neck quit dey husbands right and left and take up wid new ones, and don't stop to study 'bout no divorce. But I ain't dat sort. I'm like white folks,— I want my divoce 'cording to law."

"That's right," applauded Thomas. "Well, I reckon you won't have any trouble. You can plead desertion,— from what I hear."

"I kin dat. But what you charge?"

"I won't charge but fifteen dollars."

"*Fifteen dollahs!*" cried Josephine, with expanding eyes. "How in de name o' goodness I gwine pay you fifteen dollahs, man? You mus' think I *made* out o' money. Shoo!"

"Great Scott! you don't meant to say that ain't cheap?" retorted the lawyer. "I ought to charge fifty."

Josephine looked undone. She had never had fifteen dollars in her pocket at one time in her life, and the divorce was therefore impossible. The idea of gradual payment in smaller sums did not seem to occur to her. She made a movement toward the door, remarking with an air of great discouragement, " I'll go see dem t'other lawyers and see ef I can't git it done cheaper."

" Hold on," cried Thomas. " Maybe we can make a trade. I saw you comin' out of a certain house the other day," he continued, as she halted and turned back. " Do you go there often, — to Mrs. Lawrence's ? "

" Dat I does! Me and Miss Reba mighty good friends," cried Josephine, eagerly, hope kindling in her breast. She saw a light; she almost antici- pated the " trade." " I gits work for Miss Reba," she continued, " and I haf to go dere 'most eve'y two three days."

" You get what for Miss Reba ? "

" I — I goes dere to do jobs for her," she stam- mered, recollecting that the sewing was to be a secret as far as possible. " Miss Reba," she hur- ried on, " is de nices', puttyes' young white lady in dis town."

" She is, eh ? " rejoined the young lawyer, looking as if he admired his client's taste. " Well, Josephine, what I want is for you to speak a good word for me to Miss Reba, and if you 'll do that, and do it up brown, I 'll tell you what *I'll* do. I 'll get your divorce through for nothing. You understand ? "

"Will you, Mr. Thomas, sho' nuf?" cried Josephine, overjoyed. "Yes-sir-ee, I'll speak a good word for you eve'y time I go dere. You kin 'pend on me. I'm good at dat."

"But you'll have to be mighty careful and not overdo it," he cautioned her; "and besides, here's the point, it will do no good for you to speak a good word for me unless you speak a bad word for another fellow, who is, I'm afraid, ahead of me there. See?"

Ah! it was not so easy, then. Josephine's face fell; what if she got herself into trouble? "Who dat other one?" she asked.

"Bob Morton."

The woman now looked more troubled than ever. She had once done Morton's washing when her friend, Maum Katie, was ill, and she had pronounced him in thought "a mighty nice man." "What I gwine tell Miss Reba 'bout *him?*" she asked, stubbornly. "I ain't never h-yeared nothin' bad about him."

"Well, I don't say there is anything 'specially bad about him," replied Thomas, craftily. "He's smart and he's considered a pretty good sort of a fellow, but he used to be a wild boy and he drinks yet. Only the other night a friend of his had to carry him home. You can tell her that, can't you? Young ladies are usually afraid of men who drink."

Josephine's glance fell upon the empty beer

bottles as she rejoined, " I never yeared dat 'bout him befo'."

" You don't hear everything."

" Well, Mr. Thomas, if *you* ses so, of co'se hit 's so." Josephine was coming back to her own concerns, and the question of saving fifteen dollars represented itself. " I 'll tell her," she finally agreed, " and I 'll do my bes' for you."

" You must n't tell her that I told you, remember. You must be very careful."

" I 'll tell her dat what I year folks say."

" Don't waste any time about it, either," he called after her as she was going. " I 'll draw up your papers right away, and if I find you 've kept your part of the trade, you won't have to pay me a cent, understand."

After reiterating her promise, Josephine departed, leaving the young lawyer chuckling over his " trade." " All is fair in love and war," he remarked gayly, as he got up and walked about the room, bestowing hopeful glances upon the portraits of the four " big" men which adorned the walls.

" Well, if dat ain't mean ! " said Josephine aloud, as she went down the stairs, referring wholly to the lawyer's part in the agreement. She failed to characterize her own part. As said before, Josephine was of an easy conscience.

VIII.

ADAM BROWN lived in one of the more pretentious houses of Barcelona, which, although central, was suburban in its surroundings of trees, shrubs, and flowers, — not to mention the sugar-cane patch in the rear. One afternoon, two or three weeks after the holding of his court which has been mentioned, the mayor came home early in order to overlook the planting of fall-turnips in his vegetable garden. Having spent an hour there, he cut a stalk of cane and returned to the house, peeling and chewing it as he crossed the newly swept back-yard and dropping both peelings and pith at almost every step. On the front piazza he found Reba Lawrence with his wife and step-daughter, the subject of their conversation being Miss Black, who had just passed on horseback without a companion or attendant. Whenever she could spare a few hours from her work, the latter was known to hire a horse and take long rides on the country roads in the pursuit of health; those now commenting could well understand that she needed the exercise and the fresh air, but Mrs. Brown thought it unsafe, and the two girls agreed.

"Too many triflin' darkies hangin' around every-where now-a-days," the former was saying, as her husband appeared.

"Who's that you talkin' about, — Miss Francie Black?" he asked, after saluting Reba. "Oh, she's all right. Them Yankee women know how to take care of themselves."

"Adam, don't throw them peelin's down there in the yard," exclaimed Mrs. Brown, in distress. "I jes' had it swept yesterday." She called one of her children from within and sent for a waste-basket.

Owing to the way in which he had been brought up and had lived during the greater part of his life, the mayor was wholly indifferent to litter, and disorder in general, never seeming to see it. Not so his wife; during her engagement to George Walton, and after their marriage, she had tried hard to make herself the equal of his sister, and had in some ways succeeded. Where she had failed was in her efforts to educate herself, though even here she had made praiseworthy advance. After marrying Adam Brown, however, she had gradually relapsed into the old slip-shod manner of speech, furnishing a constant source of regret to her sister-in-law, her niece, and her own daughter, whose educational opportunities had far surpassed her own.

"I like to see 'em come — them Yankees," continued the mayor, looking after the disappearing horsewoman. "Colonel Sanford says we can never count on thrifty fureign immigrants as long as the nigger is in the way, and we want all the Yankees we can get to help us develop this country. The trouble is *they* don't want to butt agin the nigger any more than the fureigner does. Mighty few of 'em come South."

He generously offered each of the ladies a "round" of cane before seating himself within range of the waste-basket. His wife was knitting, and the two girls were looking through a magazine together; all declined the proffered sweet.

"You ain't lookin' well, Reba," he remarked, kindly. "You stay home too close."

The girl's face flushed under his keen glance and she answered quickly that she was quite well, wondering if he could detect the signs of slow starvation, although aware that she was less thin than a few weeks before. In proportion as her mother's appetite failed, Reba had eaten more and in some measure improved.

"It's time both you girls was gittin' married," Adam Brown continued, with a twinkle of the eye. "Reba, I hope you ain't as hard to please as Betty. *She* won't have Jack Sanford, and she won't have Jim Jones. A man would have to be cut out and moulded in gold to suit Betty."

"Do, papa!"

"Jack *is* too much of a boy, I reckon, but you'll go a long ways before you'll find a better man than Jim."

"You ought to see him dance!" said Betty, cruelly.

"It always seems a pity," the mayor proceeded, smiling, "for a girl to fool along till she's old and laid on the shelf. You girls ain't ugly enough to be old maids. How old are you, Reba?"

"Now, Adam, that ain't polite," exclaimed Mrs. Brown. "Young ladies ain't supposed to have no age."

The girls laughed, and Reba, with a slightly aggrieved look, mentioned that she was only twenty, and was in no hurry to surrender her freedom. The man who could persuade her to give up hers, Betty declared, was yet to appear upon the scene. At this juncture the attention of all was attracted to a passing vehicle containing young Morton and Jones, who lifted their hats in honor of the group on the piazza. They were evidently driving out of town on the same road taken by Miss Black.

"That buggy-load reminds me of Bill Arp's lecture on the 'Cracker and the Cavalier,'" said Betty.

"You mean Jim's a cracker, eh? Well, we're all crackers when it comes to that, I reckon," said the mayor.

"Speak for yourself, please," requested Betty. "My father was not a cracker, and neither am I."

" Well, anyhow the bottom rail is on top now-a-days. You can 't git around that."

" Mamma says," put in Reba, taking Betty's side, "that it may have more money, but it can never really be, on top."

" Does anybody mean to tell me that Jim Jones with all he 's got ain't as good as that po' stuck-up Bob Morton ? "

" He ain't stuck-up, Adam. I never heard that," ventured Mrs. Brown. " And they say he 's a fine young man, and smart, too."

" He belongs to that po' stuck-up crowd anyhow, and he ain't got nothin'."

" He 's a gentleman, and Jim Jones is n't," declared Betty, with an air of certainty which staggered the mayor in spite of his well-settled opinions.

The expression of Reba's eyes showed feeling, but she gladly left the defence to her cousin. She told herself that it was not for Morton's sake that she felt indignant; the " stuck-up crowd" meant in a political sense the intelligence of the community, in a social sense the old families, and her mother and Betty's dead father were as much or more included in the mayor's denunciation than young Morton himself. Mrs. Brown came to the rescue, conscious that they were verging upon dangerous ground. She had not entirely forgotten her first husband, and she believed in the old families, but she also believed in Adam Brown. Her policy was pacific always, and she hoped in

time to fully reconcile the two apparently heterogeneous elements existing in her own family. Her
method now was to bestow a warning look upon
Betty and begin to crowd her husband with questions about gardening. So was he diverted, and
the girls, left to themselves, returned to their
magazine.

After Miss Black rode by, bowing to the ladies
on the piazza, the same question which they began
to discuss arose in her own mind, — was it safe to
take those lonely rides unattended? She was
quick to answer and ride on into the country in a
perfectly tranquil state of mind. Yes, it was safe,
— reasonably so, at least. Miss Black was not
timid, and the idling, rambling negroes whom she
sometimes met on the country roads, having never
molested her, failed to excite her apprehension.
As for the white men, it seemed to her that, as a
class, they were unusually respectful toward all
women. Only a few days since she had passed an
excited crowd in Barcelona, the behavior of which
excited her astonishment. Two men were in the
midst of an angry and abusive dispute, and the
crowd about them occupied the whole sidewalk,
awaiting with intense interest the coming fight,
which promised to be no trifle. As Miss Black
paused before deciding to step into the street and
cross to the opposite side, the whisper, " A lady! "
suddenly went through the crowd, and instantly it
parted and rolled back, a small portion flattening

itself neatly against the wall, while the bulk precipitated itself into the street as from the volition of
one man. The angry voices were hushed, and the
way was clear; the lady passed, the two sections
of the crowd swayed together again, and the interrupted wrangle was resumed. Men who treated
her with such consideration at such a time could
do her no harm at any other; so Miss Black
reasoned.

She had made rather a late start, and when about
a mile and a half out of town it occurred to her
that she ought to turn back. She did not, however, being unable to resist the temptation to pro-
long her ride. She revelled in the fine October air,
the delicious odor from the endless forests of pine,
the autumn color of sky and leaf,— for along the
water courses the monotony of green pines was
relieved by other growth. Pushing on, she descended a slope which led downward through the
dense woods bordering what is locally termed a
branch. This, however, was more than a branch,
being in reality a considerable creek, and was
known as Black Swamp.

As she rounded a bend and the stream came
into view, Miss Black momentarily glimpsed the
dark figures of two men somewhere between
herself and the flowing water. Occupied immediately with the stumbling of her horse she did
not observe these two figures as they darted into
the bush; and when she again looked up, the de-

serted road caused her to wonder if she had seen aright in the first place, meanwhile continuing to advance without apprehension.

"Jim's gone to law about some land, and he give the case to Bob Morton," the mayor had remarked, as the two young men drove past his house, and it was this business which was taking them into the country this afternoon. As they drove on, they occasionally observed a horsewoman far in advance of them, but the windings of the road for the most part screened her from their view. The sand was too heavy for fast driving and before a great while they lost sight of her altogether. As they neared Black Swamp, however, they heard a faint and far cry which immediately suggested the horsewoman. It was a cry of distress, and evidently a woman's. The two young men looked at each other as if to ask, "Did you hear that?"

"A lady!" said Morton, excitedly, as the cry was heard again. He seized the whip and they dashed down the slope at a break-neck speed.

Perhaps it was five minutes later, perhaps more, when an old negro living on a small farm in the neighborhood of Black Swamp was made aware that something unusual had just taken place. He heard no pistol shots, for the two young men who had driven down the slope in such desperate haste were unarmed; but, as he was emerging from the dense woods of the swamp where he kept a partridge trap, the sound of some one running through the brush behind him attracted his attention and caused him to halt. He observed that the person who ran had set his face toward Barcelona, although it was clearly his intention to keep to the woods and avoid the road; he also observed that this person, whose face was black but too far away to be recognized, literally tore through the woods, regardless of the low, overhanging branches which whipped him as he passed, and the lightwood-knots or fallen logs, unseen in the brush, which bruised his feet and barred his way. Clearly he was a fugitive and believed that his life depended on his speed.

The old negro, commonly known in the neighborhoood as "Mingo" or "Uncle Mingo" (no one ever heard mention of his surname, if indeed he had one) made these observations in silence, then proceeded on his way, soon arriving in the neighborhood of the road. Here he halted and looked forth cautiously before exposing himself, the glimpse of a terrified fugitive having awakened vague fears for his own safety. Surveying the lonely road, he saw that it was deserted at every point save one, about fifty yards distant, where stood an abandoned horse and buggy. Before he had time to speculate as to the whereabouts of the driver, a young white man ran out of the woods, and, having possessed himself of a piece of rope from the bottom of the vehicle, hastily returned the way he had come.

Old Mingo then heard indistinct voices, and knew

well that a serious event had occurred, but did not budge from his place. After waiting but a very short time, he saw the same man reappear, accompanied by another, the two bearing a heavy burden between them. What this burden was he did not at first quite discern, but, as they lifted it and placed it on the floor of the buggy, he saw that it was a man, a negro, apparently senseless and bound hand and foot with ropes. One of the men sprang immediately into the vehicle, gathered up the reins, and drove off slowly, the other man following a short distance on foot in order to give a few parting instructions, as it seemed.

"I 'm glad it will soon be dark," he was saying, as they drew near. "You can get to the jail without attracting a crowd. Just get Dave Hardy to lock him up, Jim, and don't say a word to a soul. We must keep it quiet for her sake."

They were now very near, and old Mingo, ere he drew back among the bushes, took note that the inert body on the floor of the buggy had begun to move and groan.

"The black devil's comin' to," remarked the man who drove. "He 's bleedin' like a hog. You hit him a powerful lick with that light'ood knot."

"I meant to kill him," said the other, with eyes of fire, "when I saw him trying to pull her off her horse; but after I knocked him senseless I had enough of it."

"I tell you what, she had spunk," declared the

man in the buggy. "The way she spurred that
horse and made him jump!"

At this juncture the man afoot halted and turned
back. "Now I must see that she gets home," he
said, reflectively. "Jim, I suppose I'd better go
all the way with her—don't you think so? She
might faint again, you know," he added, in a
troubled, perplexed way.

The other called out "Yes," adding in a lower
voice as he drove on, "I'm glad the job don't fall
to me." And so they separated.

About five minutes later, having meanwhile hastened to plant his feet upon his own domain which
was not far away, old Mingo, who now more than
vaguely comprehended what had occurred, saw a
white woman pass on horseback along the road to
Barcelona accompanied by a man afoot.

Meanwhile the fleet-footed fugitive made good
his escape, having taken the alarm and bounded
away before his presence was even suspected by
the rescuers. Luckily for him the unbroken woods
continued to the outskirts of the town, and he was
thus able to run at his best pace and attract no
attention. Making a wide détour, he entered Barcelona by another, far distant road, and hastened
to compose his features, cease his quick breaths,
and show himself conspicuously on the principal
street as well as in the restaurants and other haunts
of the blacks, thus making his alibi secure. Long
before Jim Jones drove into town with his prisoner

all this had been accomplished, and the fugitive was on the lookout for his arrival, idling carelessly at a corner and covertly scanning every vehicle on the street which came in from the Black Swamp road. When at last the one he watched for appeared and quietly turned toward the jail, he boldly stepped forward and inquired if Mr. Jones wanted any more cotton pickers on his place.

"Who's that, — Mamie-Lou John?" was the response, without drawing rein. "I thought you was too stuck-up to pick cotton. You can see me 'bout it to-morrow." The vehicle was then driven rapidly on, and the crafty fugitive turned away well satisfied with his chances of escaping the halter.

It was quite dark and a whippoorwill was calling cheerfully in a neighboring dell when the horse-woman and her attendant halted where two ways met on the outskirts of the town. Little had passed between them by the way, and that little referring in no way to what had occurred. Never once did he look directly at her, and, aware of this, she by and by looked at him freely and often, — too often, she told herself afterward. His tall, sinewy form, his thin, sallow face and firm jaw, his eyes of fire, above all, the atmosphere about him of true manliness and of genuine and simple devotion to the woman in his care, combined to form a picture which would perhaps haunt her memory with a lasting and dangerous persistence.

"I'll turn off here," he said, halting, conscious

that they would attract attention if they thus entered the town. "I think you are all right now and can go on alone."

She assented, then leaned forward and put out her hand to him in the darkness. As he took it and they said good-night, she was quickly conscious that his hand was very cold. "Mr. Morton," she began abruptly, in a very low voice, "a second time — I owe to your — to you — everything —" She seemed unable to proceed.

"I must hurry," he hastened to say, with an embarrassed manner. "I am going to have a chill."

"I am so sorry," she murmured, still halting. He moved on then with another "good-night," and thus they separated.

This, however, was no subterfuge on his part, although he distinctly aimed to cut short her labored and difficult words of gratitude. Had they remained in each other's company five minutes longer she would have heard his teeth chatter. It was not his fated day for a chill, but he had got his feet wet and the cool night air did the rest. It had been his intention to stop at the jail and reiterate his wish that "the thing" be kept quiet, but, bent over and shivering as he was, he found it necessary to go directly home and put himself to bed.

As late as half-past eleven o'clock that evening a light still burned in Robert Morton's room. The chill had left him two hours since, and his mother had removed the heavy pile of blankets beneath which he lay quaking so long, bidding him good-night and expecting him soon to be asleep. But he was still awake at half-past eleven, when a light tapping on one of his windows opening on the front piazza attracted his attention.

" Who 's that ? " he called.

" Jim Jones."

" Push up the sash and come in," Morton directed from the bed, and a moment later one of Jones's long legs was thrust over the low window-sill. " Put the sash all the way down; I 'm all in a sweat," Morton added.

" This is a funny time o' night for me to be comin'," apologized Jones, crossing to the bed and seating himself; " but I thought I 'd stop and tell you all about it."

" I 'm glad to see you."

" When I come back to town with the boys jes' now I saw yo' light and I thought you was still awake. Dick Marshall said the light was in your room, and so I stopped."

" Well, what have you to tell me ? "

" Well, I told Dave Hardy jes' what you told me when I turned the nigger over to him, and he said, ' All right.' He give out the report that the nigger was caught robbin' a white lady on the big road ; but after supper I went around and told a few of the boys jes' how it was, but that you and me had decided to keep the name of the lady back, and I

did n't tell 'em who she was. Them boys was jes'
rip-snortin', every one of 'em, especially after I
told 'em it was Cicero Witherspoon, and they 'lowed
they 'd lynch him or raise hell. They jes' reared.
I 'd had enough of it a'ready, but nothin' would
do but I must go with 'em and show 'em the place.
So about a dozen of us went down to the jail without raisin' no row, and told Dave Hardy he mought
jes' as well hush up his talk to begin with, for it
wan't no use. He didn 't care nohow, — he was in
with us from the start; but of course he made a
stand jes' for show tell the boys drawd their pistols
on him, and then he give the nigger right up. Well,
we took him out in a spring wagon and the boys
swung him up over the very spot. Sam Thomas
and most of 'em took a pop at him before he
stopped kickin', but I could n't. Look like to me
hangin' was enough. The boys held a torch and
Sam wrote a notice in a disguised hand and pinned
it on the nigger's coat. He begged pitiful. It was
hard to stand. And, look-a-h-yer, Bob, that Cicero,
after he confessed it all, had the face to swear that
Mamie-Lou John was with him and got off in the
bushes just in time for me and you not to see him.
Of course I told him he was a brazen liar, and — "

"But how do we know?" interrupted Morton,
musingly. "It may be true. It seemed rather
strange to me that he should have made the
attempt alone, she being on horseback."

"But I saw Mamie-Lou John myself jes' as I

drove in town; he tried to hire to me to pick cotton. And some of the boys said they seen him hangin' round town all the evenin'."[1]

" Oh, well, then."

" I reckon Colonel Sanford will rear when he hears about it to-morrow," said Jones, at the conclusion of his brief outline of the dark tragedy.

" Yes," rejoined Morton, gloomily, " and I tell you it is a bad business, Jim, though it *does* seem to be the only way to check it."

[1] Afternoon.

IX.

COLONEL SANFORD did not "rear," as was predicted, but expressed himself freely and in forcible language as he stood in conversation with his neighbors on the street the next day. He characterized lynch-law as a relic of barbarous times, and deplored its brutalizing influence upon the youth of his community and country. He said that lynchers were no doubt actuated by a desire to see justice meted out to criminals, but at the same time they were largely dominated by race hatred and, in the case of young men especially, by a love of wild excitement which some would miscall "fun," flocking to the scene of a lynching in the sway of similar emotions to those experienced by the spectators of an ancient gladiatorial contest or a modern bull-fight. He declared that lynch-law could be called justifiable only where the courts were notoriously weak and corrupt, refusing to visit a just punishment upon the guilty, and such a condition of things was happily rare at the present day. The white race had everywhere the upper hand, and there was no possible escape for a negro criminal justly convicted. Would anybody contend that Cicero Witherspoon could have escaped punishment had he been allowed to stand his trial for robbery? He would have escaped the halter, indeed, but would have been punished to the full extent of the law.

However, when a better-informed bystander asserted that robbery was the mere incidental of the blackest of crimes — happily prevented — the Colonel's argument halted. The better class of Southern men condemn the lynching of the blacks in the case of all crimes but one. Although the name of the rescued was determinedly withheld, the real nature of the attempted crime became generally known in the course of the morning, not, however, before a flaming account of the affair as first reported was sent over the wires to the newspapers.

There is a class of people everywhere who discover an unaccountable pleasure in looking at dead bodies, whether calmly at rest in the course of nature, mangled through terrifying accident, slain in battle, or hanged on the gallows. From an early hour of the morning until night the people of this kind, both white and black, might have been seen going and returning on the road to Black Swamp. Even some of the most respectable could not rest satisfied until they had imprinted the hideous picture on their memories, ostensibly

going out to drive, but failing not to halt at Black
Swamp and look long upon the lifeless thing which
hung there, with the solemn warning pinned across
its breast : "*This is the way we protect our wives
and daughters.*"

Josephine received the news at first with incredu-
lity, and then with tears and loud lamentations.
Although she had cast Cicero off utterly and regarded him as nothing to her henceforth, although
her early affection for him had withered and died
out completely, her love seemed now to come to life
and flourish again, — now that he was dead and gone
forever. His crime did not engage her reflections;
in the tumult of her grief she was conscious only
that the father of her last children had been cruelly
put to death. The Neck resounded with her cries,
her distress increasing as she recalled the recent
attempt to " bad-mouth " or bewitch her, and recognized the present calamity as a most probable result
of the evil charm.

Later in the day she went into town and walked
through the streets with streaming eyes, calling
upon the mayor in his office. She did not beseech
or demand the arrest of the lynchers, — would
scarcely have done so, in fact, if their names had
been known; she merely asked permission to take
down and bury her dead, proposing to go out to
Black Swamp with a few of her friends in a wagon.
Adam Brown was greatly perplexed by this request. He was well aware that the authorities

could not act in the matter, they being on the side
of law and order, unless they should act against the
lynchers; but that they did not intend to do, and
therefore they were supposed to know nothing of
what had occurred.

"H-yer you come a-botherin' me again," he
complained, greatly annoyed; but a happy thought
struck him and his face cleared. "I ain't got nothin' to do with it," he declared. "It's outside o'
town, outside o' the corporate limits, and outside o' my jurisdiction. It's the sheriff's business,
the Malvern County sheriff, and the curoner's.
They tell me the curoner left town soon this mornin' before he heard of it. It's his business to take
the body down and hold a inquest. I ain't the
one to see; go see the sheriff. But if I was you,
Josephine, I'd let the body stay there tell to-morrow,
anyhow. Feelin' runs mighty high, and somebody
might stop you. People want it to hang there all
day as a warnin', you know."

The mayor spoke kindly enough, but Josephine
saw at once that he could not be persuaded to act,
and so she withdrew, wiping her swollen eyes. She
at once sought the sheriff, and being unable to find
him, returned home, her grief in a measure as-
suaged by certain thoughts which crowded upon
her. She was now free to marry another and better
husband, — one, in fact, already selected; and her
distasteful bargain with Sam Thomas, which indeed
saved to her the fifteen-dollar divorce fee, but was

likely to get her into trouble, could be repudiated
forthwith. Josephine was comforted also by the
reflection that the complete and public disruption
of all relations with Cicero had occurred several
weeks since, and that her neighbors would not
necessarily expect her now to assert herself as his
wife. In reality she cared for him no longer, and
was only moved by compassion and the recollection of earlier days.

Very different was Rosetta's state of mind. Her
love for Cicero was the uppermost passion of her
nature, and in order to win him for herself alone
she had already gone far beyond the utmost which
a more timid character would have dared. The
news of his fate overwhelmed her with a grief
which was rendered the more bitter by remorse,
by the fear that the misfortune which she had attempted to bring upon Josephine had fallen upon
Cicero, thus indirectly upon herself. After the
first paroxysm she did not shed tears and loudly
lament after the fashion of Josephine, but wandered
about the streets with dry eyes, compressed lips,
and an absent manner. She stood and listened to
what each talker had to say on the steps of the
restaurants, in the alleys, or other haunts of the
blacks,— the fearful murmurs of the old women, the
wild threats of the young men, the moderation of
their elders, — but said nothing herself, only heark-
ening and looking from side to side with the manner of one struck dumb.

She knew of Josephine's intention to go out and take the body down, and not until after nightfall did she learn that the former's plan had not been carried out.   Not till then was Rosetta aroused from her waking-trance.   She swore that the body should be taken down that night, and immediately set about accomplishing the task; she made propositions to one man after another among her acquaintances, trying first persuasion and then offering payment far beyond her means to such as would agree to go out with her to Black Swamp in a wagon.   But not one of them could be induced to go, their disrelish for the undertaking arising not so much from the fear of hindrance and possible bodily harm as a superstitious dread of encountering the dead body in the dark.   While soliciting the aid of these several persons, Rosetta was continually on the lookout for Mamie-Lou John, who was Cicero's friend as well as her own, and who might therefore muster up courage to render the assistance which she so much desired.

It was as late as nine o'clock when she sought him at the house of Parson Smith, in the Neck, whither she had been directed.   There, in conversation with the schoolmaster and the parson, she found him, distinguished by scarcely the air of one equally guilty and narrowly escaping the fate of Cicero.   They sat before an open fire which was the only light in the room.   As the evening was only slightly cool, the door stood wide, and Rosetta opened the gate, walked forward, and looked in, without being observed. After a few moments of hesitation she sat down on the steps and waited quietly. She was afraid of the parson and of the schoolmaster; besides, she was weary, and it might be that Mamie-Lou would get up and come out presently.

"I'll pay 'em for hangin' Cicero yit," the man she sought was saying, angrily. "You jes' wait tell I git a good chance — jes' watch me!"

"Oh, shet up that," said the portly parson, in reproof. "You better behave yourse'f ef you know what good for you. You better take warnin' by Cicero and go to work. Hangin' round doin' nothin' what got him into trouble. Idleness is the devil's workshop, you see it so."

"Ef I could clerk in a sto'," said the young outlaw, slightly impressed, "I would go to work, but I ain't goin' to plough nor pick cotton for nobody."

"That's where the trouble comes in," remarked the schoolmaster, who unmistakably had the most intelligent face of the three. "Soon's ever our young men git a little education they think manual labor is too low-down for 'em, and there ain't nothin' else hardly for 'em to do. Some few of us kin be teachers and some few kin be preachers, among our own color, but the rest got to pick cotton, plough, or loaf. The white man owns nearly everything, all the stores and the mills and the farms, and he controls all the government offices,

and of course he ruther have white men to fill all
the places and do all the work except ploughin'
and hoein' and sich as that.   It's mighty hard for
us, but we can't blame them, 'cause you know this
is a white man's country.   If it was a black man's
we-all 'ud do the same thing.   Co'se we would.
They do it in Hayti.   I was readin' only the other
day about how black dukes and markerses and all
sich big dogs ride over white men in the streets
there jes' like they owned 'em.[1]   They ain't bound
to recognize a white man's rights there, and they
don't do it neither."

"Whay is dat Hayti, 'Fesser Brice?   Dat's the
place for me!"   exclaimed Mamie-Lou, with
enthusiasm.

"A white man don't count for nothin' in Liberia
neither," continued the professor, ignoring the
interruption.   "The two races nat'ally ain't got
no use for one 'n other, that's what's the matter, —
'race antipathy' Colonel Sanford calls it.   We show
it jes' as much as dey do when we git the upper
hand.   We was n't made to live together in one
country nohow, and we can't do it and have peace.
The only chance for our people to prosper is to
colonize off to ourselves somewheres."

"Don't you think we could git along all right
with the Northern white folks, Brother Brice?"
asked the parson.

[1] He had read an extract from James Anthony Froude's
"English in the West Indies."

" I useter think so, but I don't no longer."

" They sot us free, you know."

" They sot us free and turned us loose, a lot o' miser'ble paupers. They forgot the forty acres and a mule they promised us. They bit off mo 'n they could chaw, as the feller says, and they dropped us. But I ain't a complainin'; I'll always be mighty thankful to 'em for settin' us free, though if I read hist'ry right that was a sort o' accident. Lots and cords of 'em wanted to see us free, — no doubt about that; but what they was fightin' was secession, and their government declared us free jes' to weaken the enemy, looks like to me. Of co'se the Southern folks did n't want us free 'cause they had all their money in us near 'bout, and they was afraid to see their country divided with a free people of a different race. And they was right to be 'fraid, too, and now they got the bag to hold, while the Northern people is way off yonder and don't suffer. Me and Colonel Sanford has stood on the street and talked it over heap o' times, and we agree that two races in one country is bad for both."

" But de Northern folks don't despise us like de Southern folks, do they?" asked the parson, not quite convinced.

" I useter think they did n't," was the answer, with a smile, " but I'm findin' out better all the time. The Northerners don't have half the aggravation. Down h-yuh nearly half the population

is black, but up there the colored people is mighty
few and scatterin'; and yit them few know mighty
well what race prejudice is. I tell you, the color
line is everywhere. That's what 'The Freeman'
says,— the paper I take; you seen it, Brother
Smith. Only a little while back I read about how
the white people in Felicity, Ohio, kept colored
children out of the schools by force, beat their
parents and destroyed their property in some cases.
They defied the law and was not punished. They
did the same thing in Oxford, Ohio. Seventy-five
leading citizens banded together, not to protect
themselves against the vote and rule of the negro,
but to prevent his children from gettin' a education. There was almost a riot in Marion, Ill.,
because a tobacco house imported some colored
men to work in their factory. I've heard of some
such outrage in almost every Northern State.
Colonel Sanford showed me a piece in the 'New
York Herald' that said that the prejudice was
stronger in the North than in the South, and yit
they don't have one-tenth the friction and aggravation up there. They can't have. That's what
makes me stop and think. No-sir-ee! No use
lookin' to the North. It's a case of white against
black in this country, North or South."

The parson sighed and Mamie-Lou John swore.

"I wish we could have a waw of black against
white," the latter declared, fiercely.

"We'd be the under dog in the fight shore's

you born, and we'd be fools to try it," declared
the schoolmaster in rejoinder. "We ain't got
organization nor nothin' yet. We can't have our
rights tell we git stronger."

"They tell me we increase faster 'n the white
folks," remarked the preacher, more hopefully.
"It's so, too; I kin see it right yuh in Barcelona."

"Yes, that's so," assented the professor, "but
my hopes is in colonization. We can't cope with
the white man; that's the way it looks to me.
We'll have to go away to ourselves. I propose
we discuss the Liberia question at the first meetin'
of our debatin' society."

Rosetta had begun to lose patience long ere
this. She now rose, walked to the gate, placed
herself outside of it, and called Mamie-Lou John's
name loudly. In a few moments he appeared at
the door, and, recognizing her voice, came out to
her. She told him why she was there, and urged
him to accompany her, but he promptly refused.

"I'll git a wagon and go out dere wid you by
daylight in de mornin'," he said, "but I can't go
to-night. I f-yeared to go to-night, Rosy."

"Do — please — come, go, Mamie-Lou," she implored, catching hold of him across the fence.
"I'll do anything for you ef you'll go."

"I can't, I tell you. Great Scott! Cicero might
come to and grab me. No-suh-ree!"

Rosetta saw that further persuasion would be
useless, and after reproaching him bitterly, she

turned away, leaving him to return to the discussion going on within. The girl walked straight through the town and out toward the Black Swamp road, vowing to accomplish the task alone, although she felt that her courage was failing steadily. It was not the lonely walk, but the thought of the dead body that affrighted her. Her father having formerly lived on a small farm out of town, she had often walked a lonely country road at night alone, minding it little.

The negro is a puzzling creature. In many respects he enjoys a livelier imagination than the white man; he cherishes a far more absolute belief in the existence of spirits, and the reality and nearness of the world which they inhabit. Particularly at night does this spirit world seem to draw near and reveal to him its secrets. To his imagination the shadowy woodlands are full of the arisen dead. Should he walk a lonely way in the moonlight and see a rabbit run across his path, he thinks he should be careful, — that is a spirit. Should he, in similar surroundings, feel the touch of a warm breath on the back of his neck, again he recognizes the presence of a spirit. The soft murmur of the forest when the wind does *not* blow, is the whisper of spirits. Should he walk in the neighborhood of a swamp and see a floating light (the *ignis fatuus*, called the Jack-o'-lantern), he thinks he should run home as fast as he can, for that is a spirit or demon " hot from hell." Woe to him if he attempt an investigation; a horseman once did so, and the terrible being turned upon him in wrath, consuming both him and his horse in its flames. And yet the average negro seems to experience less dread of unseen dangers on a lonely night walk through the woods than the average white.

Rosetta was not obliged to go alone, however, and none of these fancies engaged her imagination. On the outskirts of the town she encountered a young country darkey going home on a mule, recognized her opportunity, and seized it. The fact that he was in a semi-tipsy condition was made apparent through his loud soliloquies and occasional exultant shouts. Rosetta promptly hailed this " country Jake," as she mentally styled him, and engaged him in conversation.

" Come, go wid me out dis road a piece," she proposed to the astonished negro, as soon as there had been some exchange of compliments.

" Out dat road? Wut fur? "

" I 'll tell you bimeby. You come go wid me an' do wut I tell you, I 'll gie you a dollar," she promised recklessly, although she had not a cent at the present time.

The " country Jake " was tipsy, he liked the sound of Rosetta's voice, he liked still more the promise of a fee, and so he allowed himself to be led out toward Black Swamp without knowing where he was going, or what he was to do. The girl walked in advance, refusing to answer his questions, only

assuring herself that he followed.   Occasionally he
uttered his exultant shout after a prolonged solilo-
quy in celebration of his own greatness.   He was
a " much of a man," he could throw anybody in
the whole county; in fact, he was the very cock
of the walk; and as for astuteness, cunning, and
superior mental qualifications in general, there was
no one to equal him; he was a wonder.   Best of
all, he was n't " beholden to nobody."

"Look yuh, ain't dis fur enough?" he roused
himself to demand several times; but Rosetta
would give him no satisfaction, and if he showed
any sign of a disposition to turn back she promptly
took measures to attract him forward.

And so they drew near the swamp.   Hitherto
the full moon had lighted their path, but ere
descending into the dense woods along the creek
Rosetta felt it necessary to strike a match and
apply it to a stick of rich pine with which she had
provided herself.   Holding the torch aloft, she led
the way down the slope toward the water, with a
trembling voice endeavoring to pacify her follower,
who complained of their surroundings and threatened to go no further.   As they presently turned
at right angles from the road and penetrated the
woods a short distance, the torch-light all at once
outlined a suspended object, which caused the
mule to shy violently, and its rider to utter a yell
of terror as he was thrown headlong into the
bushes.   At this moment an owl in a neighboring

tree uttered a harsh and dismal hoot, which so
startled the already terrified Rosetta, so shocked
her unstrung nerves, that her knees gave way
beneath her and she collapsed to the earth, dropping her torch, which rolled a few feet down an
incline and was extinguished.

About midnight a childless old negro who lived
with his wife in a cabin of one room near the public road about half a mile from Black Swamp on
the Barcelona side, — the same old man who had
seen the insensible Cicero lifted into the white
man's buggy and glimpsed the form of Mamie-Lou
John as he fled through the woods, — was aroused
from sleep by a faint but protracted tapping on his
door, and the sound of some one weakly calling
his name.

"Unker Mingo! oh, Unker Mingo!" said the
voice, — a woman's faint voice. "Open de do' —
please open de do'!"

"Don't you open dat do' tell you fine out who
dere," cautioned his wife, as the old man rose,
stirred the embers in the fireplace and threw on a
stick of fat pine.

The room was soon flooded with light, and going
to the door, old Mingo demanded to know who
sought admittance to his home at such an unheard-
of hour. But there was no answer save the faint
tapping and the low cry which begged that the
door be opened. He thought he recognized the
voice. Besides, it was a woman's, and evidently a

woman who was ill — what could he fear? So at
last he unbolted and opened wide the door, leaning forward to look out.

The old man suddenly backed into the house
with an ejaculation of fear, as the light from the
fireplace outlined two prostrate figures on the low
steps, — one that of a groaning woman, the other
the stiffened form of a man with the fragment of a
rope hanging from his neck.

"Unker Mingo," implored the weary voice,
"take him in; take him in, do, please, Unker
Mingo. I can't tote him no furder. I can't tote
him to town, Unker Mingo."

"She talk like Rosetta Hightower," said the old
man's wife, getting out of bed.

Holding aloft a lighted torch, the astonished
old couple stood in the doorway and examined
the two prostrate figures, recognizing instantly
the dead body of Cicero and the living form of
Rosetta. The wife of Mingo looked searchingly at
the latter, and was not slow to comprehend that the
condition of the young woman lying helpless on her
doorstep was such as to demand prompt attention.

After a short consultation the two old people
lifted the body between them and placed it temporarily on the floor in a corner. Returning to
the doorway, intending to lift the young woman
also and bear her in, they were amazed to see her
suddenly rise to her feet, shrieking horrible oaths.

A vehicle was passing rapidly on the road and

the sound of the laughing, happy voices of a young girl and a young man entered the cabin door. There was a ball in Barcelona that night, and one of the gay dancers was now being taken to her home in the country. It was this that roused Rosetta and filled her soul with bitterness and rage. She knew from the sound of their voices that they were white, and she stood up and cursed them with her last strength. They were white and therefore honored, their pathway sown with happiness and light; she was black, dishonored, her pathway lost in darkness, and her soul weighed down with hopeless grief. The woman raged at the contrast and called down evil upon them. The burden of her curse was that hell might engulf them and all their race.

The sound of the wheels and the merry voices coming no more out of the gloom to madden her, Rosetta's strength gave way as suddenly as it had just now come to life. She fell in a heap on the steps and moved no more. They lifted her up, bore her in, placed her on their only bed, and then the bewildered old man and woman sat down before the fire and conversed in low, awed voices, while waiting for the dawn.

The body was carried to the grave next day, but Rosetta did not follow it, nor was the unhappy young woman removed to her own home until after she had suffered the pangs of premature parturition.

X.

As he walked along a street in Barcelona two or three weeks later, going to his office, Robert Morton paused to listen to Colonel Sanford and a prominent planter, who stood in animated conversation, the centre of an interested gathering of some eight or ten persons. The young man was in a troubled state of mind and had decided to appeal to his elderly friend for advice. It was this that caused him to halt, rather than any great interest in the subject of discussion.

"But when you move them out wholesale," the planter was saying, "what am *I* going to do? Who is goin' to plough my fields, and pick my cotton, and do the cuttin' and dippin' on my turpentine farm?"

"If they should go in a body, which is very unlikely, our agricultural system would no doubt suffer,—that is, until white foreign labor could be imported," Colonel Sanford admitted. "But what would that be in comparison with the evil that threatens our children and grandchildren?"

"It is my business to take care of myself, and
let Providence take care of my children after me,"
declared the planter. "Let our children control
'em as we control 'em. This is a white man's
country and always will be."

"Do you suppose for a moment that the present
state of things can remain the same indefinitely?"
asked the colonel. "It is the wildest folly to depend on that. Just wait until they have developed
capacity for organization and concerted effort, and
until they numerically outnumber us. Already
they are on the road toward it."

He went on to say that every negro child
in Barcelona, almost without exception, went to
school; every white child did not, could not. And
it had been shown that the race was increasing
much more rapidly than our own. In 1790 there
were only 700,000 blacks in the whole country, in
1860 there were 4,000,000; he had estimated that
there were now about 7,000,000, and at the same
rate of increase there would be in fifty years not
less than 35,000,000, one-half the present population of the United States. When it came to that,
the colonel thought, there would be a desperate
struggle for existence, and one race or the other
would have to go down. History would repeat
itself. It was not possible for two distinct races to
exist on terms of equality and friendship under
one government, unless they had begun and would
continue to rapidly amalgamate by intermarriage.

Would there ever be this amalgamation, this mingling of the blood of the two races, in the South? There was not a man or woman of either race in the whole country who for a moment expected it.

Colonel Sanford declared that neither would the people of the outside world for a moment expect it, if they had any conception of the silent but ceaseless and inexorable warfare that has been waging ever since the slave was set free and placed in a position to antagonize the dominant race. The inevitable conflict is in progress wherever the two races come into contact, and there is absolutely no hope that it will ever cease. Every living soul in the South, in great part unconsciously though it may be, is taking part in it continually. It enters into everything, is the one burning question, relegating all others to the background, and massing together in one unbroken army every discordant element of either race which would otherwise stand independently apart. What, then, is to be expected when the weaker race shall become able to measure arms with the stronger?

The planter could not answer, and took himself off, pleading pressing business. "The selfishness and thoughtlessness, or apathy, of our own people about this question are simply amazing," the colonel concluded. "We are willing to cut our children's throats rather than suffer from a temporary disorganization of labor."

Morton said a few words in rejoinder, substan-

tially agreeing, and then asked Colonel Sanford to
accompany him to his office. Arrived there, he set
a bottle of wine before his friend, and they cordially
pledged each other. The younger man began at
once to speak of a loss by fire which he had sustained
the night before, the elder expressing well-chosen
words of regret and sympathy. All the circumstances of the fire seemed to indicate the work of
an incendiary, and Morton found additional cause
for suspicion in the fact that some enemy was
trying to cast a spell upon him. A few days before the fire this enemy had contrived unobserved
to convey to the young man's bedroom a conjur-
ing medium similar in most respects to the one
exhibited in the mayor's court."

" Some friend of Cicero Witherspoon, perhaps,"
conjectured Morton. "I did n't help lynch him,
but I helped to catch him, you know."

" Jim Jones had better look out, then. His gin-
house may be the next to go."

" This loss embarrasses me," the younger man
continued, with a frown. " I had expected to fix
up that house and go there to live when I married,
leaving my mother and sisters in the other one. I
can't afford to build. The income from my profession is very small, as you know."

" But it will increase. It is bound to. You had
a good reputation to start with, and you have made
a good record. It is only a matter of time,
Robert." Colonel Sanford brought down his
empty glass with emphasis.

" ' Only a matter of time ' is rather an unsatis-
factory prospect to a man who is in love," said
Morton, with downcast eyes. " This is the matter
I wanted to ask your advice about, Colonel. Already I have waited a whole year to speak to — to
her, hoping that my prospects would improve.
You probably know whom I mean."

" I think I do, and there is n't a lovelier girl in
this whole country," Colonel Sanford declared,
with enthusiasm. " But don't put off speaking to
her too long. Some one else may get ahead of
you."

" I have often feared that," said Morton, gloomily, " but I have as often told myself that I was in
no position to marry. Has a man a right, Colonel
Sanford, to ask a woman to share hardships with
him ? "

" He certainly has a right to tell her that he
loves her, and let her decide the rest. No true
woman is afraid of suffering hardships in the house
of the man she loves. Women are not as weak
and tender as a young man is apt to think, and
have far more fortitude."

"I cannot bear to think of not being able to
give her every desirable comfort."

" Look here, my friend," exclaimed the colonel,
" you are all wrong. That sad story of broken
fortune and wretched poverty which has been the
story of so many of us since the war has not been
told for nothing. In the long run it will have

been good for us. You are a stronger character now than you would have been if you had been brought up in the lap of luxury. The same thing applies to young married people; I believe it is good for them to begin poor. Here's to your success, my boy," the colonel concluded, lifting his glass.

Half an hour later, as Maum Katie was slowly mounting the steps, Colonel Sanford came out of the office with a satisfied smile on his face and passed her with a friendly nod, in response to her low courtesy.

Old Maum Katie was a curious anomaly. As before indicated, she seemed to have no conception of the absorbing interests and aspirations of the younger generation, — of her grandson, the professor, and others like him, — but stood wholly aside, living in the past. So much, perhaps, for having been fifty years a slave. However that might be, it is a fact that the representatives of the old slave-holding class seemed to be everything in her eyes, while the new people were nothing. She courtesied low to Colonel Sanford, but a few minutes before when she met Adam Brown on the street she looked the other way. The mayor was not a favorite with her, however. She did not live in the Neck, but owned a little property in Barcelona proper, and refused to give it up. Although it was a low and unhealthy spot, it joined the mayor's land and he wanted it.

"Well, Maum Katie," said he, accosting her one day, "it's time for you to sell out and move back among the colored folks. I'll trade with you; I'll give you a good price for your place." The indignant old woman's reply, as reported, was quick and to the point: "I ain't advertisin' to sell, Mr. Brown. I been among nice white folks all my life, an' dat's mo'n some people kin say. *You* ain't been dere long!"

Robert Morton was putting the glasses and bottle away when this courageous character appeared in his doorway and brightly wished him a good-day. "I come get de money for de wash, Mas' Robert," she said.

"And you shall have it, Maum Katie." As he was paying her, he asked kindly about her health, complimented her on the excellence of her laundry work, and ended by presenting her with an extra coin.

"I wonder wut you'd say, Mas' Robert," she remarked ere she retired, "ef I was to tell you wut I done wid dat last fifty cents you give me."

"Well, what did you do with it?"

"I went to Mr. Parker's sto' an' I bought ten cents' worth o' sugar an' ten cents' worth o' flour an' ten cents' worth o' eggs an' twenty cents' worth o' butter."

"And you took it all home and you and your grandchildren ate it up, eh?"

"No-sir-ee!" declared Maum Katie, smiling,

but fixing her eyes gravely on the young man.
" I gie it all to a young white lady. I went down
to her house an' slipped in de dine-room an' open
de pantry do' an' poured de sugar in de sugar-dish
an' de flour in de flour-box an' put de eggs on de
shelf an' de butter in de butter-dish, an' den I come
'way an' dey did n' know nothin' 'bout it."

" Did you really, Maum Katie?" The young
man was astonished. "And what made you do
that?" he asked, looking at her with admiration.

" You mus n' tell nobody, Mas' Robert, but dem
po' people 'bout to starve, you see 'em so."

" Why — who — who can be so very poor?"

" Miss Reba Law'nce an' her ma."

"Oh, Maum Katie, is this true?" exclaimed
Robert Morton, in great agitation. " And you
really did that for them?" His sallow face had
turned a shade paler.

A tear rolled down the old woman's cheek, and
wiping it away, she explained how she had first
begun to suspect it, and how she had found by
investigation that Mrs. Lawrence and her daughter
were really in desperate straits. The young man
listened in silence, a look of great pain on his face,
which gave place gradually to an expression almost
of happiness as he reflected that under such circumstances she could lose nothing in marrying
even a very poor man. By this time the whole
story had been told and the narrator was going
over it a second time, as was her wont.

"Maum Katie," Morton interrupted suddenly, "you must do that again, and keep on doing it, and let me give you the money to buy the things with, you understand."

"All right," she agreed, her soft, kindly voice sounding like music to him.

"But you must be very careful and not let them find you out.   And — and," he continued, eagerly, couldn't you leave *money?* — put it down where they could not fail to find it, and perhaps think they lost it themselves."

Maum Katie showed that she was quite willing to try, and before she could answer Morton bounded to a little iron safe in the corner, opened it, and came back shortly with bills in his hand.

"Here are seventeen dollars," he said, enthusiastically.   "It is all I have on hand, but it will do for the present.   I want you to put this ten-dollar bill in the house somewhere and take five dollars to buy groceries with — "

"Mus' n' buy too much one time," interrupted Maum Katie.   "Dey 'll 'spicion sump'n right off."

"Do as you think best, but be sure to carry them something often.   They sha'n't suffer: I 'll spend every cent I 've got in the world first!"

"I knowd it.   I knowd *he* would n't back out 'cause she so po', like some mens would," was Maum Katie's reflection, as she folded the bills in her hand and gazed fondly at her companion.

"And take these two dollars for yourself."

" Oh, Mas' Robert — "

" Yes, you must. It's all I can give you this time, but you will have to take more than that from me before we are through with this thing. I expect you to look after them, remember, and not to say a word about it to anybody."

" I ain't tole a soul but you."

" Don't you think you had better buy something and take it down there in your basket right away? " he urged.

Maum Katie agreed and went off smiling, well pleased at this turn of affairs.

" Come and see me again in a day or two," he called after her, adding : " If they catch you at it, of all you do, don't mention my name."

As the sound of her footsteps died away on the outer stairs and his excitement began to subside, a sudden misgiving seized the young man. What if this old black woman had deceived him and gone off with all his ready money? How could it be possible that those two refined and delicate ladies, whose interests were so near to his heart, had been reduced to such an extreme of poverty without the matter becoming public? He remembered hearing of their loss through the insolvent railroad company about a year since, but it could not be that this was their only means of support. With the half-formed determination of following Maum Katie and questioning her more closely, Morton caught up his hat, but instantly dropped it. No, he would

wait.   He would trust this kind old mammy who
was agreeably associated with all his earliest recollections.   He had never known her to lie; he had
always trusted her, and would do so still.   It must
be true.

Walking out that afternoon, he saw Reba and
Betty go into the photographer's where Miss Black
was employed, and he resolved at once to take a
step which he had been contemplating for some
time.   Returning to his office and making some
slight changes in his toilet, he descended into the
street again, and walked rapidly in the direction of
the Lawrence home.   Somewhat to his surprise
and relief, for her presence there was clearly indicative that his trust in her was not abused, Maum
Katie appeared at the door in answer to his knock,
and, as she showed him into the faded parlor, informed him that she was staying with the invalid
mother while Miss Reba went out with her cousin.
Morton bade her tell Mrs. Lawrence that he had
called to see her about a matter of importance, and
that if she should not feel well enough to receive
him, he would communicate with her by letter.

Mrs. Lawrence sat propped up in bed, sewing
hard on a garment which Reba had put down when
she went out.   The sudden announcement of the
visitor excited her as only a nervous invalid who
never saw company could be excited.   A decep-
tive flush overspread her face, and she trembled
from head to foot, so that for some minutes she

thought it would be impossible to receive him, and contemplated sending him word to address her by letter. Had she been sure it was a mere matter of business, this would have been her final decision; but through some inexplicable process of reasoning she arrived at the conclusion that Reba was to be the subject of the coming interview, and she determined to see the young man face to face. Assisted by Maum Katie, she hurriedly made herself and the room presentable, and the visitor was shown in.

It was all over in a few minutes. In a very simple and manly fashion, he confessed his love for Reba and asked permission to pay his addresses to her. He said he had hesitated a long while before deciding to take this important step, and gave his reasons, stating plainly what his profession brought him at present, and being careful not to overestimate his future prospects. Mrs. Lawrence heard him out, and then made answer in the somewhat formal fashion which, it seemed to her, the occasion demanded.

"I knew your father well and esteemed him highly," she said. "I have not seen you before for some years, but I have heard only good reports of you. That is the point — the only point. As to business matters, I can well afford to say nothing. We are all poor alike now-a-days; poverty is the fashion. It is therefore a matter for Reba only to decide. Should she — like you, you may be sure of my full approval, Robert."

She pressed his hand warmly at parting, and when he was gone lay back upon her pillows trembling and more unnerved than ever, yet filled with gladness; for out of all the young men in the town this one just gone would have been her choice, could she have voluntarily selected a husband for her daughter.

Miss Black's labors at the photographer's were neither arduous nor incessant. She often had time on her hands, and on this afternoon she was writing when Betty and Reba called for her. A letter had reached her from her aunt in Kingston that morning, and she was already inditing her answer.

"I have just seen a newspaper giving an account of that horrible lynching in Barcelona," Mrs. Blossom had written. "I wonder that you are willing to live in a place where such terrible things happen. Simply because that poor colored man committed robbery — driven to it by hunger, perhaps — he was inhumanly murdered. But you know the harrowing details."

"I know the harrowing details only too well," wrote Miss Black, and proceeded to give the true version of the story. "I owe it to a hero," she added in conclusion, "that the 'poor colored man' was at first accused only of robbery, and my name was withheld from the public. No, I am not afraid to remain in Barcelona; I intend to stay and make my home among its people, because they are my friends, and I trust them and love them.   My eyes are opened, and I shall never cease to wonder at our Northern people for looking on carelessly from afar upon the desperate struggle of the two races in the South, persistently bestowing their sympathy upon the ignorant, slavish, lawless blacks rather than upon their brothers in color and blood."

Had Miss Black known what was to pass between Mrs. Lawrence and young Morton the same afternoon, it is possible that she would have expressed herself with less eloquence.   A woman's opinions are likely to take their shape and color from the circumstances immediately surrounding and personally affecting her, rather than from an extended or general view of a given situation with its manifold and conflicting phases.   From Miss Black's point of view the Barcelonans were good and kind, and in the happiness of a vague and doubtful dream she would fain have called down blessings upon them; from Rosetta's point of view they were wicked and cruel, and, in the depths of her misery, which she charged up to them, she would have visited them with the most blighting curse it would have been possible for her to conceive.

After a half-hour's chat, Miss Black followed her visitors into the street and walked some distance with them.   It so happened that as the three neared a street corner, a hurrying negro suddenly appeared around the angle and narrowly avoided colliding with the young lady from Boston, who shrank away

from him with an involuntary cry of terror. The
negro was Mamie-Lou John, and he was quick to
disappear down a side street. His face recalled a
recent occurrence which she would be glad to
forget, but Miss Black was not sure that he was the
man. Afterwards she felt glad not to be sure,
considering that, had she been, a sense of duty
would compel her to inform against him.

"I am getting nervous," she said, apologetically.
"I am frightened by almost every black face I
see."

"I thought you liked them — the negroes,"
Betty remarked in wonder, exchanging glances
with her cousin.

"I like them? I detest them!" declared Miss
Black, with such ardor that her friends were more
than ever surprised.

XI.

BEFORE calling at the photographer's to see Miss Black the cousins had spent an hour together, and Betty had communicated some important news. In the first place, she announced that she had at last agreed to engage herself to her youthful lover, Jack Sanford, and said that her decision was the subject of congratulation at home, her mother being well pleased, and her step-father, although he preferred Jim Jones, being relieved that the matter was finally settled. Jack, of course, was very happy, and she, — well, she had at last concluded that she did really love him. The chief trouble seemed to have been that he was only twenty, a year younger than herself, and though a fine manly fellow of whom she was very fond, he had seemed too boyish. During a year past she had hesitated to dismiss him, while unable to make up her mind to accept him, and so the "thing hung fire," as Adam Brown declared, month after month.

The crisis had been brought about in rather an amusing way. The young lover, who was on friendly and familiar terms with his father, had consulted the colonel and asked his advice. The advice given was that of Benvolio to Romeo; the colonel recommended his son to "examine other beauties," and to make sure that Betty knew such examination was going on. This plan being carefully and craftily carried out, at the end of two months Betty's mind was made up and she came to terms.

"When I saw him gallivanting around with other girls," she confessed to Reba, "although it was exactly what I had often told him to do, I did n't like it, and I felt that I could n't give him up. I should have known it before if he had n't been such a boy! I told him I could n't be a Lady Castlewood. The case of a man marrying a woman whom he had long hoped to have for his mother-in-law was made attractive in 'Henry Esmond,' fascinating in fact, but in real life it would be the most utterly absurd and frightful thing imaginable. The fact that I am a year older than Jack will always haunt me, but I suppose it will make no difference a hundred years hence."

Reba congratulated her cousin upon having arrived at a decision, but was not without misgivings; in her opinion there could be no room for doubts where love was real. Betty added that the news of her engagement had seemed to stun poor Jones, although she had steadfastly discouraged him from the beginning, and her step-father was solely responsible for his visits to the house. The mayor himself was commissioned to tell him, and did so, — riding out to his farm and calling on him for that purpose.

"And what do you suppose?" continued Betty; "that poor man came to town next day and *got drunk!* Papa says he was never drunk before in his life. He not only got drunk, but came down to our house in that condition. Mamma was on the front piazza alone, and he staggered in and sat down by her. She did n't get up or call, not wanting me to know it. But I saw him open the gate and I went and sat at one of the windows, so as to be near if there should be trouble. Mamma was n't a bit afraid of him, and sat there quietly and talked to him. She asked him how he felt, and he said 'Bully,' afterwards mumbling something about his liver being out of order. 'I'm afraid something else is out of order, you poor man,' said mamma, and cried a little. She was very sorry for him. He seemed to realize that he was in the presence of a lady and did not say a profane word; but he talked in a very ridiculous way, and nearly fell out of his chair several times. He tried to sing a song and talked exultantly about being 'beholden to nobody;' and once he cried out that he had 'plenty of money and no poor kin'! Finally Charlie turned up and took him off down town. 'Charles, old boy, you're my friend, ain't you?' the poor fellow repeated two or three times as they staggered off. He apologized to papa for it a few days later, and said he would never get drunk again as long as he lived. I shudder to think of what my feelings would have been if I had ever encouraged that man just for the sake of his attentions, as some girls do. Papa is to blame if anybody is. He is n't the only unhappy one," Betty continued. "You must have discouraged Charlie at the tournament ball, Reba."

"I did," was the low answer. "For his sake I thought it ought to stop then and there. I suspected it before, and I ought not to have allowed him to crown me."

"Ever since then he has shown it," Betty declared. "He stays and stays out at the place and will hardly ever come to town. Mamma cries over it and won't give up hope. But I've told her it's no use; you never would like Charlie in that way."

"I'm so sorry,— for her and for him," said Reba, tears in her voice.

"Oh, he'll get over it," was the rejoinder, with an air of large experience. "He'll get over it after a while, and Jim Jones will, too. Young men recover very soon."

On the day after her interview with Robert Morton, Mrs. Lawrence made him the subject of a conversation with her daughter, but said nothing about his visit or his intentions, fearing to influence Reba's decision. She easily conceived that a girl of the highest spirit, who proposed for herself a true marriage or none, might delusively persuade herself that she loved an attractive young man, while under the influence of a desire to extricate her mother and herself from a position so desperate as was now theirs; and to save her daughter from the consequences of such a mistake was the mother's chief concern, for she admitted no sort of doubt that such a marriage would be a mistake fraught with the possibilities of the worst evil.

When, therefore, the subject came up she spoke guardedly. She had observed for some time that her daughter seemed disinclined to discuss the young man, and took this as a favorable sign,— as indicative that she had begun to feel for him more than mere friendship; but she was not sure, and wished to see events take their own proper course. She began by saying that she regretted not to see a man so promising as Morton succeed more rapidly in his profession, and added that she had heard a good deal about his affairs from Mrs. Brown, who was fond of him. He was not making much money, in fact, he was quite poor,— not, however, because he lacked in ability or failed to exert himself. She had heard that he was particular and conscientious, and, unlike some other young lawyers in the town, refused the proffer of a good many cases after he understood their merits. This was one hindrance to his material success. Another was that there were so many lawyers, each with his little following of relatives and friends who used all their influence in his behalf, thus widely distributing the limited patronage. In a town of the size of Barcelona there could be only one or two schoolmasters and editors, a few physicians and ministers, and the law was almost the only opening for young men of ability who had neither capital nor taste for trade; for the bulk of the young men did go into trade now-a-days, farming being a lost art.

Mrs. Lawrence added that if Miss Black had an atom of wisdom she would concern herself with Morton's character rather than with his present business prospects; it was better to be poor and happy than to be rich and full of regret.

" Have you heard — anything — about them? " asked Reba, with a studied, mechanical manner which her mother regarded as suspicious.

" Oh, no; only I thought she might fall in love with him after — after that matter with Sam Thomas, you know."

" Did Aunt Matilda say anything about his tendency to drink?" asked Reba, suddenly, and for the moment Mrs. Lawrence lost all hope.

" Why, no! Who says — "

" Josephine told me ' people ' said he had been seen taken home drunk late at night."

" I don 't believe a *word* of it. Matilda had never heard such reports.. I suppose he drinks in moderation, as all gentlemen do — or used to do."

"I did n't believe it at the time," said the girl, quietly, and her mother's hope returned. "Josephine has not been here since the day she told me," Reba added. "If she does n't collect us some money soon I don't know what we 'll do."

Their struggle for existence was growing more bitter. The help persistently given by the invalid indeed lessened the burden for Reba, but hardly increased their income. Josephine was offered special inducements and brought them more work, but failed to collect a proportionately larger sum. For weeks Mrs. Lawrence had been feigning a lost appetite, and her daughter in consequence was able, as a rule, to satisfy her own hunger; but already a day had come when there was absolutely nothing to eat in the house. At breakfast Reba cooked the last egg and carried it in to her mother together with a single slice of bread without butter. Mrs. Lawrence feigned nausea and would not touch either. At noon Reba heated the same egg over and carried it in with the same slice of bread, only to find that her mother's nausea had increased. The same tragical comedy was re-enacted when the hour for supper arrived.

Reba began to comprehend that her mother was determined to starve so long as there was not food enough for both, and saw that something must be done without delay. She told herself with consternation that a person of so delicate a constitution as her mother's could not suffer hunger with impunity, little dreaming that grave mischief had been done already. She determined to go to her aunt the next day, confess their deplorable situation, and appeal for help.

Going to the kitchen at an early hour the next morning with intent to warm over the same egg a third time and toast the same piece of dry bread, she was amazed and bewildered to find butter, flour, sugar, and several eggs in the pantry. It was impossible that she could have overlooked these things yesterday. Yet what other explanation could there be? Food did not rain down from the roof of a pantry. Reba thought of the miraculous increase of the meal and the oil in the house of the widow who entertained the man of God, the prophet of Israel, in time of famine, and with a thankful heart prepared a breakfast for her mother and herself. She shrank from appealing to Adam Brown, even through his wife, her aunt, and put her visit off.

The next day Josephine appeared, as cheerful as ever, in spite of the fact that she was less than three weeks a widow. Josephine was a child of nature, and did not see the necessity of feigning a grief which she did not feel. What was of importance in connection with her visit was that she left two dollars which she had with difficulty collected, and thus absolute famine in the household was averted for the time.

One morning, a day or two after Maum Katie's

interview with Morton, Reba was overjoyed to
find a ten-dollar bill in a drawer of her dressing-
table, and ran with it to her mother, hazarding the
guess that she had put it there and forgotten it
months before. But Mrs. Lawrence looked at the
money suspiciously, recalling the recent strange
discovery of unexpected food in the pantry.

"I fear some kind person knows how wretchedly
poor we are, and is trying to help us secretly," she
said.

"It may be Aunt Matilda," suggested Reba,
after a thoughtful pause. "Betty may have found
out, in coming here. She has sharp eyes."

The discovery on the same day of more groceries in the pantry, a larger supply than the first,
served to confirm this view; and it was at once
agreed that Reba should keep on the watch, in order
to discover if possible the benefactor who was actuated by so tender a regard for their feelings. It
should be added that their pride was not as keenly
wounded as it would have been in former days,
they having reached the point where such a feeling
is well-nigh lost in the presence of graver concerns.
Still they felt uneasy. Bitter necessity compelled
them to eat the food and spend the money, but
they would gladly have refrained from so doing.

For more than a week Reba kept on the watch
without making any discovery, sitting with her
sewing in her mother's room near a window
whence she could frequently scan the back piazza

and not fail to observe any one entering the dining-room. It was often her habit while thus engaged to sing, in a soft, sweet voice, which was an unfailing source of pleasure to the invalid. Her voice was of an unusual quality, and had been much admired among her few friends; but of late Reba scarcely had the heart to sing, and was glad her mother did not request it. As she sat in the room, they talked a little now and then, and meanwhile she sewed hard and kept on the watch. At last one afternoon, as she sat listening to a mocking-bird in a China-tree of the yard and thinking of her own neglected voice, she heard stealthy steps on the back piazza, and looked up just in time to see a figure disappear through the dining-room door.

Reba rose at once and followed to the dining-room as quietly as possible. A black woman with a basket on her arm, standing within the wide-open pantry, busily engaged in emptying several small packages, was what she saw. One step nearer, and she recognized the intruder.

"Maum Katie, what are you doing there?" the girl suddenly demanded from her place; whereupon the old woman dropped her basket and came out of the pantry in great fright.

"I ain't stealin' nothin', Miss Reba. I ain't stealin' a thing," she ejaculated helplessly.

"Oh, Maum Katie," cried the girl, horror-struck, "how could you think I thought you were stealing? I *knew* what you were doing."

" Did you, Miss Reba, honey? "

" Yes, I did, and I think you are an angel of goodness." Reba burst into tears. " Come with me to mamma," she sobbed.

The two went into the house immediately, and stood together by the invalid's bed as Maum Katie made her confession. At first she made no mention of Morton, remembering his earnest charge, except to say that it was the money given her by him, out of the goodness of his heart, that she had made use of.

" And did you put that ten-dollar bill in Reba's room, too? " the invalid asked suddenly, in the midst of the confession, which had embraced only the pantry supplies.

" Ye–yes, ma'am," stammered Maum Katie, in great uneasiness.

" I did n't know there was anybody in the world as good and kind as you," said Mrs. Lawrence, overcome, a great tear rolling down her cheek. " We thank you with all our hearts," she added, looking tenderly upon their stammering benefactor ; " but you must not do any more of it, Maum Katie. How can you afford to? It must be all you can do to take care of yourself. And — and " — her pride coming to the surface — " we really don't need your help, you know. And we will pay you the money back soon."

Maum Katie was now overcome in turn, and, forgetting her promise, confessed all, — how she had acted of her own accord in the first instance, but only as Robert Morton's instrument afterward. The effect of the story on Reba was such that she fell on her knees at the bedside, threw her arms round her mother, and the two kissed each other repeatedly, in an odd frantic way, weeping softly. Maum Katie looked down upon this inexplicable demonstration with shining eyes, deducing therefrom certain conclusions which were evidently very satisfying to her.

" Tell him," said Reba, following the old woman to the piazza as she was taking her leave, — " tell him we don't need it, as mamma says, but *please* don't tell him that we know *he* is helping us."

Maum Katie readily gave the promise and departed. Then Reba returned to her mother, kneeling at the bedside as before.

" We have a friend now, — a true friend, Reba," said Mrs. Lawrence, softly. " I could die now without feeling that you were being left alone."

The girl saw no significance in this speech, and the two were happier that night than for many months. But the next morning Reba was made anxious by the discovery that her mother was weaker than usual, and really could not eat, although for the present, at least, there was no lack of good food.

XII.

MORE than half the adult population of the Neck had crowded into its small, rude public hall in order to listen to the much advertised debate on the Liberia emigration question. Parson Smith and Professor Brice smiled complacently at each other as they witnessed the gathering of the assembly and reminded themselves that the coming contest of words was the result of their efforts. They had organized the club, had selected the speakers, had put ideas into their heads, and thought they had every reason to believe that the result would be a source of pride to the race. Especially gratified were they when some half-dozen white men, Colonel Sanford being among them, entered the hall and were provided with seats on a separate bench near the door. The smiling parson and professor each wondered if even the most intelligent white people could surpass what they expected to accomplish in an oratorical way that evening, and for the moment this thought obscured in their minds the end and object of the meeting itself. A certain exuberant and almost childish vanity characterizes the educated (or half-educated) negro.

After prolonged and inexplicable delay, during which the leaders scanned the assembly with an air of conscious superiority, and put their heads together and whispered, the meeting was opened by the singing of a hymn. Then a robust young woman stood forth and recited in a sort of half-chant a long, measured narrative, which, for the want of a more accurate term, may here be called an epic poem in condensed form, describing the march of the sons of Israel from Egypt to Canaan. It was the same young woman who was wont to chant and sell her own and "the blind lady's" productions on Saturdays in the negro quarters of Barcelona. Grammar and metre were alike at fault in the present effort, but the poetess had chosen an august and stirring theme, her voice was a rich contralto, her manner was animated, at times really dramatic, and the white as well as the black occupants of the hall listened intently.

"We could n't 'a' had a better interduction to the subjeck befo' us," said Parson Smith, taking the floor as soon as the poetess had sounded the last string of her lyre and resumed her seat amid great applause. "Miss Rachel tells the old story of the Israelites marchin' to the promised lan', an' it makes me think of us h-yuh to-day who 're tryin' to see our way clear to march out of America, the white man's country, to Africa, our own country, which

God give to us long ago. Brethren, we are free, but we are still in Egypt, in the house of bondage, in the white man's country, where it's no use to try to live under our own vine an' fig-tree, an', brethren, we must *git out!* We must rise up an' go up an' march to the promised lan'," shouted the parson, already on his highest key.

"But the trouble is, some say it's too fur, an' some say they dunner whether we ever come fum there or not, an' some say one thing an' some another, an' some care more for the flesh-pots of Egypt 'n for the glory of their race, an' they ruther stay h-yuh an' make bricks for the 'Gyptians all their days. These are the faint-hearted brethren, an' the holy Book says ' a shaking leaf shall chase them.' Brethren, I despise the faint-hearted. Brethren, I say rise up! — wake up!" shouted the speaker, striking his right fist into his left palm. "Brethren, we are in a strange lan'; we was brought h-yuh by force; an' now we are free to go, let us return to the lan' of our fathers where God meant for us to be. It ain't good for white an' black to live together; it ain't accordin' to the will of God who put us off to ourselves at the start an' ' determined the bounds of their habitation.' Brethren, let us arise an' go."

After a long, rambling, and impassioned harangue in this strain, the parson became more calm and spoke with more real force of the advantages of African soil, vegetation, etc., presenting the more favorable reports as to the progress of the Liberian republic, and quoting from Bishop Taylor.

The next speaker proved to be Mamie-Lou John, appointed on the negative. He had been carefully "coached" by the schoolmaster, who wished to see both sides of the question presented, and he began by asking if the situation of the negro in America was really as bad as some pretended. He thought not. He thought the race had made considerable advance, and now had many rights and privileges formerly denied it. He raised a laugh by declaring, in substance, that although it was difficult for a negro to get into the jury-box, it was comparatively easy for him to get into the prisoners' dock. Work was furnished the negro not only on plantations, but in many industries. Many of the race had been able to accumulate a little property and were better off than a good many white laboring men. Some had even acquired wealth. He pointed out that negro children went to school, mainly at the white man's expense. In some elections, at least, the black man's vote was not only counted, but was paid for in cash.

"I reckon Brother Smith will call me one o' the faint-hearted," said Mamie-Lou, with a laugh, "but I want to know mo' about Liberia befo' I go there. I don't want to make bricks for the white man no mo' 'n he does, but I 'd ruther stay in Georgia where I kin git biscuits an' cabbage than to go to Liberia an' have to eat lizards. That 's what they tell me. An' I don't want none o' them wild, naked Africans to ketch me an' swing me up over burnin' red pepper, or tie a rock roun' my neck an' fling me in the river, like they done Dave Green 'cause he stole somethin' from 'em. That's what Jake Hart says, an' he's went there an' come back. But ther's one thing 'bout Liberia I do like," the speaker admitted: "They say you kin buy one them native niggers for ten dollars. That would suit me. I would n't mind ownin' one ef I could git 'im so cheap." After a pause he concluded: "But I'm on the other side this question, myself, an' you ought to put me there to start wid."

"Den I think you better set down," said the chairman, whose voice was drowned in a roar of laughter, coming chiefly from the white bench.

The next speaker was a young man who had enjoyed a collegiate education, or what passed for one, in Atlanta, and he delivered a passionate and intemperate address in favor of wholesale and immediate emigration. Stripped of its flaming rhetoric and tiring repetition, its profuse reference to the " burning intellect of the brain," the " mental force of the mind," etc., with which the black man was insistently declared to be endowed equally with the white man, " and often superior," his speech was in substance as follows: —

" This is a white man's country, and always will be, right or wrong. The power of might triumphs over the power of right. The white man is boss, and the negro is 'nowhere.' The negro is his horse,—his very dog. And the shame of it is that the negro is willing. Why, when some of these white men wake up in hell they'll expect to hold a nigger between them and the fire, and the nigger will be afraid to say no [laughter]. A few of us can be preachers, and teachers, and merchants, and doctors, and editors among our own people, but what are we among the white people but hewers of wood and drawers of water? What are we but porters, butchers, hod-carriers, draymen, coachmen, butlers, barbers, waiters, and cooks? What career is open to us but that of an inferior serving a superior? We cannot advance beyond the bounds set for us, even though we be the most skilled and learned in the whole community in which we live, which often happens [!]. The best and most intelligent of us are not fit to sit in the presence of the most ignorant and low-down white man. At no table, public or private, is there a place for us. We are, indeed, allowed to see the inside of the finest hotels, but only when we are willing to wear the white man's livery, and stand behind his chair.

"My blood boils when I remember that my race contributed 250,000 soldiers to the armies of the Union in the late war, and up to this date not one genuine negro holds a commission in the military or naval service. Only one colored — almost white — man has as yet reached and held the grade of a mere lieutenant. Alas, the poor negro! Wher-

ever he goes, whatever he does, he is hounded by
prejudice, and there is absolutely no door of escape except that of the grave. Were he a snow-
white leper instead of being merely covered with
the black skin which God gave him, he could not
be more completely cut off from all fellowship
with the whites. Our fathers tell us that there is
a thousand times less real sympathy and friendship
between the two races now than there was before
emancipation, and you will notice that it is our
humble old people to whom the white man now
shows kindness. This means that the white likes
the black well enough as long as he knows his
' place,' as long as he is willing still to be a slave,
still to fill his old lowly position without complaint;
but just let the young freeman assert himself, and
there is war!

"Friends, countrymen, and lovers, are we to
stay here and allow this to go on? Are we to
remain forever the white man's waiter, day-laborer,
wage-earner, when we want to be and ought to be
lawyers and judges and congressmen and senators
and presidents, — when we want to and ought to
own factories and steamboats and railroads and
banks? Is it right for us to forever be the under
dog, the bottom rail, when we might be on top and
have got just as much right to be the cock of the
walk as anybody? A thousand times no! In
Hayti the black man controls everything and the
white man *ain't nobody*. What a contrast! Here

we have no protection for our wives and daughters or even for our lives. The case of Hayti shows that we can become great if we only will. Then let us leave this country, where we are nothing but dogs, and return to the land of our forefathers, where a great destiny surely awaits us. Friends, Romans, countrymen, and lovers, do not be faint-hearted. Rouse ye ·from your apathy! Awake to the bugle blast of freedom! Strike for your altars and your fires, God, and — the land of your forefathers ! "

After the applause had subsided a mulatto rose to speak for the negative. He said it was interesting to hear both sides of a question, but, for his part, he wanted to stay in America. And he was n't afraid to stay, either for himself or his family. The whites would not catch him and hang him unless he committed some terrible crime, and that he expected to be careful not to do. As for his wife and daughters, no white man had ever insulted them, and as long as they respected themselves he believed they would be respected and would be safe. He would say the same thing for the women of the whole race; as long as they behaved themselves properly, which they did n't always do 'by a long jump,' they were as safe as the average white woman. He ventured to assert that those who wanted to emigrate to Liberia in order to become judges and congressmen and senators and presidents would not find those positions lying around loose; he thought there were thousands of white men in this country who would like to have such positions, but who would never secure them, for the simple reason that the "burning intellect of the brain," which the young man from Atlanta referred to so often, was lacking. Granted that this was a white man's country and Africa the black man's, and there must be a complete separation, he would like to ask where was he and other "colored" men to go? This sort of arithmetic could only result in assigning them a place in the middle of the Atlantic ocean, and they had all better learn to swim at once. He thought it a fortunate thing that there were now fewer mulattoes than before the war.

The schoolmaster, known as Professor Brice, then spoke. He said he had been deeply interested in the sentiments expressed with so much force by his young friend from Atlanta. It was all true, but there was another side to it. The white man was indeed unconquerably determined to ostracize the negro; he had notified him in unmistakable terms that thus far he should approach and no further. The negro had learned his lesson pretty well on the whole, and those who forgot it might expect to be taught it anew most effectively and without delay. But still there was another side to all this, namely: every intelligent and candid black man knows that he would do practically the same thing in the white man's place. The best, the most intel-

ligent and high-spirited of the race do not desire
close contact with the whites, and prefer to stand
apart as a separate body. Race antipathy may
possibly be more intense among the whites because
the blacks have been their slaves, but it is strong
enough on both sides. This — he declared — was
not an argument against but for emigration. The
history of Hayti shows how the black man is
inclined to treat the white when he has the power;
it also shows, just as conclusively as does the negro's condition in America, how impossible it is
for two such heterogeneous races to live in peace
under one government.

"Our people made a big mistake about this
thing," continued the speaker. "We thought the
Northern white man loved us and was ready to
take us to his bosom, and that only the Southern
white man hated our black skin, but we've found
out better. We profited out of a white man's
quarrel, that was about all. As long as the Northerner stayed mad with his Southern brother he tried
his level best to put us on top, but he ain't mad
now no more, and he's done quit tryin'. He bit off
more 'n he could chaw anyhow. We can't blame
him; he's a white man and sooner or later he's
bound to take the white man's side against the
black. You notice that all of 'em that comes down
h-yuh to live mighty quick takes the white man's
side and gives us the cold shoulder. We all vote
the Republican ticket in national elections, and

that's right because that party freed us; but it
ain't goin' to pay for us to forget that as far as *we*
are concerned it ain't a question of party, but of
race in this country. I could tell you of many
cases if I had the time, but it's gettin' late, of
outrages against the black people in the North,
which prove that race prejudice is jes' as strong up
there as down h-yuh. It's high time for us to stop
puttin' hope in the North and begin to depend on
ourselves. If we ever do anything h-yuh we've
got to do it ourselves, and if we ever go to Africa
and make a nation we've got to do it ourselves.

" We can't do it h-yuh, — that's settled. The
very man who wrote the emancipation proclamation — God bless him! — said before the war broke
out that there was such a difference between the
white and black races as would forever prevent
their living together on terms of social and political equality. In this thing, hist'ry only repeats
itself, as they say. Birds of a feather must flock
together. It is the everlasting decree from on high
that the races of men as well as birds and beasts
should collect together 'after their kind.' The
black people belong to Africa, the yellow people
to Asia, and the white people to Europe and
America. God never intended for these people to
live in one country. All Europe is mixed up in
the United States, of course, but then all Europe
is white; it's one race. The Chinese, they like to
come h-yuh, but not to stay; they want to make

money and go back. And Uncle Sam is tired of
'em a'ready and is fixin' to shut 'em out. My
friends, it ain't a question of whether we ought to
go or stay; that was settled ages ago when we
was made black and the white man white. The
question is how to go, where to go, — whether to
Liberia or the Congo, — and when. Go we must.
If the national government will help us, so much
the better; the thing will be easier and quicker
done. If not, then we must work and wait and
plan and save and go anyhow! I propose that at
the next meetin' we debate on the means to carry
out the great scheme."

As the schoolmaster resumed his seat, Colonel
Sanford was seen advancing down the aisle.

"If you have no objection, I'd like to say a
word or two," he said to the chairman as he
approached.

"Suttenly. We be glad to hear you, Cun'l."

"I cannot subscribe to everything that has been
said here to-night," began Colonel Sanford, looking about him upon the assembly, "but I have
heard much that has pleased me and I have been
deeply interested, — especially so in the remarks
of the last speaker, who, I believe, hits the nail
squarely on the head. Better than anything else
he said, I think, was his advice to you as a race to
cease to look to the North for help and go to work
to help yourselves. In this African emigration
question which is of vital importance to both you

and me, but especially so to you, I would advise
you as he has done, not to wait to see whether the
North will help you, or the South, but to *help yourselves*. The North has already done more for you
than you could have dreamed of expecting. When
it suddenly admitted to the suffrage a million of
recently freed slaves, belonging to the least civilized race in the world, — I speak frankly, — it did
for your sake what no nation or country has ever
done before in the history of the world. After
that most extraordinary leap in the dark, after that
too precipitate if not reckless assumption of untold
risks, the final results of which no man now living
can foresee, and the present aspects of which fill
with alarm many even of its former advocates, the
North will likely be slow about making further
sacrifices for you on a large scale. Yet in the end
I believe North, South, and West will combine to
help your movement, because your going will be
for this country's good as well as your own. A
government whose revenue from whiskey and
tobacco alone in two years would doubtless more
than pay the expenses of the immediate transport-
ation and settlement in Africa of your entire race
now in this country, a government which has spent
$800,000,000 on pensions alone within twenty-five
years, is surely in a position to countenance and
give at least a measure of material aid to a movement which must prove of vast benefit to its own
citizens.

" But do not make the mistake of waiting until
that is done. All the important emigrations of
history were the voluntary movements of spirited
and enterprising men who were anxious to better
their condition. The two greatest emigrations in
the history of the world, those of the Irish and
Germans to this country, were accomplished without any government aid whatever. The total cost
must have been enormous, but was borne by the
emigrants themselves, although most of them were
very poor men. Do you, then, follow the exam-
ple of these; work hard, live frugally, put by your
savings, and when the time arrives you will not be
left behind. Most of you have little to leave
behind, and a very small sum comparatively would
suffice to carry a family to Africa, build for them a
house as habitable as most of you now live in, and
maintain them for a year. Liberia is not your only
chance. The great Congo Free State has now
been opened to the world, and its charter offers
splendid opportunities for the founding of an
empire by determined colonists. The climate
would perhaps be trying for a white man, but it
could hardly be so for you. The mean tempera-
ture is really never excessive, seldom rising above
ninety-one degrees even in the hottest months, from
January to April. The country is divided between
mountains, plains, and lowlands, is dotted with
lakes abounding in fish, and is intersected by innu-
merable rivers, the greatest of which is the mighty

Congo, a stream nearly three thousand miles in length, and not less than ten miles wide at its mouth. There are vast tracts of the country covered with seemingly boundless forests interrupted only here and there by clearings around the villages and farms. The best of the negro races are said to be found in the Congo basin. The present scattered inhabitants of this region are said to be peacefully inclined, to be good farmers, and to have a taste for trading. There is already a trade in precious spices, ivory, gums, and dyewoods; and rich iron and sulphur mines, and gold and silver deposits, have been found. The soil is exceedingly fertile, and many useful trees and plants, as coffee, grow wild, and as many as three crops a year of some vegetables can be produced. Besides many native fruits unknown to you, the grape, the orange, the lemon, the pine-apple, the cocoanut, the banana, etc., flourish there, and manioc, millet, sugar-cane, tobacco, hemp, etc., are cultivated. Indian corn, wheat, rice, and the potato could no doubt be introduced, if this has not already been done; for in the opinion of eminent scientists, the Congo basin is destined to become the granary of the world. With the exception of the elephant, the hippopotamus, the chimpanzee, and a few others, the animal life in general differs but little from that of our Atlantic seaboard. But I can't stop to tell you about all these things. You can find them out for yourselves. I only speak of

them because, to my surprise, so little has been
said of them here to-night.

"One would think your race here would rise
up as one man to embrace any opportunity to
escape degrading social conditions in a country
belonging to another race, especially when a rich
and desirable country is open to you, where, if
anywhere, you will be able to realize the dream
of prosperity and greatness which some of you
doubtless entertain. I believe there is an appointed destiny for races and nations, and surely
it would seem to be yours to go back to the ancient
seat of your race, and carry the blessings of civi-
lization which you have at least in a measure
acquired during your long enforced sojourn in a
strange land. A more glorious, soul-stirring prospect has never been set before the eyes of any
people.

"Will you advance and embrace it? Are you
worthy of it? If you are, you will be prompt to
bestir yourselves. Your leading men will be tire-
less in their effort to awaken the masses of the race
to the importance of this question. They will
agitate it far and wide in this country, and cease
not until there has developed an overwhelming
sentiment in favor of it among your people, — until
shipload after shipload of your friends and neighbors have forever left American shores, — and all
this whether with or without the white man's
help."

It was now half-past twelve o'clock, and on concluding his remarks Colonel Sanford did not wait
to hear more. Turning, he walked quickly down
the aisle as he had come, and then out at the door.
The bench reserved for the whites was long since
deserted. Two or three white men were standing
just outside, however, and as the colonel appeared,
one of them, who was a large planter, stepped forward and demanded : —

" Colonel Sanford, do you know that you are a
labor agitator, sir? "

" I 'll tell you what I know, sir," was the haughty
reply. " I know that I 'm trying to save your grandchildren and mine from inconceivable political
ruin."

" He 's a regular old crank," said one of the by-
standers, as the colonel walked on, disdaining to
discuss the matter.

" If Sam Thomas and some of the boys was here,"
remarked another, " that young Atlanta nigger
might have some trouble before he got home
to-night. He 's about as sassy as they make
'em."

Colonel Sanford soon left the precincts of the
Neck behind, and entered Barcelona proper. The
streets were now absolutely deserted, and, although
the freshening wind shook the China-trees and
scattered their yellowed leaves abroad, the midnight stillness and repose were no less perceptible
and impressive.

As he advanced into the glare of an electric light in the business quarter, the colonel's attention was attracted to the figure of a woman shuffling noisily and hurriedly over the brick sidewalk. As she drew near, she called his name eagerly, and he recognized Maum Katie. She breathlessly informed him that Mrs. Lawrence was dead, and asked if he would not go to the house, no one being there but Miss Reba and the doctor. She was now on her way to tell Mrs. Brown.

"She was tuck sudden," the old woman explained. "I des happened to be dere, an' I run fer de dawcter, but he ain't mo'n git dere a half-hour befo' she was gone."

Colonel Sanford said he would go instantly, and the two separated. Upon arriving, he found the front door open and the hall dark, but light streamed from a chamber door which stood ajar, and after some moments of hesitation he approached and entered softly. The doctor turned from the bed at the sound, and the two men stood together near the door and whispered, their eyes fixed on the young girl who knelt beside the couch of death, her face buried in the pillows, her hand clasping that of the dead, her form quivering but sending forth no sound.

"It is a very strange case," whispered the doctor. "She must have suffered from a sort of nervous dyspepsia, for she has evidently wasted away for the want of proper nourishment."

In a short while hurried steps were heard in the hall, and Mrs. Brown appeared, being followed into the room by her daughter and Maum Katie. Betty went instantly to the bed and knelt down there, clasping Reba in her arms.

"Oh, doctor — colonel —" faltered Mrs. Brown, with streaming eyes, looking from one to the other appealingly, — "it 's so sudden — so dreadful! We did n't none of us know a thing ailed her more than common. Po' Reba! po' child!"

XIII.

On the morning after the great debate, in which he modestly believed he had achieved distinction if not greatness, Mamie-Lou John left the town in the company of a young negro called Riley Martin, who had succeeded Cicero as his favored friend. Tired of hanging about the haunts of the idle in the Neck and Barcelona proper, they had some days since planned a change of scene, and only waited for the night of the debate to come and go before taking the highway for Putnam, situate twenty miles away in the adjoining county of Richmond.

Cheerfulness is one of the negro's most pronounced characteristics, and these two reckless vagabonds, who had no prospects in life, and who, indeed, would be lucky to escape the halter, did not fail to enliven their long tramp with jest and laughter, gossip and song. At one o'clock they halted in the negro settlement of a plantation, drank water at the well, and met a friendly welcome, but were not offered food, the dinner hour

being long past. However, they did not suffer,
having found wild grapes in a forest by the way,
foraged a field until they secured a phenomenally
late watermelon, and later in the day invaded a
farmer's sugar-cane patch. The average negro is
accustomed to scant and irregular meals, and these
two were by no means inclined to complain of hard
fare that day.

Arrived before nightfall in Putnam, a less considerable town than Barcelona, they looked up old
acquaintances, made new ones, stood about the
fires which the blacks burned out of doors in the
back streets, made themselves agreeable, and were
invited to supper. Later they lay down to sleep
on the bare floor before an open fire in the cabin
of an acquaintance, their host occupying the small
inner apartment with his wife and family. This
was only a slight inconvenience to Mamie-Lou and
Riley, and they thought not of complaining even
to each other; they were enjoying their visit, and,
but for an important circumstance, they might
have returned to Barcelona in a day or two no more
guilty than when they started on their journey.

The important circumstance was the sight of a
young white man with money. It was at an early
hour of the next morning that they saw him go
into an express office in Putnam and count and
re-count a roll of bank notes preparatory to having
it inclosed in an express envelope and sealed.
They kept an eye on him all day as he went about

13

doing business and collecting more money, and when about mid-afternoon they overheard him say that he was going to ride to Barcelona that night, they put their heads together and whispered.

The young man was a fine, handsome fellow, barely of age, and was none other than Betty Walton's youthful lover, Jack Sanford. The old colonel had hoped to see his son study law, and was disappointed when he developed an eminently practical turn and a great liking for business. However, when Jack declared that he would rather be a successful merchant — and he believed he could be in time — than an unsuccessful lawyer, which would be inevitable, his father wisely allowed him to follow his own bent. After serving two years in the establishment of a prominent merchant of Barcelona, he was now second only to the head clerk in importance and value, having developed uncommon aptitude for the business and risen rapidly. An absorbing desire to marry Betty Walton as soon as possible was unquestionably the leading inspiration of his untiring efforts, and now that she had engaged herself to him he worked harder than ever.

During the past year it had been his practice to spend a week about once a month in visiting the smaller towns in Malvern and one or two neighboring counties in order to solicit orders and collect accounts, and this was his present business in Putnam. The vicious, the lazy, and incompetent are prone to cherish feelings of envy and malevolence toward the worthy, the intelligent, and industrious. When, therefore, Mamie-Lou John and Riley Martin saw Jack Sanford counting his employer's gains, they asked themselves what right had this young white man to all that money when they had none; and, as they meditated their dark design, their only scruple took the shape of the fear of detection and punishment. They resolved to act, but to act warily.

It was six o'clock before Jack Sanford had finished his business and was ready to start. He had his choice between going to an hotel or the house of a friend for the night, waiting for the morrow to start home; but he did neither, preferring to take the lonely night ride. His reasons were simple and sound. He had been absent five days and felt that almost an eternity yawned between the present and his last glimpse of Betty, and if he went straight home without loss of time, he knew that he could see her the same night. There was to be a ball at Barcelona, and, knowing nothing of Mrs. Lawrence's sudden death, he counted on the presence of Betty among the dancers. Without pushing his horse too hard, he calculated that he could reach home by half-past nine; by half-past ten, or at the latest, eleven, he could present himself at the ball, and even though her card should prove to be taken up, he could at least see Betty in her beautiful evening dress, and have a few words with

her between dances. The ardent lover did not go
over all this twice before deciding to start.

There had been not a few cases of murder and
robbery within his recollection on lonely roads at
night in Malvern and Richmond counties, but as he
went on his way Jack Sanford did not recall one
of them or think of a possible danger. The night
was clear and the high-sailing moon rained plentiful light along the winding road, the coarse, heavy
sand of which glistened here and there with the
brilliancy of diamonds; but deep shadow envel-
oped the forests of pine on either hand, and none
could know what evil might lurk there. Jack did
not even recall with a sense of satisfaction that he
had taken the advice of friends and carried a pistol
when starting on his tour; his mind was occupied
by a single picture, — that of Betty whirling grace-
fully in the dance, clothed in soft garments of white,
and more beautiful than the watchful moon-goddess
herself.

About five miles from Putnam, at a turn of the
road, he was suddenly aroused from his absorbed
contemplation of this alluring picture by a flash of
red light only a few feet to the right of him, and
the sound of a pistol-shot close at hand. There
was no time to draw his own weapon and defend
himself or put spurs to his horse and flee; a second
shot immediately followed the first, and by the time
Jack had grasped his pistol his horse had plunged
madly forward and was sinking beneath him.

As the wounded animal went down, falling heavily upon its side and pinning its rider to the earth, two dark figures materialized at the borders of the road and leaped upon their prey. Jack's pistol had gone off at random, but was still in his hand, and he strove to spring to his feet and defend himself. While struggling frantically to withdraw his leg from beneath the horse, unable to rise or see his assailants, with the harrowing thought in his mind that he might be murdered and see his Betty no more, he was conscious of a heavy blow on the head accompanied by a sharp intense pain. And then, in a moment, all things became a dark, formless waste before his sight and before his mind.

A short while later two strangers presented themselves at a negro cabin on the same road and less than a mile from the scene. One of them halted to drive a bloody hatchet into the gatepost, while the other mounted the steps and knocked. An old man opened the door, and a middle-aged woman and a young man just grown came and looked over his shoulder at the visitors. Mamie-Lou and Riley announced, with every appearance of innocence, that they were walking from Barcelona to Putnam, that they were tired and cold (the night was a little frosty), and asked permission to stop and rest by the fire for half an hour.

The privilege was readily granted, and they were soon warming themselves before the bright pine-knot fire and engaged a in friendly conversation with the old man and his son. It was past the hour of supper, but they were invited to help themselves to some sweet potatoes which had just been raked out of the hot ashes, and did not fail to do them full justice. Their host felt that politeness forbade his asking questions, but he permitted himself to inquire what " mought be" his visitors' "entitlements," whereupon Mamie-Lou glibly mentioned a false name for himself and another for Riley, who looked somewhat disconcerted. The old negro then mentioned that his own name was Jerry Carter, and his son's was June. In the course of their conversation he also stated that they were farming for themselves on rented land; they held a small eighty-acre farm belonging to Colonel Sanford of Barcelona, and were on good terms with their landlord. The visitors, as they were from Barcelona, of course knew who Colonel Sanford was.

" Mister Jack, de cun'l's son, stopped by yuh to see us 'bout de rent yistiddy," said old Jerry, little dreaming that his two visitors had heard the last sigh of the young white man named within the hour.

After warming himself thoroughly and eating a couple of potatoes, Riley became uneasy and restless, evidently desiring to be gone, but Mamie-Lou lingered, laughing and joking in the most careless manner. A gold ring on his little finger attracted the notice of old Jerry and his son, the latter inquiring if the owner would sell it. Mamie-Lou pretended that he could not be induced to part with it, but presently offered it for the sum of ten dollars, and finally agreeing to accept one dollar for it, the money was paid and the ring passed to its new and proud owner. This business completed, the two travellers said good-night and departed. Had June Carter been able to read, he would doubtless have inquired what was the meaning of the name "Betty," which was so prettily engraved on the inside of the ring.

It was near nine o'clock when the murderers left the cabin and took the road in haste for Barcelona, fifteen miles distant. At every sound they halted, squatted in the grass by the roadside, or hid themselves in the bushes until the way was clear. The first five miles were covered within less than an hour, so great was their hurry, but after that they lagged from weariness, having been on their feet all day; and it was one o'clock when they saw the lights of Barcelona. Failure to make a fair division of the spoils was a fruitful source of angry words during the journey, and a serious struggle would have ensued if, at the last moment, Mamie-Lou, who had seized the money in the first place, had not come to terms and surrendered to Riley what the latter regarded as his rightful share. Much to their chagrin, the sum of twenty dollars only was found on their victim, the bulk of the collections having been forwarded by express.

The sound of music and happy young voices

arrested their attention as they passed through the quiet streets of the town. The ball at which Jack Sanford had expected to find Betty was still in progress, but some of its gay company was now going home. Riley Martin's impulse was to slink away in the night, particularly after sighting two policemen at the door of the "opera" house; but Mamie-Lou John walked boldly forward, calling upon him to follow. The latter had saved his neck from the halter by his coolness before, and had no intention of letting slip so good an opportudity as this to secure an alibi.

"Quit crowdin' me, nigger!" shouted Mamie-Lou, giving his friend a rude push, as they stopped to watch some half-dozen couples streaming out into the night air.

Riley took the cue and a slight struggle ensued, attracting the attention of all. The crafty Mamie-Lou thus succeeded in catching the eyes of several swallow-tailed young white men who knew him by name.

"Go on off from here right straight, or you'll git locked up," ordered one of the policemen, after demanding the cause of their presence "up town" at that hour of the night.

"Who, me?" shouted Mamie-Lou, with a guffaw. "*I* been to a party." And off they went.

As they separated to go to their respective homes in the Neck, Riley was thus cautioned by his more talented friend: "If you know what's good for you, you git up soon in de mornin' an' show yourself. I aim to be up town by daylight myself, an' stand round dat fire in front o' 'Liza Simmons's."

Riley Martin overslept, but his energetic friend, true to his word, not only exhibited himself on the streets at an early hour next day, but figured among the crowd which pressed forward to get a glimpse of Jack Sanford's body when it was brought from Putnam on the midday train, and transferred from the stretcher to the waiting coffin, amid the horror-stricken whispers of the spectators.

Before going down town after breakfast that morning Colonel Sanford spent an hour looking through his mail, which consisted of several business letters, a leading Georgia daily newspaper, and the latest issue of the London " Saturday Review." The letters were promptly put aside for a fuller examination later on, and the larger portion of the hour was expended on the newspaper and the periodical. The room in which he sat was called by the colonel's daughter the library, by his wife the sitting-room, and by the colonel himself his " home office." Its most pronounced feature was the book-shelves covering two-thirds of the wall space, containing the remnant of a once comparatively extensive library, or such a portion thereof as still remained after years of depredation on the part of the conscienceless, who borrow and never return.

It was while the colonel sat tranquilly reading

in this student's paradise that a message addressed
to him came over the wires from Putnam and was
written out in the Barcelona office. Had he sat
there ten minutes longer the message, which was
promptly sent out for delivery, would have reached
him in his own house, but the sudden recollection
that he had intended to call at the stricken Lawrence home early that morning caused him to drop
his papers and hurry off. He found Betty on the
Lawrence piazza and sat down there with her, asking news of Reba.

"She bears it as well as could be expected,"
the girl told him. "It is very hard for her; she
had no one else — but us."

"Betty, do you think she is engaged to Rob
Morton?" asked Colonel Sanford, thoughtfully.
"I am sure he loves her, and if he had spoken
before this happened, she would not now feel so
wretched and alone, — that is, if she loves him."

"I don't think they can be engaged," said Betty,
quite willing to tell all she knew to her prospective father-in-law, who was a familiar friend. "I
think she likes him, but I am not sure. She is
very reticent."

"I wish we could have seen them married before
this happened," mused the colonel.

While they were still talking, a negro boy opened
the gate and approached, holding a small yellow
envelope in his hand. "Dey tole me dey seen you
come down yuh," he remarked, delivering it to

Colonel Sanford. The boy breathed hard, as if he had been running.

Betty saw that it was a telegram and that it had already been opened. As Colonel Sanford unfolded it and absorbed its contents, she observed a sudden convulsive movement of his hands. A glance at his face revealed to her that her friend's soul was occupied with a most intense anguish, and without waiting to be bidden she bent over and read the message. It was then evident that the same intense anguish occupied her own soul. With a low, broken cry she fell on her knees and looked up frantically into the colonel's eyes. A moment later they were clasped in each other's arms, each uttering inarticulate murmurs and desolate sobs.

"Dey tole me to tell you to come dere," ventured the negro boy, after waiting uneasily during some moments. "I taken de message to yo' house fust an' Mis' Sanford an' all of 'em read it, an' when I was comin' 'way, Miss Kate she run out atter me an' tole me to go fetch you. She say please hurry up an' come dere right straight, her ma 'bout to go deetracted."

Colonel Sanford staggered to his feet, kissed Betty on the forehead, and hurried down the steps. Then the girl turned promptly and entered the house, putting out her hands before her as if to feel her way. The negro boy picked up the telegram which had fallen to the floor, and followed the colonel down the street.

Miss Black was standing in the photographer's doorway when her honored friend passed by. She offered him a bright smile, but he did not seem to see her at all, and she observed that he looked ill and staggered slightly at every few steps. She involuntarily stepped into the street and looked after him anxiously; observing which, the negro boy, who still followed, stopped and gave her the telegram to read. A few moments later, almost blinded by her tears, Miss Black was asking leave of absence, and having put on her bonnet, hurried away in the direction of the Sanford home.

A Richmond County farmer, starting at daylight for Putnam, had discovered the body. He also observed the bloody hatchet sticking in Jerry Carter's gate-post and leaped to a conclusion, pausing not to consider that such thoughtlessness on the part of the murderer or murderers was incredible. The alarm soon spread. While the coroner went out from Putnam and took charge of the body, the sheriff and a posse also fared forth and led the old negro and his son to town, regardless of the screams of the wife and mother and the reiterated story of the visit of the two strange negroes the night before. The costly ring on the finger of young Carter at once excited increasing suspicion, and, it being presently identified by a friend of Jack Sanford, the public mind was irrevocably made up. It was known what business re-

lation existed between Colonel Sanford and the
Carters, and it was now surmised by some and concluded by others that Jack had been murdered and
robbed soon after collecting the rent.

The two unhappy negroes were forthwith
lodged in jail, and it was soon being repeated from
mouth to mouth that nothing short of lynching
would mete out to them a full measure of punishment and satisfy an outraged public.

Toward the close of that day, which was so
darkened by grief and tragedy for two families in
the town, a young man was seen moving about the
streets of Barcelona, stopping here and there and
unfolding a written paper which he read aloud and
then handed around for investigation. The young
man was Sam Thomas, and, as a rule, he showed
his document, which evidently excited great interest, to men of his own age and such as he thought
suited to the business in hand.

At length, while standing in conversation with
four or five young men, Thomas saw Robert
Morton approaching, and, without giving any
reason therefor, he surprised his companions by
abruptly folding up the paper and putting it into
his pocket.

"I'm looking for somebody to sit up with me
at Colonel Sanford's to-night," said Morton, his
eye travelling round the group.

"I heard John Wellington and Gordon Marshall

say they were goin' to offer," remarked one of the young men by way of rejoinder.

" Do you know where they are? " asked Morton, about to move on.

Some one answered, and the first who had spoken detained Morton with the question: —

" By the way, has Bob seen it? "

" What? "

" That letter from the boys in Putnam. Show it to him, Sam. A friend of Sam's sent it over."

Sam Thomas then produced the paper, and unfolding it gave it to Morton without remark. It ran thus: —

PUTNAM, GEORGIA, Dec. 10, 188-.

If any friends of Mr. Jack Sanford would like to join us in a neck-tie party, come over to-night on the ten o'clock train and we will meet you. We will have every-thing arranged. Feeling runs high and we are going to do it up brown.

HEMP.

" Well, boys," said Morton very gravely, as he folded the letter and returned it to its owner, " I don't know who's going and who is n't, and I 'm not going to ask. It is none of my business. But I want to tell you what Colonel Sanford said to me not half an hour ago. He said, if I heard any talk of lynching, to say — from him — that he *would not countenance it*, and he hoped his wishes would be respected in the matter. He said he begged the young men of this town not to add to

his misery by lynching two negroes who possibly
may prove to be innocent of the murder of his
son."

"Well, if the colonel feels that way, of course —"
began one of the young men, evidently moved by
this appeal.

"He won't feel that way a month from now,"
interrupted Sam Thomas. "Of course he's all
broke up to-day."

"I wish you boys would mention to everybody
what the colonel says about it," concluded Morton,
decisively, omitting Thomas as his eye went round
the circle. He then moved on his way, the others
lingering to discuss the matter further.

The message of the stricken father was not without its effect on a number. Nevertheless a small
contingent made ready, went over on the ten-
o'clock train and joined the Putnam forces, and the
"neck-tie party" took place in due course. Jerry
Carter's gray hairs, his frantic prayers and protestations of innocence, and the bare possibility of
a doubt, induced the lynchers to spare him. The
next morning it was known that he had been left
in the jail to stand his trial, but that his son hung
by the neck close to the spot where Jack Sanford
had heaved his last sigh, and that the bereft
wife and mother went about from place to place,
wailing piteously and seeking comfort where there
there was none.

XIV.

THOSE were sad days which succeeded in three
households of Barcelona. Colonel Sanford was not
a man to surrender himself to grief and helplessly
deplore the calamity which had befallen his house,
— a hopeful striving to recognize a Providence
in all the events of life being with him a leading
characteristic. Nevertheless the loss of an only
son in such an unforeseen and horrible manner was
a crushing blow. He staggered beneath the weight
of it, but did not fall. He alone in his family
maintained a composure, and he outdid his minis-
tering friends in devising means of diverting his
stricken wife and daughters when in the first ago-
nies of their grief. The news of the unlawful exe-
cution of the suspected murderer, which reached
him promptly, so far from gratifying or comforting
him, caused his face to contract in pain as the fear
fell on him that innocence might have been offered
up in the stead of the guilty, in which case the
latter was now escaped beyond detection.

"They ought to have listened to me," he said wearily to Morton. "They assumed a fearful responsibility and may live to rue their action. In any case, it was unnecessary, and therefore wholly unjustifiable."

The other two stricken households were now merged into one. The Lawrence house was shut up, Reba having been induced to go to her aunt's, where a double grief now reigned, the poignancy of the one, however, perhaps in a measure softened through sympathy with the other. On the day after the second funeral Mrs. Brown gave a touching account of the two girls, her minister having called.

"They don't do nothin'," she tearfully asserted, "but sit and cry and put their arms round one 'n other, and then talk a little and then cry again."

But it was not all crying. Now and then they spoke hopefully of the future state of the mother and lover, of their probable meeting, which had perhaps already taken place, and of their life in that new, super-material world which is a logical and necessary complement of the wondrous miracle of creation already visible to our natural eyes. Overhearing this, Mrs. Brown's own heart was momentarily eased of much pain, but she shook her head doubtfully as she recalled the teachings of her minister, with which such ideas did not agree. Calling in order to give her consolation, he had told her that the precious dead for which they mourned would sleep until the last day, which might be a thousand or a million years hence, — nobody knew, — and that finally the dissipated body would again clothe the awakening spirit and the dead would live again. To further comfort her, he stated, in substance, that it was the opinion of some that the bodiless spirit floated about in the air, or ether, in a state of partial or full consciousness, waiting, waiting, through the interminable cycles of time for that deliverance supposed to arrive only after re-conjunction with the vanished body.

This picture of exquisite torture had been painted for the two sorrowing girls also in former days, but they now refused to contemplate it; with the unperverted perception of hopeful youth, they preferred to remember the visions of poets, and such applicable portions of Holy Writ as lived in their memory. The " To-day shalt thou be with me in paradise," from the Lord's own mouth, was to them an unfailing beam of light transpiercing their cloud of sorrow and pain.

But at the end of three weeks they both looked wasted and thin, and Mrs. Brown decided that something must be done for them. She consulted with her husband, and it was proposed to send them to visit a relative who lived in Chatham County, by the sea, a change of scene being always the best of medicines. After some coaxing they agreed to go, and Mrs. Brown hurried them off. Thus, by a few weeks spent on a rice plantation by the unfa-

miliar sea, were they in a measure diverted from
their sorrows, returning home much the gainers in
health of body and cheerfulness of mind.

While they were away Reba received a letter
which brought sudden bright color into her pale
cheeks. She was walking alone on the sands,
looking wistfully out over the quivering yellow
marshes and the blue leaping ocean, when a negro
boy attached to the house ran toward her with a
sealed missive bearing the Barcelona post-mark.
She knew the chirography at a glance, having received a number of brief notes in the same hand
asking the "pleasure of her company" at a ball or
for an afternoon drive. As soon as she was alone
Reba read this important letter, reread it, and then
prolonged her walk far beyond the limits first proposed, seeing always wherever she looked, out over
the marshes or the sea, one image, — the young
man of the sallow face, the square jaw, and the
haunting eyes.

"I have just heard of your departure," he wrote,
"and not knowing when you may return, or what
may happen, I am unable to resist my desire to
communicate with you. I longed to go to you
immediately after your great loss, but felt that I
had not the right, and since then I have been waiting, not with the patience of a philosopher, but
with the doubts and fears of an unhappy lover,
until such time as I could approach you without
intruding upon your grief. I think you must have

seen long ago that I cared for no one but you. For two years past the greatest and most constant ambition of my life has been to make you my wife, and it is my steadfast purpose to win your love if that be possible. I know not how to plead my case, how even to express my feelings, but there is one thing I know, and that is that I love you. I have absolutely no reason to hope that you will ever return my love, and I tremble to think of what your answer may be, but I know that you will be considerate and kind if you cannot love. For the present all I ask is that you give me time and opportunity in which to try to win you."

By way of postscript, the following was written: " I asked your mother's permission to address you, and it was granted."

To this simple, manly love-letter a brief answer was despatched a day or two later. " I thank you for the great compliment involved in your letter," Reba wrote. " In reply I can only say that no woman is ever unwilling to give 'time and opportunity' to a man whom she respects and has no reason to dislike. When we return, in a few weeks, my cousin and I will be pleased to receive you at my aunt's."

The encouragement that could be read into these lines was certainly of a very moderate nature and there was little to build real hope upon, but the young man to whom they were addressed was made almost deliriously happy on reading them.

To him they meant at the very least that no other man was preferred. Betty had ere this made up her mind that her cousin loved Morton. Supposing there were reasonable grounds for this conclusion, the cause of Reba's epistolary impassivity and reserve, her manifest determination to keep her lover in suspense until a future season, must be sought for in the mysterious and inexplicable operations of the feminine mind.

On the day after the two girls returned home, Mrs. Blossom and her maid appeared unexpectedly in Barcelona. The Philadelphia lady explained to her niece that homesickness had cut short her stay in Jamaica. As long as her nephew, Paul Shepherd, had remained at Kingston, everything had pleased her, she declared, but later on, when loneliness began to prey upon her, everything became equally displeasing. A Christmas enlivened only by the remarks of her maid and the nods of a few acquaintances when she drove out, was the finishing touch to the dreary picture, and she had determined to pack up at once and take all the risks of the Northern winter and spring. The weather happened to be particularly fine when she halted to rest in Barcelona, and her proposed stay of a day or two was prolonged to two weeks, during which time she several times came in contact with Reba and Betty, who were now Miss Black's acknowledged friends. Toward the last she twice took Reba and her niece driving.

Her interest in the former steadily increased, and she soon determined to act on her nephew's suggestion and invite the girl to visit her in Philadelphia.

"I want her on my own account as well as on Paul's," she said to her niece. "I am fond of her already. Really it is difficult to understand how a girl could grow up so refined and well-bred, and be in every way so lovely, in the midst of such poverty as you say was hers."

"'Blood will tell,' perhaps, as people say here," suggested Miss Black. "It is considered a fine family, and her mother was said to have many accomplishments."

"Sometimes it 'tells,' and again it does n't," rejoined Mrs. Blossom, stroking her prominent nose and reflecting. She was hardly to be called a handsome woman, although distinguished by a strong and pleasing presence.

"Paul does n't care for ordinary society life in the least," she continued. "He actually shuns it. He has n't shown himself at an Assembly ball in years. But I could see that he was unusually interested in this girl. It was n't her mere beauty, I 'm sure. I should like to see him marry a girl of the right sort, and Miss Lawrence impresses me favorably."

"He would be lucky to get her," declared Miss Black, so irreverently that her aunt was filled with indignation. They were alone in the photographer's little parlor, Miss Black at work examining

newly mounted portraits, and Mrs. Blossom standing near the street door, looking out.

"She ought to go now, with me," the latter
continued presently. "She needs a change. But
what could I do with her, socially, so soon after
her mother's death? However, she would be
there during Lent."

"She is n't wearing mourning," said Miss Black.

"By the way, I noticed that. It is n't *possible*
that she does n't know any better!"

"Mr. Lawrence objected to it, I believe."

"How foolish! What were his reasons, pray?"

"I heard that he said it was the very essence of
vulgarity to be continually holding up a sacred
private grief to the view of the public, and that is
what mourning apparel does."

"Well, upon my word, I never thought of it in
that light before," exclaimed Mrs. Blossom, almost
as if indignant that such an idea had heretofore
been withheld from her.

Miss Black added that Miss Walton was her
authority, she having reported that her uncle had
requested his wife and daughter not to wear mourning for him. He said the practice had come down
from the ancient Pagan world, and was in its very
nature more Pagan than Christian. The true
Christian being supposed to believe in a blessed
future state, nothing but the most consummate
selfishness, or the most absolute unbelief, could
justify him in mourning indefinitely for the de-

parted friend. Mrs. Blossom remarked that all this sounded very well, but she desired to be told how any respectable person was to carry out such an idea in the face of established custom.

"I want to see more of these new friends of yours whom you have elected to love so much," she had said to her niece on the day after her arrival, — "not only Miss Lawrence and her cousin, but this Colonel Sanford, and especially that young — Morton? — that knight of yours. Francie," she boldly demanded, " are you engaged to him?"

"Why, Aunt Mildred!" exclaimed Miss Black, with heightened color. "Did you think *that* was the reason he acted as he did when I first came here and had no friends? I scarcely know him. He *never* calls on me."

"Oh? Then I misjudged you, Francie, and failed to give him his due. So, then, your 'eyes are opened,' and you sympathize with the poor white brother, and not with the 'poor negro,' contrary to prevailing sentiment and tradition?"

" Exactly."

" Well, I can't say that I am personally fond of the 'poor negro' myself. He positively sickened me in the West Indies. I'm glad enough that one-half the population of Philadelphia is not black."

A few days later her curiosity was satisfied. She contrived to have Morton presented to her, and engaged him in conversation for half an hour.

" He may be an excellent young man," she told
her niece afterwards, " but he is too stiff, or too
haughty, or something.   He needs social training.
How sallow he is !   But for those strange, those
really beautiful eyes, he would be positively ugly.
If he only looked more like Paul.   He is insignificant in comparison."

At this point of the discussion Miss Black's lip
curled, to the intense indignation of her aunt.
Colonel Sanford would have laughingly quoted
" De gustibus," etc., and Mrs. Blossom herself would
have lightly said, " Chacun à son gout ; " but Miss
Black allowed her lip to lift itself in scorn, disdaining words.

" I really believe you consider him a finer type
than Paul ! " exclaimed the elder lady, critically
surveying her niece.

" I do," said Miss Black, boldly taking the bit
between her teeth ; whereupon her aunt's wrath
waxed so hot that she would not trust herself to
speak.   It was evident that her nephew was her
idol.   The two ladies were driving at the time, a
week after Mrs. Blossom's arrival.

" How I enjoyed those rides I used to take
through these pine-woods," said Miss Black anon,
breaking the silence.   " I never go now."

" I should suppose so."

A few minutes later, turning a bend of the road,
they came suddenly upon a phaeton driven by
Robert Morton.   At his side sat Reba, her face

alive with color, and in her hands a cluster of the beautiful bell-like yellow jessamines now just beginning to put forth and perfume the woods. Mrs. Blossom forgot her annoyance, so charmed was she by the vision of happy youth which the two presented. Had she known of the letters which they exchanged a few weeks before, she would have readily comprehended that they had now come to a full understanding and pledged themselves to each other; for their faces were suffused with a soft glow, and a tender, indescribable light shone in their eyes. Even without knowing anything of this, she was struck by the atmosphere of peace and happiness which seemed to surround them.

"They look like lovers," she remarked, with surprise, after Reba had bowed and smiled, Morton had lifted his hat, and the phaeton had passed them.

"Perhaps they are," was Miss Black's slightly constrained answer.

"I shall invite her to visit me anyhow," Mrs. Blossom continued, after a moment's reflection. "It may not have gone very far yet, and if Paul should really fancy her she will think twice before she refuses him for a young man who has nothing in the world."

"She will not think twice if she knows and loves Mr. Morton," said Miss Black, with decision. "His poverty will be the last thing she will think of."

" You are as perverse and foolish as your
mother was before you," declared the elder lady,
severely. "*She* lost her head about a penniless
young man, and as a result of it her daughter is
now a working-girl in a photographer's shop. I
had more wisdom."

" My mother has never known actual want, and
she has been a happy woman ever since her marriage," said Miss Black, with flashing eyes. " I 'd
far rather be a 'working-girl' and know that she
tenderly loved my honored father, than to be rich
and know that they hated each other."

" What do you mean?" exclaimed the elder lady,
looking round sharply.

But a record of the family quarrels, misunder-
standings, or mistakes, with which these two women
were concerned, of a marriage of outward ease and
inward heart-burning and regret on the one hand,
and another distinguished by much external hard-
ship and interior happiness, is not within the scope
of this brief tale.

" Really, Francie," said Mrs. Blossom, returning
to the subject of Morton, as they were on their
way home, " I 'd advise you to be careful. It is
unwise for a girl to allow her thoughts to dwell on
a young man who pays her no particular attentions."

This thrust caused Miss Black to bite her lip
and answer haughtily: " Do not be alarmed. I
shall be able to take care of myself."

The invitation was given and pressed, but for the present, at least, was declined. Reba felt that the eccentric Northern lady, whose liking she returned, really wished her to go, and did not dismiss the matter as a mere compliment. She showed a due appreciation of such unexpected kindness, and readily agreed to the proposal of a correspondence until such time as she might desire to accept the invitation. The recent death of her mother, and the fact that she was without money would have been sufficient ground for her decision, but this was not all. Having of late entered upon a new and great happiness, which any indefinite absence from home would seriously mar, she felt no desire to leave Barcelona. And so her new friend went North without her.

XV.

THE January election of municipal officers was a season of no little excitement in Barcelona, and the struggle for the office of mayor especially was hard fought and productive of animosity between the adherents of opposing candidates. There being less than half a dozen white Republicans in the town, and the white voters possessing a safe majority, the negroes did not put forward a candidate, and as there were two opposing Democratic factions, the blacks for the most part sold their votes to the highest bidder, possibly arguing that, the office being beyond their reach, it was only fair that they should have a share of the salary.

Thus the negro practically holds the balance of power in local elections. But unfortunately it never seems to occur to him to use it in the interest of good government. The prospect of personal gain appears to occupy his whole attention. The candidate who, through his close friends, will pay the highest price for the services of a dozen of the most experienced black " workers," will control the election. As for the rank and file — give a negro a pint of whiskey, or send him to the polling-place in a carriage, and his vote is secured. Still, there is usually some room left for the display of demagoguery, and the more shameless of the two candidates always poses as the especial friend of the black man.

Adam Brown did not scruple to appear in this rôle, he being a candidate for re-election. Opposed to him was the best element of the town, with a really respectable candidate,—one Harvey, a lawyer of ability and known integrity; but intelligence, ability, and integrity unfortunately appeal only to the intelligent and upright, and are everywhere derided by those free American sovereigns who offer their votes for sale. Such qualities are especially useless when the contest is complicated, it should rather be said debauched, by the participation of a horde of ignorant and venal blacks, whose thoughts and aspirations are apparently scarcely able to rise above the mere bodily senses and appetites. Adam Brown had indeed a white following among the less intelligent class, and among his familiars and beneficiaries, but without the cajoled and purchased vote of the vast majority of the blacks his election would not have been even remotely possible.

As the circumstances were, it was certain from the outset. All day long his hired carriages were driven through the streets, loaded with semi-tipsy and wholly senseless negroes, monarchs for a day, going in state to deposit a purchased ballot. Everywhere his "workers" were active. Here a grinning, dusky sovereign, with a ballot upside down between his fingers and a pint of whiskey in his pocket,— if not already in his stomach,— was led forward by the arm. There another, who had greedily sold himself to both sides, was paying the penalty of a public exposure, an opposing "worker" grasping each arm and dragging him back and forth with loud and abusive wrangling. As neither would be disposed to surrender, the only equitable arrangement which could suggest itself to an impartial observer was to divide the guilty sovereign in two, and vote each half. If not this, one contestant must knock the other down and bolt with the prize; and indeed such developments were more than once imminent, when the appearance of the police would put an end to the struggle. The saloons were all shut according to law, but the mayor's whiskey had been purchased in advance, stowed away at unseen and convenient distributing points, and now flowed freely among the happy darkies, who shouted, "Hurrah for Brown!" until the surrounding atmosphere was permeated with a perceptible flavor of alcohol. The opposition, the friends of candidate Harvey, made a determined effort, some of them indeed succumbing to the general demoralization to the extent of making a few indirect bids for the votes of the blacks; but on the whole they were the sort of men who will surrender before they will stoop too low, and the result was inevitable.

Among the more quiet negroes who stood about the court-house square in small groups and conversed, Parson Smith and Professor Brice were conspicuous. The parson had been easily and speedily corrupted, but the professor obstinately refused to entertain the overtures of the Brown forces, much to their astonishment and disgust. His attitude was partly due to his superior knowledge and character, and partly to the influence of Colonel Sanford. In all matters social and political, with the exception of questions involved in national elections, the professor sought instruction from his honored white friend, and was a willing pupil. Only a few days since they had discussed the coming election, and Colonel Sanford had eloquently urged it as the duty of every good citizen to support the most worthy and capable candidate, regardless of party, of reward, or the fear of censure. The professor had not failed to be impressed, and being sufficiently astute to perceive that Brown's protestations of especial friendship for the negro were hollow and insincere, he determined on the course above indicated.

" Who you goin' vote for, Mr. Smith? " asked a young black man, as he joined the group surrounding the parson and the schoolmaster.

" Well, I think I 'll vote for Mr. Brown," said his

Reverence, unconsciously smacking his lips at the recollection of a recent dram. "I ain't got nothin' against him, an' they tell me he's the friend o' the po' man an' the cullud man."

"Yas-sir! *he's* de man to vote for," cried the first speaker, with enthusiasm. "He willin' to pay for it, you see him so. He got de money an' he willin' to pay it out. I done voted, merself. I wish I could vote 'bout six times mo'. I'd be willin' to vote eve'y day in de week if dey pay me."

"He ain't the friend o' the colored man any mo''n Harvey is — not one bit," said the professor, stubbornly. "You listen at all that! Neither one o' 'em is the friend o' the colored man. Colonel Sanford the best friend the colored man got I know of, — he don't tell us no lies. Adam Brown make out like he do anything for us to-day, but jes' wait tell to-morrow."

"Den you won't vote for him?"

"I voted for Harvey — if you want to know. An' I'll tell you why: I done it because he's got the most sense an' the most education, an' I believe he's the most apt to do the right thing for white an' for black. I'd ruther trust him. You don't see him rushin' round makin' us promises he don't aim to perform. That shows he's honest. Adam Brown can't pull the wool over my eyes as easy as he can some niggers."

"Sorry to see you so sot in yo' mind, Brother Brice," said the parson, shaking his head in disapproval. "Colonel Sanford a nice man, I don't dispute it, but it won't do to let him 'suade you too fur."

"I ruther be persuaded by common-sense 'n by boodle," retorted the professor.

"Wut 's dat?" asked one of the by-standers.

"Some call it whiskey, some call it spondulix," was the quick response; whereupon there was a laugh from all who saw the point, the parson, how-ever, participating only to the extent of a "dry grin."

Conspicuous figures on the streets and about the court-house square throughout the day were Mamie-Lou John and Rosetta Hightower, the for-mer being one of Mr. Brown's most enthusiastic "workers," and the latter one of the idling black women who stood about in small groups, looked, listened, gossiped, and "rubbed" snuff. Josephine Witherspoon was also frequently to be seen, slowly navigating her large person from one group to another. Cicero had passed from the scene less than six weeks since, and already Josephine was in her third honeymoon and talked gayly of her pres-ent "old man." With great hilarity and good-humor she accosted Sam Thomas on the street, informing him of her new estate and demanding tribute.

"I got ma'ied 'way week fo' last," she said, re-proachfully, "an' you ain't gim-me nothin' yit."

"If I 'd known you were goin' to strike me for a

wedding present," he retorted, laughing, "I'd 'a' dodged you."

"Would n' 'a' done you no good, *I'd* 'a' caught up wid you," she declared, with a great laugh, bending her body and spreading her arms in the extravagant African shrug, which may be fitly compared with the evolutions of a crab.

"And so you are married again already? How long has Cicero been an angel, for goodness' sake?"

"Oh, you hush dat. You got nothin' to do wid dat." She seemed to wish to resent such impertinence, but laughed in spite of herself. "Anyhow, you owe me sump'n for tellin' all dat tale to Miss Reba Lawrence."

"Well, here's half a dollar," he said, and having delivered a significant threat behind the mask of a smile, passed on. She was made distinctly to understand that if she told any one of their little conspiracy touching Miss Lawrence and Robert Morton, she would be made to pay for those divorce papers which he had drawn up at her request.

Rosetta was less gay, but she, too, had already consoled herself with another love, the unlawfulness of which appeared to disturb her no more than in the first instance. The present recipient of her favors was none other than the crafty Mamie-Lou John, who, like Cicero, had a neglected wife in the background. Rosetta was fast becoming reckless in more ways than one, as an incident of the election day showed.

Josephine had collided with the unfortunate Mrs. Simpson within the boundaries of the Neck with absolute impunity, but when Rosetta similarly insulted a prominent lady on a principal street of Barcelona, she exposed herself to possible consequences of a serious nature. Among the whites it was a matter perfectly understood that no lady would be seen down town on the day of an election; but necessity — as was afterwards stated — had compelled the mother of Robert Morton to break this unwritten law on the present day, and while passing hurriedly through the business quarter she was tempted to halt a moment and look into a shop window. It was then that Rosetta, moved by her hatred for the race in general and for Morton himself in particular, passed rapidly by, deliberately running against the unwatchful elderly lady and knocking her off her feet so effectually that nothing but the proximity of the wall of the shop prevented her from falling prostrate.

Rosetta walked on laughing, but a policeman had observed the whole proceeding, which was nothing short of a deliberate assault, and he now promptly arrested the young woman, who attracted much attention as she was led away by her noisy declamation and curses. Within a few squares of the jail, however, the defiant captive was set at liberty, after being warned that if she did not be-

have herself in future she would be put on the
chain-gang and made to work the streets. The
cause of this unexpected clemency was that the
jail was already full of negroes awaiting trial for
grave or minor offences as the case might be.

"Lockin' you niggers up and feedin' you in
the winter time is too good for you," declared the
officer, in a disgusted tone. "Looks to me like
some of you *try* to get locked up. The chain-
gang is the only thing to take the starch out of
you, and if you don't look out you'll get your fill
of it."

And so Rosetta returned to the court-house
square in triumph. About the middle of the
afternoon, or somewhat later, a negro boy sought
her with the information that "Cun'l Thomas"
desired to see her at his office, and curiosity carried her thither. All lawyers were gratuitously
dubbed "colonel" by the ignorant in Barcelona,
greatly to the disgust of such men as Colonel
Sanford who had served for their titles on the field
of battle.

Sam Thomas felt jubilant over the now clearly
foreshadowed result of the election, but as regards
his personal concerns he was rather downhearted.
In the race for money he had unquestionably left
Morton "'way behind," as he would have expressed
it, but as to prosperity in affairs of love, it was
painfully clear that his rival was forging ahead.
Certain developments of late, or evidences of them,

had alarmed him, and the conviction forced itself upon him that something decisive must be done, and done promptly, or all was lost. It was such reflections as these which incited him, as he now sat alone in his office, to unlock a drawer, take out an old letter, and begin imitating the chirography therein for perhaps the hundredth time.

"I've got it at last," he said aloud, after some minutes of careful effort. "He wouldn't be able to tell the difference himself, and how could she?"

"What you want wid me?" demanded Rosetta, appearing in the doorway.

"Oh, there you are, eh? I want to see you," responded Thomas, being careful to put away the papers on which he had been writing.

"What fur?"

"We'll come to that directly. What made you slam against Mrs. Morton that way this morning?"

"Any yo' business?"

"Oh, I ain't goin' to quarrel with you about it. I know why you did it. You did it because you hate Bob Morton, and you hate him because he knocked Cicero down and brought him to town that day, — him and Jim Jones."

"Well, if you was so wise, what made you ask me?"

"Don't be sassy now. I've got a little proposition to make to you. How would you like to make — well, say a dollar — and spite Bob Morton at the same time? I thought that would fetch you," he added, seeing the young woman's eyes leap in her head and her lips involuntarily fall apart.

" How I goin' do it? " she asked eagerly.

" I 'm goin' to put up a little job on him, — just a joke, you know, no real harm in it, — and you can help it through if — "

He checked himself at the sound of a step on the stair. Going to the door, he saw that it was Colonel Sanford, and, turning, hurriedly dismissed his companion. "I can't tell you about it now," he said softly. " Come again in about an hour, or come to-morrow."

" I thought we might take up that Abial Richardson matter this afternoon and have done with it," said Colonel Sanford, as he walked heavily from the head of the stairs to the office door, not appearing to observe the retreating figure of Rosetta.

" All right, colonel," said Thomas from the doorway, with an air of great importance. " It won't take long, once we put our heads together. This is the first time we 've been associated on a case, ain't it? "

" Yes," rejoined Colonel Sanford, coolly, as if he trusted it would be the last. He looked older and grayer since the death of his son, and his manner of seating himself showed that he was feebler.

" Well, what do you think of the election ? " asked Thomas some time later, when their business was practically completed.

" I think it is a public scandal."

" They tell me Brown is 'way ahead," rejoined the young lawyer, promptly, with a cheerful smile.

" I referred to the manner of the election," said Colonel Sanford, an expression of mingled disgust and pain on his face as he lifted his eyes to the portrait of George Washington on the opposite wall, " but my words are equally applicable to the success of the candidate himself. From your manner, I should judge that you voted for him."

" Yes, sir, I did. Between you and me, colonel, I think Harvey is the man for the place, but I could n't afford to antagonize Brown and his crowd."

" In my opinion, a man can afford to do anything that is right," was the curt rejoinder.

" But, you see, I get too much business out of 'em. We 've got to look out for number one in this world."

Colonel Sanford disdained to continue the discussion, and there was a pause.

" I wonder what Washington and Jefferson and the other founders of the Republic would say if they could see such an election," he remarked after a few moments. " Sometimes I almost wish our independence had been delayed fifty years, for in that case slavery with us would have come to an end by that act of Parliament in 1833 which caused it to cease in all the British dominions. Thus the South would have been saved from a disastrous war and the terrible financial depression and distressing social evils which followed it. For, not only would the English have voted us the same indemnification awarded the slave-owners in all their colonies, but they would never have perpetrated the gigantic mistake of conferring the suffrage suddenly, without preparation or discrimination, upon millions of slaves, the vast majority of whom were as incapable of casting an intelligent vote as their fathers were when they were led down in coffles by their own countrymen to the African coast and sold. Even now, after twenty-five years of freedom, the vast majority are as unfit to vote as ever. What the end of it all will be no man can foretell."

" Oh, the nigger is all right as long as you can control his vote," said Thomas, lightly.

" How are you going to control his vote after he is decidedly in the majority? Either there will be revolution, war, or the most ignorant and profligate race on the face of the earth will govern the most intelligent. I could give you statistics showing the negro's increase that would startle—"

"That's easy enough," interrupted Thomas, as lightly as before. "Even when they are in the majority it's no trouble at all to control their vote."

"Do you mean by intimidation?" asked Colonel Sanford, surprised. "I have never seen that done yet, and I have always been inclined to regard the accusation as a campaign lie pure and simple."

" I have no doubt it's been done," said Thomas, confidently, " but I don't believe it ever was neces- sary. There are too many other ways of cuttin' down the nigger vote. The poll-tax alone prevents thousands of 'em from votin'. In most Northern Sates the poll-tax is only fifty cents, but we have been wise enough to make it a dollar. When there's no white man who wants their votes to pay their poll-tax for 'em, lots and cords of niggers will give up voting before they 'll pay a dollar for the privi- lege. I've seen 'em back out many a time.

" The niggers have a big majority in Carleton, but when I lived there the whites always knew how to manage 'em. They had a separate ballot-box and ballot for every candidate, and it was the law for every voter, black or white, to walk in by him- self and deposit his own vote, and if he put it in the wrong box it could n't be counted. More than three-fourths of the niggers could n't read and of course they put most of their votes in the wrong boxes. To meet this, their managers would take the voters and arrange the ballots between their five fingers, and tell them to put in first this, then that, and so on, beginning at the right or the left ballot-box, as the case might be. This would work for a while," concluded the young man, with a great laugh, " but the white managers would catch on mighty quick, and go in and *shuffle the boxes*, and then there would be more confusion than ever.

"There are lots of others ways," he continued.

" For instance, the law in some places which pro-
vides that the polls shall be opened at a certain
hour or the precinct be thrown out of the election
count. I've known of heavy nigger precincts
being thrown out in this way, the white managers
being careful to oversleep and open the polling
place after the appointed hour."

" I thank Heaven that no such tactics need to be
resorted to in the community in which I live,"
said Colonel Sanford, gravely; " but I confess that
I should regard almost anything as justifiable that
would prevent this ignorant, profligate, and im-
moral people from getting control of our local
governments. It *must* be prevented. But don't
you see," he continued, gloomily, " that such ex-
pedients can work temporarily only? The rank
and file of the negroes are learning to read, and
learning fast. They don't learn much more, as a
rule, but they all seem able to learn that much and
to do it quickly. I tell you a serious struggle for
supremacy will fall to the lot of our children, perhaps to be followed by a struggle for existence
later on."

" Then, all I 've got to say is, Look out, nigger ! "

" You may be right; in the end he would
doubtless go to the wall. The negro has never yet
been able to cope with the white man, so far as I
know, except in the single instance of Hayti. But
what we should do is to take measures to avoid the

inevitable conflict at the outset by colonizing him."

" *We* might gain by that, but don't you think the negro would lose? In my opinion he 'd become a howling savage in no time."

" He *might* lapse into his former state in the course of time," said the colonel, reflectively; " there's no telling. The case of Hayti is not encouraging. I was reading Froude on the subject of the negro in the West Indies yesterday, and he does not take a hopeful view. He says the result of leaving the negro nature to itself is more and more apparent. As long as they were slaves they were docile and partly civilized, but now there is not the slightest sign that the masses are improving either in intelligence or moral habits, and the steady tendency is back toward West African superstitions. Immorality is so universal that it almost ceases to be regarded as a fault. In spite of schools, missionaries, etc., seventy per cent of the children now born are illegitimate. The young people make experiment of one another before they will enter into any closer connection, and the generality of the people are mere good-natured animals. The similarity is so striking that the reader almost forgets and begins to imagine that the historian is writing of the negro of the Southern States.

" If our negro should settle in the Congo basin and relapse into the state of some of the African

tribes, it would certainly be the worse for him.
Some of the evils found among certain tribes are
too shocking to be named. The Bushmen regard
fratricide as perfectly harmless, and have only one
word to signify girl, maiden, and wife. They con-
sort together like cattle, and the men exchange
their women freely. They regard lust and glut-
tony as the acme of earthly felicity. According
to Bastian, in all negro languages the word 'belly'
is one of immense importance. Politeness requires
that one ask of his neighbor at every meeting if all
is well with this organ, and the Kroo negroes assert
that it ascends into heaven after death. According to Campbell, the Bechuanas have less regard
for the aged than for cattle, leaving them to die in
helpless misery; and their neighbors, the Coran-
nas, expose the old people to wild beasts, — they
being, as they say, no longer of any account, only
serving to use up the provisions. Among other
tribes, also, the daughter is often said to turn her
old mother out of the hut, and sons put their
fathers to death with impunity.

" But this horrible picture of the aborigines is
offset by the encouraging reports received from
time to time from the Liberia colonists," Colonel
Sanford pursued, " and I can't help feeling that the
negro might really be better off if left to himself.
He constantly furnishes evidence that, in the mass,
he absorbs our vices rather than our virtues, and it
was surely never intended for the two races to live

together as one people. At any rate, we've got to look out for ourselves and our children. It is a case of *sauve qui peut*, as with the French after Waterloo. We must shake the old man of the sea from off our back, but, while doing it, let us help *him*, if we can."

The colonel cut himself short here, and rose abruptly. He had called on Sam Thomas to do business, not to discuss what his friends called his "hobby;" he regarded it as a useless waste of time to talk seriously to such a man about a question involving no personal gain.

As he went heavily down the stairs and out upon the sidewalk of manufactured stone, he observed a young negress hanging about, and recollected absently that he had seen her before and that her name was Rosetta. Had he looked back a moment later, he would have been made aware that she had disappeared, and, if he had walked more lightly himself, he would doubtless have heard her footsteps as she ascended the stairs.

When Sam Thomas appeared on the street an hour later it was growing dark, bonfires were beginning to burn, an addle-pated negro stood on a wagon endeavoring to address a crowd of deriding listeners, and far up and down the street elated black "workers," with some money in their pockets and more alcohol in their brains, staggered here and there, and with a hollow, bought-and-paid-for enthusiasm shouted and shouted again, "H'rah for Brown!"

XVI.

As a matter of course, the result of the election
was the source of much congratulation in the
Brown household. The mayor never tired of discussing the theme, and his wife listened to him
with equally unfailing interest, but Betty and Reba
were more moderate in their enthusiasm and their
expression thereof, each being silently aware that
the defeated candidate would have brought more
dignity and ability to the position.

On the afternoon of the day after that of the
municipal struggle Adam Brown came home early,
and finding the three ladies on the piazza, launched
afresh into the story of the contest, introducing
new details, rehashing others, and serving up for
the second or third time all the complimentary
speeches made to him by this friend and that
friend, apparently expecting his listeners to show
as keen an appetite for the same as he did himself.
Betty was the first to weary of this and withdraw,
wandering aimlessly out to the wide, tree-embow-
ered back-yard, and finally seating herself on a

bench under a crêpe myrtle, and entering into conversation with two of her young step-brothers, who were busily stuffing themselves with sugarcane.

Reba also presently retreated beyond the reach of the mayor's eloquence, retiring to her room, and engaging herself with a favorite book. Rest and the cessation of the wearing daily anxieties which had been hers for so long; the passing of the acute stage of her grief for the loss of her mother; above all, her arrival at the entrance-court of a new and great happiness, — were not without their affect on her appearance, and she was now a more pleasing and lovable object to the eye than ever before.

She was still alone in her room when a knock sounded on the door, rousing her from the absorption in her book. Inviting the visitor to enter, — from her seat, and without laying aside her book, — the door opened and a flashily dressed and comely young negress appeared.

" Mis' Brown tole me to step down the entry to yo' do' an' knock, explained the visitor, staring about her at the pleasing objects of the apartment with an air of very great interest. " I come to pay you for that dress you made for me last fall," she added.

" Which one was that?   Are you — "

" My name Rosetta Hightower. Josephine brung de cloth to you."

" Thank you, Rosetta. Better late than never, you know."

" I' d 'a' paid it befo'," declared Rosetta, with her most amiable manner, stepping forward and putting several pieces of small silver into the outstretched hand of the young lady, who still sat, her book upside down in her lap, — " I 'd 'a' paid it 'way yonder before Christmas, but I could n't spare it. Bet you can't guess who gim-me that money," she added, retreating a step and smiling mysteriously.

" I don't think I 'll bet," said Reba, lightly. " I suppose you earned it. The best money is that which is honestly earned, don't you think ? "

" Mr. Bob Morton gim-me that money jes' a while ago," said Rosetta.

This was not a part of Sam Thomas's " little joke" which had no " real harm in it," but an amplification thereof originating in Rosetta's own fertile brain, and utterly without foundation in fact. Seeing the easy expression of her companion's face suddenly stiffen and become cold and repellent, her courage failed her and she dared not proceed in the direction previously traced out for herself. She acknowledged to herself afterward that there was something about this young white lady as she sat there in silence with that expression on her face, and especially that look in her eyes, which disarmed her, thwarted her, compelled her to abandon her design.

" He — he-e — owed me dat money," she has-

tened to add, uneasily; " an' I stopped by his office
to git it this evenin', an' he gim-me a letter to give
to you." (She began to open a reticule which she
carried.) " I tole him I was comin' on down h-yuh,
an' he said I might jes' as well carry it as for him
to hire a boy. An' so he give it to me, an' h-yuh
it is."

As Reba did not put out her hand to take it, the
letter, after a moment's hesitation, was dropped on
a table near her elbow. She sat quite still as before,
the repellent expression still on her face, her eyes
fixed steadily on those of the young negress.
Rosetta felt more uneasy than ever, and wished
to be gone, but halted, recollecting something
which she had been particularly instructed to say.

" He was writin' two letters when I went in, an'
the other one had Miss Maud St. Clair's name on
it. I seen it with my own eyes, an' I can read as
good as anybody," she declared, with peculiar
emphasis.

As this gratuitous piece of information was received without comment, Rosetta concluded that
there was nothing more that she could say or do.
" Well, I must go," she said, with a somewhat
baffled air, and surveying the room once more,
departed.

" It is his writing — his surely," was Reba's
thought, as she took up the letter and looked at
the superscription, " and yet that girl looked as if
she lied in every word. . . . What, then, could

he have been writing to Miss Maud St. Clair about,
— if there were two letters as this girl claimed?
Now I recollect, he was quite attentive to her at
one time, — several years ago, before I was grown
up and when he was very young.   But that was
long ago."

The letter, which was opened immediately, was
as follows : —

DEAREST MAUD, — I write to ask if I may come this
evening.   You were cruel to write as you did.   You say
that my explanation is not sufficient ; then let me come
and add to it.   Let me swear before your face that I
love you only, and will always.   I freely admit that
I was temporarily fascinated by Miss Reba Lawrence,
and that the circumstances of her sad situation touched
my heart.   And as a friend of the family, I felt that I
could not stand altogether aloof after her recent bereavement.   My attentions meant no more.   I beg you to
believe me, and to forgive the past weakness of your
devoted lover,

ROBERT MORTON.

"It does not sound like him, and yet it is certainly his writing," thought Reba, in a fever of
agitation, as she read the letter through, forgetful
that it was not addressed to her.   " He was writing
to us both, then, and enclosed her letter in my
envelope. . . . I cannot believe — it is incredible
— he must have lost his reason ! . . . No, I trust
him — I refuse to believe — there must be some

mistake. . . . But — but do I not know his writing? . . . He loves *her*, then, and was only ' fascinated' by me. . . . The 'circumstances' of my ' sad situation,' — can this refer to our extremity of need, and his assistance through Maum Katie? . . . It is a lame plea, and he will have to do more than this to convince her. . . . He is deceiving her. . . . He really prefers me, — how else could he have persuaded me that he so deeply loved? . . . He — ah ! can it be for that, — for that money she has recently inherited? . . . Oh, what baseness ! . . . And I have loved that man ! . . . Who knows? — what, after all, if he be fickle and have really changed?   In either case it is the same to me. . . . The end has come, — the end of a bright, foolish dream. . . . Yes, there is no room left for doubt. . . . I would   doubt — summon   him — speak to him — if I could. . . . But these are his own words. . . . It is true — oh, it is too true ! "

And thus, with an indignant, breaking heart, she read the cruel letter again and yet again.

At nine o'clock the next morning Betty Walton sought her mother and anxiously conferred with her.

"Something has happened to Reba," she announced with a grave face. " I went to her room a little while ago to see why she did n't come to breakfast, and found her lying across the bed in her clothes. I could see that she had passed the night so without moving; the feathers had not been pressed down anywhere else. I knew something dreadful was the matter, and I lay down on the bed by her and rubbed her hand, and after a while she whispered, 'Betty,' like a person too tired to speak, and that was all. I asked her what was the matter, and she said, 'Nothing.' She meant she was not sick; I knew that. I could n't see her face, but I could *feel* how it looked. She had the air of a person stunned, bruised, beaten, broken — I can't describe it! I wanted to push up the shades and let the light in, but she would n't let me."

"Why, let me go to the po' child," cried Mrs. Brown, overflowing with sympathy and tenderness.

"I would n't — yet," said Betty. "It's too dreadful for sympathy. She wants to be alone."

"What do you reckon it is, Betty?"

"It may be a quarrel with Robert Morton. But it seems to me it must be worse than that."

Two days later the object of their conjectures himself appeared. He asked for Reba and showed the liveliest concern when told that she had been confined to her room for several days and had tasted no morsel of food. Betty studied his face with all the keen, perceptive scrutiny of a good woman, and was more puzzled than ever. On leaving, he said that he would call or send every day for news, taking for granted that Betty understood what his relation was with her cousin.

The next morning Colonel Sanford was the bearer of unexpected good news. He said he had known for some time that the insolvent railroad was adjusting its difficulties, but not until the previous day that the stockholders would receive their interest so long overdue. The colonel looked happier than Betty had seen him for many a day when he opened his breast pocket-book and produced a check in Reba's name for all unpaid dividends.

This news seemed to produce a remarkable effect on the stricken girl, for an hour after her cousin had informed her she rose from her bed and let the light into the darkened place. Early in the afternoon, hearing continued movements in the room, Betty knocked at the door and was invited to enter. She saw at once that Reba had recovered her spirit; she looked older, paler, thinner, Betty thought, but there was firmness in her step and fire in her eye.

"I have written to Mrs. Blossom proposing to visit her at once," she immediately announced, "and I expect to start as soon as I receive an answer."

"Reba Lawrence!" exclaimed Betty, helplessly.

"I hope Aunt Matilda won't object, because I am determined."

Betty felt hurt at being left out of her cousin's confidence, — for the first time, as she thought, — and contented herself with saying, after a pause: "And what will *he* say? He was here yesterday."

"That is why I am going," was the reply, with a trembling lip. "Oh, Betty,"— they were in each other's arms now,—"I am so miserable. Only a week ago I told you that we were engaged, and already — already I — I have discovered that — that it ought never to have been — that I — that I don't — trust him — don't love him."

"Reba!"

This explanation did not satisfy Betty, and she subjected her cousin's face to the most piercing scrutiny. "But you are going to explain to him?" she said finally.

"Yes. I can't see him, but I will write."

Betty ended another ·pause by asking: "But how on earth can you get ready? You have no clothes ready."

"I want the dressmaker to come to-morrow. I have some money now, you know. I'll have one dress made, and the rest can be done in Philadelphia."

"He'll probably come to-morrow and inquire about you. What shall I tell him?"

"Nothing."

"Have you decided how you will have your dress made?"

"No, not yet."

"Then you don't want him to know you are going?"

"No — no — not till I write to him. And please help me, Betty, with Aunt Matilda, who

will object of course. For really I must go at
once."

"I will, dearie, and I 'll help you plan your
dress. I don't quite understand all this, but I 'll
help you in every way I can. I see you are terri-
bly in earnest."

Seated in his office a week later, endeavoring to
work, but accomplishing little because tormented
with thoughts of Reba, her strange malady, and
the inevitable misgivings of an ardent lover, Robert Morton was handed a note by a negro boy, who
retired without waiting for an answer. He saw at
a glance that it was from Reba, and opened it in
great haste.

"I have come to see that our engagement was a
mistake," she wrote, "and that it will be better
for us both if it be immediately dissolved. In
imagining and admitting that I loved you, I fear
that I deceived both you and myself. Fortunately
I see more clearly now. I therefore ask to be
released, and that everything be considered at an
end between us henceforth."

Five minutes later Morton rushed out of his
office and lost himself in the streets of the town,
wandering he scarcely knew whither and seeing
only his perplexity and pain. The aspect of the
whole world seemed to have changed. The very
voice of the gay birds was mournful and the brilliant sunshine a ghastly, inexplicable mockery.
For him, and for the time, the world had practi-

cally come to an end and chaos reigned. He first
strayed out beyond the suburbs, but returning an
hour or more later, mechanically directed his steps
toward the railway station, oblivious of the straggling professional loafers preceding and following
him.

The latter, who might with propriety be called sta-
tionary tramps, being distinguished by all the characteristics of their peregrinating brother, with the
notable exception of the love of travel, were now
shifting their basis in order to witness the arrival
of the express train. These worthies were habitu-
ally much averse to exertion of any kind, but at
the appointed hour always forsook their "up-
town" haunts and submitted themselves to the
inconvenience of walking three hundred yards in
order to observe the crowd, the bustle, and commotion, to gaze with ever renewed interest upon
the puffing locomotive, and perhaps to wonder at
the energy of steam. In general appearance, except that the majority of them were negroes, they
much resembled those seedy specimens of mascu-
line humanity who in spring and summer haunt
the squares in Northern cities, sitting languidly on
the wooden benches and staring vacantly before
them. The latter specimen has the advantage of
the "bracing" climate, but in his own person does
not seem to exhibit any corresponding superiority.

The express train was late and the loafers disposed themselves about the long platform of the

station-house in sullen silence, too much effort
being involved in any adequate expression of the
annoyance which they felt at being obliged to wait.
Others were impatient as well. Eight or ten negro
children looked anxiously up and down the railroad and when the train finally appeared they
showed their beautiful teeth in the rapturous cry,
"Yawnder she come!" These little rag-a-muffins,
dressed in odds and ends patched, torn, and blackened almost to the hue of their skins, were professionals, too, but not loafers. They were minstrels,
and came to sing under the windows of the passen-
ger-cars. During the fall and winter, when Northerners were passing on their way to or returning
from Florida, they gathered a harvest of pennies,
nickels, and dimes not to be despised, but in
spring and summer the business declined, the pas-
sengers on board being usually from parts of the
country where singing negroes were as common
as mocking-birds.

Morton had scarcely devoted more than a glance
to these or other juvenile minstrels heretofore, but
to-day as he stood on the platform waiting he knew
not for what, his restless eyes, which for the most
part saw nothing but the inward pain, now and
then lighted upon them and lingered until they
were clearly outlined and their voices were heard.
Their very laughter seemed sad to him, and there
was an unspeakable pathos in their movements, as
they hopped about like birds on a frosty morning,
and looked hungrily down the vacant railroad.

Across the way from the station was a rambling
frame hotel, and on its broad veranda were seated
several sojourners lazily watching an Italian with
hand-organ and tiny monkey on the frost-bitten
grass in front. The poor little red-jacketed beast
skipped about tremblingly, as if in mortal terror
of its swarthy master, and, receiving his commands, began climbing up one of the veranda
columns to the balcony above, where some ladies
were looking down. For this was a novelty in
Barcelona as yet, while the little negro minstrels
were commonplace in the extreme. The latter
may have been aware of this, but all envy of the
rival combination was swallowed up in wonder and
pleasure, and not even the most commercial perhaps found time to speculate on the possible advantage of having a marmoset of his own to send
into the car window after pennies. They indeed
forgot their own concerns in the intensity of their
interest, as the Italian, after gazing hungrily at all
the upper windows, drew in the line, and the trembling little monkey delivered to its master a dime.
Morton saw all this as through a mist, and every
movement or sound was to him the futile expression of an inward despair. The hand-organ was
" cracked " and out of tune, its notes resembling
the broken and quavering tones of an old man tot-
tering on the brink of the grave, and when the
giddy Fishers' Hornpipe was turned off, and the
hackneyed but always touching " Ah che la morte "

of the *Trovatore* was turned on, it seemed to one listener that the sound which floated on the air expressed the condensed, insufferable anguish of a thousand worlds.

This mellifluous misery was presently cut short, being drowned in the roar of the arriving train. Commotion began in the station, clerks rushed out of the baggage office, and the loafers pricked up their ears, looking as if they took an interest in life once more. The little black minstrels took their places and did not wait for the roar to subside before they began lustily to shout, rather than to sing, while running along beneath the windows of the moving sleeping-car. At length there was comparative quiet, and the monotonous repetition of their brief strain could be distinctly heard:

> " I belong to de ban',
> I belong to de ban',
> I belong to de ban',
> Halleloo ! "

A coin was presently tossed out, striking one of them on the head and rebounding into a puddle of water left by a recent rain. Then down on their hands and knees and into the water they went, one and all, shouting and scrambling and splashing, until the lucky one found and gripped the coin in a vise, whereupon they were all on their feet in a moment and lustily singing again. To the occupants of the car this was very funny, and another coin was tossed into the puddle in order to cause the scramble to be repeated, but the observer from the platform saw in it only a suggestion of the wan and sickly smile which may cover desperation and unutterable grief.

A carriage drove up in haste, two ladies were assisted out of it, and a few moments later Reba's pale face was suddenly outlined before Morton's absent eyes. With a convulsive movement of the heart, a stopping of breath, a paralysis of hand and tongue, he became aware that she was being assisted upon the already moving train. It seemed to him that he cried out to her, with outstretched hands, as in the first moment he longed to do, but he stood as immovable as the platform itself while the train moved slowly away.

XVII.

Mrs. Blossom had despatched a prompt and carefully worded reply to Reba's letter, and the latter felt relieved of any uneasiness respecting the nature of her reception; but after her hurried flight from Barcelona was accomplished, and her dread of meeting Morton was removed, the unhappy girl had leisure to reflect upon the precipitancy of her action, and during the journey, as often as her thoughts were diverted from the one great and absorbing interest of her life, she became a prey to apprehension. Immediately upon her arrival in Philadelphia, however, her doubts were set at rest, the welcome extended to her being most cordial and genuine; and the new and agreeable phase of life to which she was now introduced soon furnished that diversion so needed by one in her state of mind.

She found that Mrs. Blossom's mode of life was more luxurious and aristocratic than she had had reason to suppose. Though scarcely to be called attractive from without, the house was situated in

the heart of the fashionable quarter, and was
filled with rare and costly, but tasteful and not
overpowering collections of *bibelots*, pictures, and
eccentricities of decoration and furniture, the
" gimcracks," to employ the language of the irreverent, having been gathered from the four quarters
of the world. A liveried Irish flunkey stood in
the hall, two stately, silent, black men in evening
dress served in the dining-room, and besides coachman, footman, and cook, the establishment boasted
a superfluity of maids, French and otherwise. All
this in the house of a childless couple struck Reba
with amazement, and she involuntarily contrasted
such luxury with the narrow and painfully straitened existence to which she and her mother had
so long been accustomed. She thought her new
friend must live a life of lonely magnificence
indeed, but for the guests who came and went so
often; for Mr. Blossom, with whom Reba never
became well acquainted, was seen in the house but
little. Indeed, the visitor soon suspected the existence of a coldness between him and his wife, as
otherwise it appeared unlikely that he would spend
every entire day in business speculations, rarely
returning even to dinner, and his evenings at his
club or elsewhere, leaving his wife to receive her
guests alone.

Reba thought these guests for the most part
delightful people, but amazingly unlike the human
specimen she had expected to encounter. From

what she had read of the popular literature of the
Northern States she had derived a fixed idea that
even the wealthy and most highly cultured classes
there were nothing if not democratic in all their instincts, that the feeling of caste was practically unknown, although, as a matter of course, every one
reserved the right to select his own associates, and
that matters of ancestry, barring the case of mettle-
some horses, could be mentioned only in secluded
corners and with bated breath, except at the fearful risk of being covered with ridicule, even as was
now more and more the case in much-mixed
Barcelona, where the triumphant bottom rail was
on top.   Her surprise amounted to astonishment,
therefore, after her introduction to the " old Philadelphia families," among the representatives of
which element Mrs. Blossom counted her friends.
Here, she found, the query, " Who was your father?" was of equal if not greater importance than
in Virginia and certain quarters farther south, and
the question of genealogy was as much a matter
of course as the multiplication-table.   Indeed, the
doors of this society were as irrevocably closed
against the *nouveaux-riches*, or other aspirants with
no background in the past, as was ever the entrance to the inner sanctuary of the old-time
Southerner, who counted his ten generations and
his hundred cousins.

Reba did not spend her days listening to the
history of near and remote relationships, however.

She saw a great deal of life, for one who heretofore had seen so little. The season of Lent, as well as her recent bereavement, imposed restrictions on her social experience, but Mrs. Blossom saw to it that she was present at many quiet dinners and gatherings, where persons distinguished for more than blue blood were sometimes to be met.

In the course of her visit Reba made the acquaintance of a few statesmen, poets, and authors whose names had been familiar to her for years, although the majority of these were not residents of Philadelphia, and while listening to polite speeches from their lips was still sufficiently mistress of herself to observe that they were, after all, very much like the average undistinguished person of the intelligent class. Mrs. Blossom being both literary and musical, her young guest was accordingly taken to the meetings of a Browning society that she might hear the enigmas of a cult-producing poet expounded ; to the Contemporary Club gatherings that she might hear disquisitions from learned and famous professors on scientific and literary subjects; to a reform club where questions of local importance were discussed, Mr. Paul Shepherd taking an active part; to an "Orpheus" club in order to hear a remarkable chorus of young men; besides public lectures, the opera, theatre, etc.

In the latter, the opera especially, Reba at first took more interest than in the doings of society itself, as a consequence of her possession of a

very keen appreciation of music and of having
been able to gratify her love of it but little heretofore. She was not critical, but her naturally
correct dramatic instincts received an unmistakable
shock on beholding a lyric artist of the Italian
school come twice out of a tomb after life was supposed to be extinct, in order to repeat her *aria* in
response to an enthusiastic encore. Mrs. Blossom
smiled at the inexperienced girl's objection to
these conventionalities of the operatic stage, but
Mr. Shepherd, who visited the house constantly
and often acted as the escort of the two ladies,
heartily agreed with her that mere concert in cos-
tume was not true opera. He declared that when,
in the last scene of *Semiramide*, the queen is
stabbed by mistake in the dark, she ought to act
is if really stabbed, and ought to fall, regardless of
a dirty stage floor and a handsome gown; that
when, with a musical shriek, she spreads herself
out comfortably on a cushion which by no sort of
chance could have been ready in the dark before
that tomb, the illusion, but faint at best, is utterly
dispelled; hero, heroine, villain and all the para-
phernalia of Babylonian court life disappear, and
nothing is left but the Academy stage and a few
masquerading Italians, with the high-priced Patti
in the centre enjoying her mock death on an impossible cushion. It was not until she witnessed
presentations of *Siegfried, Tannhauser,* and *Lohengrin,* with leading German singers in the cast, who

acted with as much energy and intelligence as
they sang, did Reba feel that she had seen real
opera.

Her unusual interest in music was occasioned by
something more than the mere desire of gratifying
her delight in it. Within three weeks after her
departure from Barcelona she had begun to think
seriously of a musical career for herself, having
proposed in mind such a plan after much anxious
thought concerning her future. For she now
believed that she would never marry, that she
could not be dependent on her aunt or live permanently in the house of Adam Brown, and that
she must have employment, both because her
income was narrow and because she had no desire
for an idle life. When her visit was at an end,
instead of returning home, although homesick
already, she determined to find a boarding-place
and prosecute her musical studies under a master,
and, before her purse was quite empty, engage
Colonel Sanford to sell the railroad shares. If
nothing more were accomplished, she might at
least, return to Barcelona and teach music. But she
did not wish to return to Barcelona, and hoped to
accomplish more. The operas and concerts of the
higher class which she had enjoyed of late stirred
her deeply with a love of song and she dreamily
pictured to herself the possible career of a singer.

Up to the date of her father's death she had
received regular instruction in music, and had

been celebrated for the unusual beauty of her voice within the small circle of her friends. More cultivated musically than these, however, were her new friends; and she wondered and doubted if their verdict would be favorable. To test the matter, partly so at least, while alone with Mrs. Blossom one day she seated herself at the piano unasked, and after playing a few chords, sang one stanza of the simplest song she knew with all the feeling and quality of tone of which she was capable, afterwards rising and moving away indifferently.

"Why — why did n't you tell me you could sing?" asked Mrs. Blossom, with great interest, her eye-glasses tumbling from their perch on the bridge of her prominent nose.

"Do you think I really can?"

"Do I think you 'can'? Your voice is *beautiful.*"

Then Reba confessed her plans, hopes and fears. They were ere this on quite intimate terms. At the outset Mrs. Blossom had been outspoken and ready with friendly counsel. " You have been well brought up," she said on the day after Reba's arrival. " Your people were evidently the right sort, and did their duty by you. I shall not be afraid for you in any position likely to be yours here; but you have seen little of society, and I must give you some practical hints." And the hints were given from time to time, and taken with becoming gratitude. Reba was now the more ready, therefore to avow her aspirations. Mrs. Blossom listened with astonishment.

"That is quite another matter," she remarked, at last. "Of course I meant that your voice was beautiful for an amateur, — just the thing for singing to one's friends in a parlor."

"I was not confident," faltered Reba. Her face had fallen now. "I thought I might at least teach music."

"Nobody can tell," said Mrs. Blossom then, unexpectedly. "Your voice might be built up. It could hardly be more sympathetic and sweet, and it *might* be made stronger and louder by proper training."

"I thought of going to see a professor," ventured Reba, more encouraged.

"Yes, and I'll invite some musical people here, and we can find out what they think. But your friends in Barcelona would not like to see you go on the stage, I know, nor should I," added Mrs. Blossom gravely.

"They would be horrified," said Reba, with conviction. "But I had only thought of concerts, and that is not quite the stage."

"There is a slight difference, but — but you are a girl who ought to marry, Reba."

"I'm sure I never shall."

"That is absurd. You cannot fail to have good offers. I know a young man who is already unusually interested in you. It was partly on his

account that I invited you to visit me, — because
I saw that he fancied you. I speak of my nephew,
Paul."

"Oh, Mrs. Blossom! if you really think — "

"I may be too hasty," said the elder lady, with
solemnity, "and I should not have spoken but for
this unexpected plan of yours. After that I felt
that you ought to know. He really is not very sus-
ceptible, and it may not go as far as I hope it will,
— and, by the way, it is not every girl that I would
deliberately advise to set her cap for my nephew,
— but if it should, you could n't do better,
child."

"I am flattered that you should wish it," faltered
Reba, astonished, "and I do admire him, but — "

"He is fine-looking, he has an independent fortune, he is not absorbed in what he calls the trivialities of society, he has ideals, and is one of the
most honorable of men. What more could any
girl desire?"

"Love," said Reba, solemnly.

"Any girl could learn to love such a man."

"Do you really think so, Mrs. Blossom?" the
girl asked, looking directly into her friend's eyes.

"Certainly."

"The poets have been deceiving the world for
ages, then."

"Nonsense. I enjoy a good love-story as much
as anybody, but real life is different. The love the
poets describe is pure fancy, my dear. Where a

little of it does exist, or seems to, it soon wears off."

Reba thought, from all the indications, that it must have worn off very promptly in Mrs. Blossom's own case, and wondered if a woman whose experience had been such was really in a position to judge.

As had been intended and as was but natural, this conversation was the source of serious reflection on Reba's part, reflection made poignant by uncontrollable recollections of the past. A tall form, a thin, sallow face and firm jaw, beautiful, haunting eyes, courage, manliness, integrity, were elements in the picture which would rise up before her in spite of her efforts to forget it, in spite of her belief that the Morton of the picture was not the true one. It was perfectly clear to her that Paul Shepherd would be everywhere regarded as a desirable suitor, but as for herself, not even in the most mercenary of moods could she so regard him — for a long while to come, at least. His appearance, his manners, his ideas, were all pleasing to her, and she felt that she could trust him, and yet she reflected and reflected again, only to shake her head.

He displeased her only in one way, and that was not a personal matter, and she did not lay it up against him. Mr. Shepherd owned a large interest in a prominent newspaper of the city, and did some active work in connection with it, — she never knew exactly what; and this newspaper, she observed, criticised almost every act of the first Democratic administration which the country had seen for a quarter of a century. Reba had no clear grasp of political questions, but as a matter of course thought her old friends in the South were right and these new friends were wrong, and that the party in power deserved its success, well remembering what great joy was manifested after the election by everybody in Barcelona except the poor deluded negroes, many of whom supposed that the change meant their return to slavery. And so, while heartily approving of Mr. Shepherd in every personal way, she still more heartily disapproved of his paper.

The subject came up between them once in a casual way, and after some good-humored sparring, he took pains to make her understand his position.

"So far as I am concerned, at least, and so far indeed as any of my friends are concerned," he assured her, "the enmity toward the South is no longer personal, but political. The South exercises a preponderating influence in the Democratic party, — it apparently does not, but it really does, — and the principles and proposed reforms of that party are not such as we can sympathize with. Therefore we criticise."

"But you are a reformer yourself," she said. "I liked the ideas you expressed in your speech at that reform club meeting."

"Thank you. Yes, I am a reformer in my own small way. I hate public abuse of power; I scorn the mere partisan who stands for a certain party simply for party's sake and nothing else; I think dishonesty in politics is even more criminal than dishonesty in private life, and should be more rigorously punished; I detest what is called the spoils system; there are many abuses which I should like to see stamped out, not only in national politics, but in the government of my own State and city. But people differ, you see, and there are reforms and reforms. Those advocated by the party now in power at Washington appear to me to be the result of a superficial study of the public needs and to be based on fallacies; therefore they are calculated to do harm. I think you see what I mean."

"I do, and I think you are right — from your standpoint," said Reba, heartily. "My father, I remember, always said that a man must act according to his own convictions, but at the same time be willing for those differing with him to exercise a like privilege. I shall think of your paper's criticism in a different way hereafter."

"As to the negro question," he told her later, "I am inclined to sympathize with the opinions of your friends, or those of Colonel Sanford, so far as I have heard him express himself. But I doubt if there be much hope for his scheme for some years to come."

" I don't think he has much hope himself," said Reba.

" The trouble is, the negro question is still too much involved in politics. And then, on account of the *ante-bellum* sympathy for the slave, and the *post-bellum* sympathy for the freedman believed to be ill-treated, as well as on account of sentimental illusions in regard to the character of the black man which have formed a part of our early education, we Northerners instinctively take the side of the negro. When the question shall have successfully shaken itself loose from politics, if the time ever comes, then the whole country may be willing to take it up and consider it on its own merits. Then perhaps it may be possible for the colonel's scheme to be developed and accomplished."

On the day after the conversation with Mrs. Blossom outlined above, Reba received a long letter from Betty which temporarily obliterated from her mind all thought of her prospective new suitor, but caused her later to reflect upon the matter more seriously than ever. After detailing household news and making some reference to what Reba had written about her experiences in Philadelphia, Betty touched on the subject of Morton. " He has not been near us since you left," she wrote. " Mamma and I feel rather hurt, considering that he formerly came so often. I think he must have been dreadfully cut up by your letter. I have only seen him once and he looked miserable; I never saw him look so. He was sitting on the St. Clairs' piazza the other afternoon when we drove by. Maud was not there. He was talking with John St. Clair. By the way, he asked papa for your address yesterday."

There was no mistake, then. The vague, fugitive hope which Reba detected in her heart now and then that there was something wrong, that her idol had not fallen, that that horrible, villanous letter might be explained, was only weakness and folly which should be determinedly shunned. He was now visiting Miss St. Clair as a matter of course; and if he looked miserable, it was because his chills had returned — nothing more. Nevertheless, when, on the following day, his own letter was handed to her, Reba opened it with trembling hands.

" Your letter was received more than three weeks ago," he wrote, " and I beg to apologize for not answering before. My excuse is that only now have I obtained your address, and that at first I was too occupied with surprise to think of asking for it. I was like one struck dumb and blind and did not know what to do, but the less said of that the better. You say that you have discovered that you were deceiving yourself, and you ask to be released. Although this change was so sudden and unexpected, I have no right to blame you or to feel resentment, and I do not. As for myself, I wish I

could change as easily. I fear that I can never
change, but I freely release you. God bless you
and good-by!"

This letter, which was far more suggestive of the
sad farewell of a breaking heart than the courteous
response of a fickle lover glad to be released,
aroused feelings in Reba which she acknowledged
with abject humiliation and terror. She told herself that it was well she had run away, for this man
could persuade her even in the face of proofs, —
this ruin of the noblest of men. In spite of her
struggles, she recalled and dwelt upon the many
qualities she had formerly admired in him. How
strangely conflicting must be the elements of his
character! — for she had had reason to know how
he once scorned dishonesty, deceit, sycophancy,
mercenary motives, and self-seeking in general;
she had always expected him to develop into
such a man as Colonel Sanford, and even his
superior.

But what could be meant by such expressions as
"struck blind and dumb," "can never change,"
coming from a man who had avowed his love for
and was paying court to another woman, unless
they were written purposely to deceive and from a
desire to appear consistent and honorable? Could
it be that he had not yet discovered his error in
sending her Miss St. Clair's letter? Or was the
error only a seeming one, and a part of his plan to
obtain his release? Bewildered amid such vain

speculation, and humiliated by the consciousness of her own weakness, Reba put Morton's letter away and hurriedly sought companionship and diversion; and during several days Mrs. Blossom observed that she seemed troubled and absent in mind.

XVIII.

THE musical people came by appointment a few days later, each prepared to contribute to the evening's entertainment. There were not more than a dozen of them altogether, and the majority were either wholly or semi-professional. They were not members of " society," but were all personally known to Mrs. Blossom. First in importance was Signor Blondinera, an insignificant-looking little man, who enjoyed the highest reputation as a music-master of the Italian school. After him ranked a lady whose name was sometimes printed on local concert programmes as " prima donna contralto," and after her a young man somewhat less distinguished as a tenor. Among the non-professionals were a Dr. and Mrs. Kolbe, celebrated for their devotion to the great German masters, and a young lady pianist of unusual talent.

Signor Blondinera "opened the ball," playing an exceedingly erratic and florid composition, which he was prevailed on to acknowledge as a "trifle" of his own. The prima donna then sang an effective contralto solo passage from one of Verdi's operas, and a simple English song in response to an encore. The lady pianist gave a stirring rendition of a Chopin nocturne, and was followed by the tenor in some beautiful selections from *Lohengrin*. After a recess the German doctor and his wife sang a Mendelssohn duet, and played together a severely classical selection from Brahms. Everybody applauded after the last, but it was probable that nobody understood it but the Kolbes themselves, who smilingly declared that they had played it together every night for seven years. Italian courtesy compelled the great Blondinera to applaud, but a composition so quiet and profound was unintelligible to him, being quite antipodal to the fire and glow of the beloved music of his native land.

Reba's turn came last. Full of dread in advance, she was surprised to find herself so self-possessed when the moment arrived. Mrs. Blossom had chosen for her a simple lullaby of Mendelssohn's, and the girl now sung it very sweetly, with apparent ease and without affectation. When it was over she was made very happy, for the moment, on discovering that she had pleased these critical people. It was clear that the applause and the expressions of gratification were genuine. Even the professionals were generous of their praise.

"I told you once that you had the true dramatic instinct," said Mr. Shepherd, who had appeared in time to hear her song. "Now let me add that I think you have the true musical instinct as well."

"If I had your voice I'd do nothing but study music," said Dr. Kolbe, and poor Reba's inexperience led her to believe that all this meant a great deal more than was intended.

Signor Blondinera said nothing to her, but at eleven o'clock when coffee and light refreshment were served, as he sat apart with Mrs. Blossom he looked now and then toward Reba as if she occupied his attention.

"I tell-a to you her voice will-a be good," he was saying. "'T is sweet, 't is r-rich, 't is r-round; myself, I did enjoy to hear it."

"I am glad you did. I wanted you to hear her. Do you think she could make a successful singer?"

"Such a voice, it is at once successful. Certainlee."

"But I mean, — as a *public* singer."

The *maestro* shrugged, and Mrs. Blossom saw that she would receive no direct or satisfactory answer to this question. "Who can-a tell?" he remarked. "The voice, 't is char-r-ming most certainlee."

"You don't think she could become a rival of the greatest singers, then, — Patti, for instance?" laughed Mrs. Blossom.

The Italian started, smiled, and elevated his eyes heavenward. Was it Patti who had been re-ferred to?— Patti the divine, the incomparable! "Madame," he said, excitedly, careless of his use of that horrible English which he had tried so hard to learn, " dere eez but de one Patti in de wor-r-ld, — de one prima donna what git five tousand dollah de night!"

Before taking their afternoon drive in the park the next day Mrs. Blossom stopped with Reba at the houses of several 'professors of vocal culture.' The first was a German, Franz Meissner by name, a heavy, thickset man, with dark, restless eyes, who shocked his callers by receiving them in dressing-gown, slippers, and a collar which appeared to have been worn two weeks. Reflecting that this was perhaps the eccentricity of genius, they felt in-clined to forgive all but the last item. Mrs. Blos-som stated that her companion thought of a singer's career, and they would like him to try her voice; Signor Blondinera had heard it and ad-mired it greatly.

"Blondinera — piff!" ejaculated Herr Meissner with a shrug so gigantic that he seemed in danger of dislocating his neck. "Blondinera, eh?" his expression seemed to repeat, — "that miserable Italian who tinkered at music! Come, let us see," he said aloud, and led the way to the piano.

Striking a few chords, he half lost himself in a revery over them, then rousing himself he put a

sheet of music against the rack and called upon
Reba to sing.   It happened to be something
with which she was familiar and she sang without
hesitation.

"She duss not know how to open her mouth,"
he announced, stopping abruptly in the middle of
the piece.   "She vill have to vork, vork, vork."

"But what do you think of the quality of her
voice?"

"Her voice is goot, but it iss not str-rong."

"Mr. Blondinera thinks he can build it up,"
ventured Mrs. Blossom.

"Built it up, — Blondinera?" cried the German.
"He vill built it up so foolish ass he can.
Young laity" — turning to Reba, — "if you vill
come to me andt vill vork, I vill teasch you to
sing."

"Do you think she could succeed as a public
singer?" insisted Mrs. Blossom.

"She can do anyt'ing if she vill vork," — after
another mighty shrug.

They next called upon a lady teacher, an
American, who indulged in much flattery, promising great things for "such a voice," — at once
exciting suspicion of insincerity.   Mrs. Blossom
led Reba back to the carriage without waste of
time.

"American teachers are best," they were confidently assured, as they moved to go.   "There is
too much affectation about these foreign teachers."

" The safest plan would be, I think, to go to the one who promised the least," said Mrs. Blossom as they drove on toward Fairmount Park. " I don't trust this woman. As to the others, it is a question which one was the more guarded, the Italian or the German."

Reba unhesitatingly declared that she personally preferred the former, and her friend agreed, adding : " That conceited, vulgar German may be more thorough, but how could you endure him ? Blondinera is much more respectable."

A few minutes later their attention was attracted to the following legend in a window which they were passing, " Signor Wilkini, Teacher of Singing and Piano," and the coachman was told to stop. Mrs. Blossom did not know of this instructor by reputation, but proposed to call on him by way of experiment. An agreeable-looking gray-haired lady opened the door and ushered them into the parlor, where, after a few moments, the supposed Italian appeared, — rather a young man, not in the least foreign, and speaking without accent.

" Are you Signor Wilkini ? "

" At your service. You are thinking that I have the appearance of an American, and perhaps you are right. Most of my life has been spent in this country, although I am an Italian."

" Ah ? Well, we wanted to — " and Mrs. Blossom explained.

Reba's voice was again tried, and this time most

recklessly flattered. It was a remarkable voice;
yes, indeed. Such a voice was bound to find its
way to the stage. He inquired if the young lady
had studied dramatic action; she should do so by
all means. He taught this as well as vocal culture.

" Do you really think she could succeed on the
stage ? "

" Yes, indeed," declared Signor Wilkini, with
enthusiasm. " To get started would be the only
difficulty. But I could arrange that. An opening
is easily managed by one of the initiated, you
know. I gave one of my young lady pupils a
brilliant start last fall. She was only studying
dramatic action, however. I got her in at one
theatre to go on in a minor part for nothing, and
she made a pleasant impression. And while it
lasted — while it lasted, mind you — I went to another manager and told him that she was getting
fifty dollars a week, but that I would prefer to
have her in his company for less. He wanted
another lady, and we finally came to terms at forty
dollars ; and so I started her off at a salary of forty
dollars a week through just a little business diplo-
macy, you see."

The two ladies exchanged glances and concluded that it was time to go.

" I wonder if that man thought I would consent
to such fraud," said Reba, when they were seated
in the carriage. " How disheartening all this
is ! "

" Don't think of his odious talk," said Mrs. Blossom. " He 's not respectable; his low prices show
that. Signor *Wilkini*," she added, in disgust.
" I believe he is a native Philadelphian, and his real
name is Wilkins. I suppose he sails under false
colors for the sake of Italian prestige in musical
matters. He is a musical quack."

Signor Blondinera was again consulted the following day, and it was definitely determined that
Reba should study both vocal and instrumental
music under his direction. Mr. Shepherd showed
plainly that he applauded her resolution to make
herself independent of her relatives by fitting
herself for lucrative employment, but took occasion to warn her not to be over-sanguine of
success.

" I think," he said a few days later, when calling
her attention to " Charles Auchester," a musical
novel, " I think from what my aunt tells me, you
may have been led to expect too much. Success
on the lyric stage is very difficult to attain, I imagine, and I fancy the average ' professor of vocal
culture ' is not much troubled with pangs of conscience. I have heard shocking stories of deception practised on ambitious young American
aspirants in Italy, who are led on and fed upon
encouragement until the years have slipped by
and their money is all gone, only to find that they
can accomplish nothing. I doubt if the average
teacher in this country is really much more trust-

worthy, except perhaps where he has more pupils
than he wants.   I hope you will take this suggestion," he added, " in the spirit it is offered."

Reba expressed sincere thanks, assuring him
that she knew better than to expect too much.
After all, she thought seriously only of going
South to teach music; the other was a mere dream.
" I have n't fully made up my mind that I should
want to be a singer if I could," she added; whereupon he showed pleased surprise.

" I am glad to know this," he said frankly, " for
really I doubt if there is much hope.   I have
heard many singers, and it does not seem to me
that your voice could ever be powerful enough to
fill an opera house.   It is sweet, sympathetic,
beautiful indeed — to me," he added softly, " but
I don't think it was ever intended for the public."

This and similar conversations established between them a certain degree of intimacy which
had not existed hitherto, and which was a source
of great satisfaction to Mrs. Blossom, that lady's
eccentric fancy for Reba having ere this developed
into a strong affection.   What with her studies
and her social engagements, the girl was henceforth very busy, and a few weeks later Betty
wrote complaining that her cousin had forgotten
Barcelona.

It was now near the end of March, and, having
spent two months under Mrs. Blossom's hospitable
roof, Reba contemplated securing a boarding-place

at an early day, in spite of the vigorous protest of
her friend, who wished her to stay where she was.
She dreaded the change, but was convinced that
her visit should not be further prolonged, and that
she would make more rapid progress in her studies
if distracted by less social life.

"Mamma thinks the idea of your singing on
the stage is simply frightful," wrote Betty. "She
cannot see how it can be even respectable, nor
can papa. It is amusing to hear him talk about it.
He says he always thought Aunt Mary was 'awful
particular' about you, but he has come to the
conclusion that she was n't particular enough; she
certainly ought to have taught you that it would
not be lady-like and seemly to make a 'show-
woman' of yourself. Papa has a great deal of
shrewd common-sense, and knowledge too, in his
own range, but he does n't know that there is
any difference between Nilsson and the common
song-and-dance 'show-girl,' and probably thinks
the opera is similar to the unbearable 'concert'
which comes after the circus is over. I overheard
mamma telling Mr. Straitlace about it, and he shook
his head solemnly, reminding her that you had
never been 'convicted of sin.' You had thus wil-
fully exposed yourself to the wiles of the Evil One,
who will always take an ell if you give him an inch,
or words to that effect. He generously offered
to pray for you every day, and I trust you will be
duly grateful, you hardened sinner! So much for

going off to the ends of the earth and consorting
with Yankees.   After he was gone I found mamma
crying.   That put me in a 'state of mind' at
once, and I was irreverent enough to declare that
the Rev. Jonathan Straitlace was a backswoods
country cracker and did n't know what he was
talking about.

"I have some news for you about Charlie.   He
gave you up long ago, of course, and now you will
be glad to know that he is on the high road toward
consolation.   That is the way with men.   One rose
seems to be as sweet as another to them, — that is,
after a slight interval devoted to sighs and gloomy
reflection.   I mean that Charlie has gone to Amanda Turner for comfort, and will no doubt get it.
I always felt that she liked him.   My greatest fear
is that he will make too easy a conquest, — a
dangerous thing for all concerned.   He took her
out in his buggy yesterday, and when he came
back he was in a better humor than I have seen
him for a long time.   I 'd like to see him marry
Kate Lawton, but Amanda is a nice girl, and I
suppose one's brother must choose for himself.

"If we can trust appearances, another young
man is seeking consolation, too, but I am not so
sure that he will get it.   Who do you suppose?
None other than my quondam admirer, Jim Jones,
the immortal 'knight of the plough.'   The object of
his constant attentions is — you would never guess
— Miss Francie Black.   At one time I suspected

that she thought too much about that enigma, Rob
Morton, but it may have been only my imagination.
At any rate, she accepts Mr. Jones's attentions, and
they seem to have become great friends. He drives
out with her frequently. She seems to be trying
to cultivate and improve him, poor fellow. She
told me that she had persuaded him to take a
Chautauqua course of reading. He certainly is
manly and has a good heart, and if she can stand
his clumsiness and his 'sweaty' hands, his 'I
taken' and 'I ain't got no,' etc., etc., she may be
happy with him. It will be the last match in the
world I should have predicted. Philip Gordon
is paying her particular attentions also, and it
looks as if she will be able to take her choice
of the two. Phil is at least a gentleman, and in
other ways seems to me worthy of the really fine
character Miss Black is.

" I know a fourth young man who apparently is
not seeking consolation. When I saw him at the
St. Clairs' that day, six weeks or so ago, I thought
he was, and that the next thing we knew he would
be visiting Maud regularly and taking her out to
entertainments. But he has n't done it. They say
he scarcely goes anywhere at all. If you have
changed, he has not, — or so it seems. His case
is doubtless more troublesome than the ordinary,
— the wound went deeper, and it will take time
to cure him. Reba, dearie, why is it you and I
are so hard to please? It has slowly been re-

vealed to me that, after all, I did not love poor dear Jack as I should have done. I loved him rather as a brother or a dear cousin, and in that way I mourn for him now. It is best to be candid with one's self, don't you think so? I fear I shall be an old maid; but you, Reba — you must n't! If you can't love Robert Morton, there are other fish, etc. Perhaps your fate may be that young Philadelphian whose remote ancestors presumably tended sheep. I liked his looks when I saw him here at the tournament. He looked like a *man*, — not more so than the one you have rejected, however."

On reading that part of the letter which referred to Morton, Reba was again stirred with conflicting emotions, and certain feelings came to the surface which she believed she had conquered. But she soon summoned the resolution and strength to put them down, telling herself that the only reasonable explanation of Morton's reported behavior was to be sought in the probable failure of his designs. Miss St. Clair had doubtless not been satisfied with his plea, had suspected his mercenary motives, and perceived the insincerity of his protestations. So had he failed, and now deservedly suffered from disappointment and humiliation.

Of late it had been more and more clearly indicated to Reba that Paul Shepherd intended ere long to ask her to become his wife, and although she studiously avoided giving him encouragement, she gradually was more inclined to dwell on the

matter in her thought. In proportion as she strug-
gled successfully to shut her mind to every tender
recollection of her former lover, she smarted the
more acutely under the indignity which she believed he had put upon her, and was the more
ready to contemplate the character of another
suitor whom she respected and admired. Involuntarily she contrasted the worldly aspects of life
as the wife of a poor Barcelona lawyer and a rich
Philadelphian of the leading class. The former
would be narrow, perhaps even straitened, and
socially dull; the latter would be one continuing
scene of luxury, social triumph, and opportunity
for every species of mental exhilaration and expan-
sion, — an existence for which she was fitted by
nature and inherent tendency.

The one cloud which darkly overshadowed this
alluring picture was the fact that her heart was
cold. She regarded young Shepherd with respect,
admiration, and friendship, but the fear haunted
her that she would never love any man again.
But — after all — what if love were mere fancy (as
Mrs. Blossom claimed), which soon deserted its
helpless victims and left them to the horrors of
disillusion and regret? Did not respect, admiration, and friendship form a safer basis to start from
and fall back upon for those who must take the
terrible leap in the dark? The question repeatedly
propounded itself in her mind as to whether it
could be the part of wisdom to surrender all that a

marriage with Shepherd involved for the sake of a
bright, foolish dream which had ended in the discovery that her idol was made of clay instead of
gold.

The temptation was persistent and strong, but
she never quite yielded to it, even for a moment.
" I would rather see you in your grave than see
you marry for anything but love," her mother had
said, and she had not forgotten.   Nor — try as she
might — could she as yet shut her mind completely
to the recollection of Morton.   And so, when,
about ten days after she received the last letter
from Betty, Paul Shepherd came perilously near a
declaration, and she needed only to give him a
word or even a look in order to bring him to her
feet, she took care to overlook his meaning and
divert him from his aim.

Returning from the opera under his escort, on a
Saturday evening within a day or two of this occurrence, she found the following telegram awaiting
her : —

Charlie Walton, Sam Thomas, and George McLeod
killed in riot with negroes.   Jim Jones and Rob Morton
dangerously wounded.   Matilda hopes you will come.

ADAM BROWN.

XIX.

Reba found the telegram lying on the table in her chamber and was alone when she read it. Five minutes later Mrs. Blossom was summoned. Miss Lawrence was very unwell — so declared the excited maid; she had fallen on the floor and now lay in a deep swoon. When they reached her she was already recovering consciousness and needed only to be assisted to a lounge, where they insisted on giving her something to drink, and endeavored to make her comfortable.

"You are tired, Reba," said Mrs. Blossom. "You have been doing and going too much, and you must have absolute rest for a few days."

"I never fainted before," said the girl, almost in a whisper. "The shock was so — terrible! The telegram — " Her voice failed and the muscles of her face contracted in pain.

The maid picked up the bit of yellow paper from the floor and presented it to her mistress, who swiftly absorbed the words: "Charlie Walton, Sam Thomas, and George McLeod killed in riot with

negroes. Jim Jones and Bob Morton dangerously
wounded. Matilda hopes you will come."

" My poor darling ! — and these are your friends,"
murmured Mrs. Blossom, horror-struck.

" One of them, Charlie Walton, is my cousin, —
almost my brother. You saw him — he crowned
me," said Reba haltingly, with the manner of
one stunned. Her thought leaped at once to another one, — the last mentioned, — but she said
nothing of him. " Aunt Matilda — his mother —
wants me, and I must go," she added.

" Yes, dear child, you must go." Mrs. Blossom
embraced the girl tenderly. " And after a few
weeks you will come back to us and — go on with
your studies."

" I must go by the first train," said Reba, apparently not hearing her friend's last words.

" Yes — if you are strong enough."

" I'll be strong enough in a few minutes."

" I suppose it will be safe to go? The fighting
will probably be over by the time you arrive."

" I will go anyhow."

" Marie," said Mrs. Blossom, addressing the
maid, " call Powell and tell him to go instantly to
the Broad Street station and find out when the next
through train goes South. Tell him to ask about
the sleeper, — a Savannah sleeper."

The butler returned in half an hour with the
information that a train had just gone, and that
another would not go until 7:20 in the morning.

It was now midnight. Mrs. Blossom, who had received this intelligence at the door, returned to
Reba's couch, and it was at once decided that the
latter would take the early morning train.

"You had better come with me to the room
adjoining mine and try to get some sleep," proposed the elder lady after a few moments. "The
maids will be busy here packing your trunks. Get
Ann to help you," she added, addressing the woman
who was present, "and tell Powell to be sure that
they are at the station in time."

Ten minutes later the butler was again summoned
by the mistress of the house, who gave him a sealed
letter. "See that Mr. Shepherd gets this to-night,"
she said. "It is important, and if he has already
retired he must be wakened."

· At seven o'clock next morning a handsome carriage driven by a coachman in full livery, and distinguished by a coat-of-arms emblazoned on its
panels attracted the attention of the passing stream
of pedestrians as it drew up in front of the Broad
Street station. A few halted in order to see the
occupants of this uncommon turnout, but were
evidently disappointed on beholding two veiled
and quietly dressed ladies descend to the pave-
ment. Entering the station, these promptly ascended to the ladies' waiting-room, where they were
at once joined by a young man.

"You have just ten minutes before the gate
opens," said Mr. Shepherd; and then in a few well-
chosen words he expressed to Reba his regret for

what had occurred and his sympathy for her and her friends.

"I am coming to the conclusion," he said afterward, "that we Northerners know less about those race troubles in the South than we think we do. We have long been disposed to think that all such troubles have their origin in politics, but it seems more and more clear that it is not a struggle of one political party against another, but is one of race against race, in which immemorial history repeats itself. All this bloodshed could scarcely have resulted from the mere act of an infamous outlaw in resisting arrest in a country inhabited by one homogeneous people. It is race antipathy which originates, aggravates, and continues this conflict."

"Let us not discuss the question now," said Mrs. Blossom, rising. "I am going out there to get some of those flowers," she announced, and took her way to the larger general waiting-room. She seemed in no hurry, bending over the flower-stand and deliberately inspecting each variety exhibited there, and asking the price. Fully five minutes had elapsed before she returned.

"At such a time," Paul Shepherd had said to Reba, "you can hardly conclude definitely as to your future plans, but I suppose — I hope — you intend to return to Philadelphia and continue your — "

"I suppose so," faltered the girl, with a quivering of the lip which was hidden by her veil. "But I can't tell. I can't think."

"At least,—I hope," he said, with lowered voice, "that if you do not return I may — may visit you at your home in the South?"

Reba heard him dreamily, her thoughts being full of him she had loved, and who was now perhaps dying, and she answered with an effort: —

"Certainly. It will always be a pleasure to see you. After Mrs. Blossom you have been the kindest of my friends here, and I should be very sorry if you were to pass through Georgia without stopping to see us."

He was disappointed in this reply and checked himself. He had meant her to understand that he would desire to travel a thousand miles solely on her account; she doubtless so understood his words, but preferred to appear to think of his proposed visit as a mere incident of a journey to Florida. He looked at his watch, and said the train was probably in by this time. At this juncture Mrs. Blossom appeared and presented Reba with a small bouquet of white roses. A few moments later the crier announced the train, and they rose and moved forward.

Reba was settled in her seat, had finally bidden both her friends good-by, and the train had begun to move slowly out of the station, when a newsboy hurried down the aisle shouting: —

"Morning papers! All about the horrible Southern outrage! Southern race war!" etc.

Reba stopped him and bought a paper, asking

19

for the " Philadelphian," with which Mr. Shepherd
was connected. But the boy was running risks,
and in his haste to supply her, and afterwards run
and jump off, he gave her the " Partisan" instead.
One glance informed her that the third column of
the first page was devoted to the " outrage," nearly
a quarter of a column being taken up with " scare-
heads," as follows : —

BUTCHERED IN A RACE WAR.

WHITE RESIDENTS OF A GEORGIA TOWN EXTERMINATING COLORED PEOPLE.

TEN COLORED MEN KILLED.

COLORED PRISONERS OF THE COUNTY JAIL THREATENED BY THE MOB.

POOR WOMEN BRUTALLY BEATEN.

TERRIBLE BATTLE IN A SWAMP.

After the foregoing, it was somewhat surprising
that the last sub-head, in the smallest display type,
should have read as follows : —

THE RIOT BEGUN BY A COLORED OUTLAW SHOOTING DEAD A WHITE MAR- SHAL WHO WAS ATTEMPT- ING HIS ARREST.

· The "special dispatch to the ' Partisan ' " from Savannah ran thus :

"The town of Barcelona, about a hundred miles from this city, is in the throes of a race riot. As yet only meagre news of the outbreak has been obtainable. The trouble is supposed to have started about four o'clock this afternoon.

" *The Killed.*

" So far as heard from, the killed are : GEORGE McLEOD, assistant-marshal ; CHARLES WALTON, farmer ; SAMUEL THOMAS, lawyer ; and from eight to ten colored men.

" *The Wounded.*

"Those wounded among the whites are : ROBERT MORTON, lawyer, dangerous wound in abdomen ; JAMES JONES, farmer, serious wound in shoulder; ARTHUR BARNWELL, marshal, shot through both legs.

" It is stated that the trouble was precipitated by an attempt to arrest a colored outlaw, Josh Bostwick by name. At six o'clock Bostwick and his followers were located in a small but dense swamp near the town, and a hundred white men have surrounded the place, and are now on picket duty, holding the blacks at bay. During the first outbreak, the pursuit of the colored men, and their retreat to the swamp, many shots were exchanged, with the result in killed and wounded as stated above. The colored men are expecting rein-forcements from Barcelona and the surrounding country, and more serious fighting is looked for.

" In response to a telegram from the Governor, the Georgia Hussars, a cavalry troop of this city, will go

immediately to the scene.   The infantry companies of
this city, which could muster three or four hundred men,
are also holding themselves in readiness to move at a
moment's notice.   An infantry company from Brunswick
is also expected to move at once.   Advices from that
point state that colored men of that town have also
become excited, and demand that they be furnished a
special train to carry them to the assistance of their
friends.   They threaten to burn the docks if the train
is not furnished.

" Later despatches from Barcelona confirm the above
reports and add some particulars.   Josh Bostwick, a
noted desperado and fugitive from justice, Mamie-Lou
John, and Riley Martin, notorious loafers and bad characters, entered Barcelona at noon to-day with guns on
their shoulders, as though returning from a hunting
trip.   About four o'clock they attracted attention by
their shouts and curses in front of a saloon on a back
street, the desperado Bostwick firing off his gun, to the
terror and imminent danger of persons in that vicinity.
Marshal Barnwell and Deputy McLeod attempted to
arrest Bostwick, who resisted, — the other two colored
men encouraging him, and Rosetta Hightower, a woman of infamous notoriety, who was in their company,
egging them on to the struggle which ensued.   Robert
Morton, a young white man, was passing, and being
summoned, ran to the assistance of the officers of the
law ; not, however, until Bostwick had freed himself
from the grasp on his collar, raised his gun, and fired,
killing the deputy.   Riley and John promptly followed
his lead, and both Barnwell and young Morton were
shot down.

" The alley was soon alive with people, and the three outlaws were fired upon and began to retreat, calling upon their friends to join them in their battle with the whites. Some fifteen or twenty colored men responded, and the combined forces, including the woman, retreated hurriedly out of town toward a small but dense swamp, exchanging shots as they went with the growing body of their pursuers. During this skirmishing, at pretty close quarters, Charles Walton and Samuel Thomas, white, and six colored men were killed, and James Jones, white, was wounded. The odds now against them, the colored men turned and fled to the swamp, near which Riley Martin, one of the outlaws, was brought to earth, badly wounded. The Hightower woman was overtaken and whipped with switches. When released, she ran into the swamp and joined her friends.

" To-night two other colored women of notoriously bad character were set upon by unknown persons in the suburbs of Barcelona and severely whipped. The excitement is at fever heat, and negro criminals in the county jail are trembling for their lives.

"The latest despatch from Barcelona states that the swamp is surrounded by white men on picket duty, and that the colored men who have made threats of another uprising in the town are overawed, and there is now no fighting going on. Those besieging the swamp are waiting for daylight. At nine o'clock a colored man was shot by a picket while attempting to leave the swamp. The ball took effect in the right breast, but the wound is not fatal. It is believed that he was acting as a spy."

Reba read and re-read this meagre account of the riot, and as her glance returned to the misleading " scare-heads " her eyes filled with angry tears and her heart throbbed with indignation.

" The despatches show plainly enough that the negroes precipitated the riot," was her thought. " They were altogether in the wrong, and yet these people sympathize with them at once, and never think of *us* at all. I wonder how such good people can be so cruel and blind. Mr. Shepherd's own paper, too, and he talked this morning as if he knew better: '*Butchered in a race war. White residents of a Georgia town exterminating colored people (!) Poor women brutally beaten (! !)*' How can he have written such dishonest headings, manifestly intended to prejudice the reader in advance?"

At this point, she observed with great relief that it was not Mr. Shepherd's paper she was reading, but a sheet called the " Partisan." Putting it away from her promptly, she sat in troubled revery until the train stopped at the next station, where she beckoned a passing newsboy and secured at last a copy of the " Philadelphian." Mr. Shepherd's paper contained the same dispatches, but they were not adorned by the " Partisan's " flowery headlines, the unvarnished facts of the occurrence and nothing more being outlined.

On the inside of the journal, which in more ways than one seemed to show a regard for simple truth

and justice far too uncommon, the following edito-
rial appeared : —

"Judging from the despatches describing the riot at
Barcelona, Georgia, this latest 'race war' is of a character to arrest the attention of the thoughtful, showing as it
plainly does that other factors beside hatred of the freed
slave enter into these troubles. It becomes more and
more evident that the Southern whites have a grave problem on their hands, and that they are deserving of at least
a measure of the sympathy which hitherto we have lav-
ished entirely upon the blacks.

"It seems quite clear that the whole trouble was precipitated by the infamous acts of a negro outlaw. Blood
once shed and innocent blood quickly following, as it
always does, public excitement naturally led to indiscre-
tions and half a score or more of lives have paid the
penalty. It ought to be quite impossible for anybody to
make political capital out of this tragic incident. Every
good citizen, white or black, North or South, cannot but
earnestly desire the suppression of outlawry wherever it is
found. The trouble is that such men as Josh Bostwick
are too often tolerated in a community, instead of being
put away for their crimes at an early period in their worse
than useless careers. They are allowed to be at large and
to work mischief among the other degraded characters ;
and such is the brutality of some human natures that des-
peradoes of this kind can always summon followers ready
to go with them any lengths in resisting the mandate of
the law. One lesson of this riot is that the law should
always be enforced, that men whose place is behind the
bars should be kept there. Another lesson, perhaps, if

we of the North are ready to heed it, is that our early
conception of the Southern situation, as one continuing
spectacle of a white foot on a black neck is, to say the least,
out of date and wanting in revision."

"That sounds more like Mr. Shepherd," was
Reba's thought on reading this; and she felt very
grateful to the fair-minded man who had so
thoroughly won her esteem, if not her heart.

The long day dragged as if toward an eternity.
The speeding train seemed to creep, as the girl lay
back upon her cushion outwardly calm, but restless
and ill with waiting, hoping, fearing, and now
and again shedding scalding tears behind her
veil.

XX.

ABOUT the hour of that Saturday night when
Reba's trunks were being packed in Philadelphia,
a little past midnight, several white men stood and
lounged about a fire in the open pine woods between that part of Barcelona called the Neck and
the swamp which was surrounded by pickets, and
in which the remnant of the rioting negroes lay
concealed. The moon rode high in the heavens,
and sufficient light filtered down between the tops
of the straggling pines to enable the pickets to
distinguish any moving figure within the distance
of a hundred yards, and effectually prevent escape
from the swamp.

The place in which the fugitives rested at bay,
however, could hardly be called a swamp at all, as
it covered only three or four acres. It was in reality
a cypress pond, for the most part "gone dry," as
it is said locally, and was grown up not only with
old cypresses and young pines, but with dense underbrush and young poplar-trees now well covered
with the fresh green leaves of spring. The fire was

more than a hundred yards without the circle of the pickets, and the half-dozen men who stood or sat around it were unconcerned in manner, being well beyond the range of bullets from the swamp. Their faces were serious and stern, however, and the tenor of their conversation showed that the outlaws at bay need expect no mercy.

There were some inaccuracies in the associated press despatches concerning the riot, but in the main the account was correct. As stated, the trouble had grown out of the attempted arrest of the black desperado Bostwick and the killing of the white deputy. The marshal himself and Robert Morton, called to the aid of the former, were shot down by Mamie-Lou John and Riley Martin, whose former exploits will be remembered. The three outlaws were then fired upon by white men gathering to the scene. The color line being drawn, the law-breakers were immediately rein-forced by all the more desperate characters of their race within hearing of the conflict. It being Saturday, an almost universal holiday among the negroes, many idlers were on hand to take part. The woman, Rosetta Hightower, now notorious as an abandoned creature, was present and incited the blacks to resistance by shrieks and curses, afterwards accompanying her friends in their re-treat and flight. Although overtaken on the borders of the pond and whipped by an enraged white man called Simpson, her spirit was not broken, and when released, instead of returning to the town, she ran boldly into the pond where her friends were concealed, tempting for the moment some of the more rash of the pursuers to fire upon her. Her sex, however, protected her from such a fate.

The pond being promptly surrounded by white men crowding to the scene, and certain spirits of the Neck who loudly threatened a fresh uprising being presently overawed, the mayor in the course of the evening telegraphed the troops in Savannah and Brunswick not to move until further notice. There had been no further developments in the situation up to twelve o'clock, at which time such of the besiegers as were not on picket duty were lounging about the fire as described.

" Colonel Sanford advises moderation," said a young man, evidently belonging to the educated class, who stood leaning on a Winchester rifle. (His name was Gordon and he was a cousin of Jack Sanford.) " He told me he would come down here and talk to you boys himself if he were well enough to get out of bed. He says when we close in on them in the morning, we ought not to fire a gun unless they fire on us first. He thinks they may be disposed to surrender, and that we ought to take them alive if possible, and let them be tried and convicted according to law."

" Shucks ! " exclaimed a man named McLeod, a brother of the dead deputy-marshal, " that sort o'

talk will do for babies. What! — give them niggers a chance for life after all the good white men
they 've shot down like dogs?" His lip trembled
for a moment or two, but steadying himself, he
added, with a solemn oath: "The first black face
I see in them bushes I 'm goin' to shoot at, —
that 's settled!"

"Adam Brown said about the same thing when
he was down here with that crowd at nine o'clock,"
spoke up a man reclining on a bunch of wire-grass.
(This was the bricklayer, Simpson, of New Jersey,
husband of the unfortunate "pond-gannet" whose
persecution at the hands of Josephine may be
remembered.) "He said the niggers in town had
quieted down and he did n't expect any more
trouble to-night, and maybe none to-morrow, and
he wanted us to take them black devils in the
swamp alive if we could. But how could we, if we
wanted to?"

"We can't do it," declared McLeod.

"They 'll shoot as soon as ever they see us comin',"
continued Simpson, "and more 'n likely a passel
of us 'll be picked off before we git a shot ourselves. Who 's goin' to try to take 'em alive, then?
Humph!"

"What do you say, sheriff?" asked another reclining figure.

"We 've got to take 'em, dead or alive, that 's
certain," briefly replied the sheriff, a heavily built
man who sat before the fire with a rifle across his
knees.

" Who 's that?" some one exclaimed, as two men were seen approaching the fire from the direction of the Neck. The sheriff sprang to his feet and called out, " Halt! "

" Don't shoot! " cried one of the two approaching men, both having halted. " We come on a peaceable errand."

The voice was unmistakably that of a negro, and recognizing it as such, the white men about the fire exchanged glances, suspicion entering the minds of all.

" Come ahead, then," said the sheriff after a moment.

The new-comers proved to be Professor Brice and a very old negro, known in the Neck as " Uncle Billy." The latter appeared to be too terrified to speak, and the former also looked about him with some show of apprehension as they entered the circle of firelight.

" I tried to git preacher Smith to come with us," said the professor, smiling nervously, " but he was afraid you 'd shoot him. I told him you would n't shoot him, gentlemen."

" What do you want? " demanded the sheriff.

" I — I — wanted to see if we could n't make some arrangement — "

" ' Arrangement! ' — ' arrangement '! " broke in Simpson, angrily. " We don't want no sassy educated niggers around here — and no ' arrangement.' " (Simpson could not afford to send his ·children to school.)

"Let him alone," said the sheriff, in rebuke.

"This old man has a son in that pond," continued the professor, without replying in any way to Simpson, "and I thought maybe if you'd let him go in there, and let me go with him, we might talk to them boys and get 'em to give up — surrender. They know they ain't got no chance nohow," added the schoolmaster, forgetful of his learning in his excitement, "and looks to me like we could persuade 'em. It would save a heap o' bloodshed, gentlemen."

"Don't do it!" cried Simpson and others, as the sheriff hesitated. "No tellin' what them two niggers are really up to."

"We've got better sense, I hope, than to let reinforcements walk into that pond right before our eyes," said McLeod, angrily.

"We ain't tryin' to fool you, gentlemen," replied the professor, mildly. "We got better sense. We mean honest."

"Be for yo' good, too," ventured old Uncle Billy, in an unsteady voice. "Dem boys is desp'ate, an' when you rush in on 'em a-shootin', dey'll sho' kill some o' you."

"Let 'em try it!"

"You can't do it to-night, anyhow," said the sheriff, still undecided.

"I think if Colonel Sanford were here he would advise us to let them try it," said young Gordon.

" If you come here by sun-up in the mornin',
we'll see about it," said the sheriff, finally.

" All right, sir," said Brice, looking disappointed,
" I hope you won't charge in on 'em before we
git h-yuh."

" That's *our* business," growled McLeod, and
the professor and old Uncle Billy turned sadly
away, moving off toward the. Neck.

The schoolmaster's proposal was discussed pro
and con for half an hour, and then silence gradually fell on the group about the fire. The soft
sigh of the wind in the pine-tree tops was for some
time all that was heard.

" Hello! what's that?" said one of the men at
last, and guns were gripped on every side.

The figure of a woman suddenly appeared from
among the dark shadows of the pines and stood
near them. As the light fell upon her they saw
that she was white-haired and old.

"Why, it's old Mammy Nanny," declared the
same speaker. " She lives right over yonder."

"What do you want here this time o' night?"
asked the sheriff, suspiciously, when the old sorceress had walked boldly into their midst.

" Wud I want?" she repeated in her peculiar,
husky voice. " I want to keep some you white
mens from gwine to hell bright an' early to-morrow mornin'. Some o' you sho' gwine."

The crowd saw the grim joke and took it good-
humoredly, several laughing outright. " She means

there's to be more fighting and some of us will 'sho' kick the bucket," some one explained.

"Ef you know wud good for you, you'll lem-me go down in dat pon' an' talk to dem chillun an' make 'em give up," continued Mammy Nanny.

The old discussion was now re-commenced. Some thought she had been sent by Brice, and that the "whole thing was a plot" to help the besieged out of their trap. Others doubted this, and asked her why she thought she could persuade the outlaws to surrender.

"Dey do wud I tell 'em," she replied confidently. "You des wait an' see; des wait an' see."

"Don't let her go," advised McLeod, the brother of the murdered deputy. "One woman too many in there now. We don't want to shoot women."

"I reckon we better let her try it," said the sheriff. "She can't do any harm, and if she can make 'em surrender, all the better."

And so it was finally decided. The nearest sentinels were notified and instructed not to fire, and then the fearless old woman walked down the slope and into the underbrush of the pond. As she disappeared from view, her voice rose upon the night air, becoming peculiarly shrill when pitched on a high key: —

"Mamie-Lou! Josh! Rosetta! Don't shoot! I'm a-comin'. 'T ain't dem white mens. It's me — Mammy Nanny!"

Shortly after this incident two white men ap-

proached the group about the fire from the direction of Barcelona. "Riley Martin died about a
half-hour ago at Thompson's drug store," one of
them announced. "Dr. Fisher got the bullet out
of his lung, but he did n't live long after it."

"And what do you reckon, boys?" said the
other new-comer. "He confessed that he and
Mamie-Lou John killed Jack Sanford. It was n't
that young Putnam darkey after all, and now I
reckon they 'll turn loose his old daddy, — old
Jerry Carter."

"*They* robbed and murdered Jack Sanford — the
same devils that killed my brother!" exclaimed
McLeod, starting to his feet, almost mad with rage.
He declared that he would charge the besieged at
that moment, and called upon all hands to follow
him into the pond. But every one objected, and
the excited man was prevented from rushing to his
certain death, at first by force, and then by persuasion, finally agreeing to wait for daylight and the
co-operation of his friends.

"You may do what you please with the rest,"
he declared, "but if we take Mamie-Lou John and
Josh Bostwick alive, they 've got to swing."

As the gray light of dawn began to steal through
the tops of the thin-leaved cypresses and penetrate
the deepest shades of the little swamp, four human
figures were gradually outlined, seated on a log
beneath a tall, branching poplar. Their position
was near the centre of the so-called pond, and, a

short distance in front of them, a bog or quagmire a few square yards in extent was the sole relic of the vanished waters which in wet weather covered an acre or two. The human figures were those of Mammy Nanny, Rosetta, Mamie-Lou John, and the desperado Bostwick, and these were the sole occupants of the pond. The besiegers were under the belief that six or eight armed negroes besides the notorious Bostwick and John were at bay, not knowing that all but the two latter had passed through the little swamp and escaped into the extensive pine forests beyond, the afternoon before, while fighting was still going on and before the place was surrounded. When Rosetta was overtaken and whipped on the outskirts of the swamp Bostwick and John halted to fire on her assailant and their pursuers, and so when they attempted to follow their escaping friends they found the place invested by white men on every side. It was during the whipping of Rosetta, which occasioned the last exchange of shots, that Sam Thomas fell.

"It ain't no use," said Bostwick, sullenly, rising from the log and peering about him in the uncertain light. "I done tried it a hundred times since yistiddy ebenin'. Dey got us hemmed in too close. No chance to git out o' dis place."

The crack of a rifle resounded through the woods. It was doubtless the signal for the besiegers to advance from every point, and the other three figures started up from the log in terror.

" You boys better tek care yo'self! " exclaimed Mammy Nanny, in a shaken voice. " Dem white mens be yuh in five minutes."

" Can't you hide some'rs? " suggested Rosetta, eagerly.

Cold sweat stood out in great beads on the foreheads of the two doomed men. Nevertheless, Bostwick exclaimed, with a fierce oath, " I bet I 'll kill two of 'em fo' dey git me. Dey can't shoot *me* down like a dog."

" Nor me neither," echoed Mamie-Lou, although with chattering teeth.

A shout was now heard, and answering shouts followed from different sides of the pond. The circle of the pickets was contracting. Bostwick and John looked at each other significantly, abject fear stealing into their hearts.

(The professor and old Uncle Billy had not turned up in time, and the former's proposition had been forgotten by the besiegers in the excitement of the hour. Mammy Nanny's failure to reappear, however, would have made them reluctant to permit further attempts at mediation.)

Suddenly Bostwick ran over to a neighboring bay-tree, muttering to himself as he went, " Look to me like dere 's a hollow up dere in dat big dead pine."

A huge old pine stood very close to the bay and towered above it; Bostwick's idea seemed to be to climb up the bay and attempt to jump a yard or two to the lowest branch of the pine, and thence make his way into the hollow. It was not a promising plan, — ten to one, if he succeeded in reaching the hollow at all, it would prove too small; but nothing else suggested itself, and he felt that he must act. He had climbed up the few feet of bare trunk and swung himself into the branches of the bay by the time the others understood what was his intention. His helpless comrade moved to follow, but Mammy Nanny stopped him.

"You, Mamie-Lou! Wait! Come yuh — I'll fix you."

He was the grandson of her sister, and it was to save him that the old sorceress had braved the objections of the besiegers and entered the pond. Repeatedly calling on him to follow, she ran out on a rotting log which lay across the mud and water of the quagmire.

"Git in an' lay down," she then commanded. "I'll fix you so dey won't find you."

"Lay down in dat cole water an' mud?" objected Mamie-Lou, with a shiver.

"Do wud I tell you, you fool you!"

"Moccasin come from under dis log an' bite me," cried the terrified and reluctant negro.

"Moccasin' bite ain't bad ez white man' bullet. Look yuh, boy, is you crazy? Git in, I tell you!"

The man seemed paralyzed with fear, and made no movement. With angry speech, she laid hold on him, and, losing his balance, he stepped off the log against his will. Then he submitted like a child as she forced him to lie down in the mud and water and rest his head near the log.

"Moccasin ain't gwine bite you," she declared, coaxingly.

Once she had placed him in the desired position, she deliberately stepped upon him, and, by standing tip-toe and then coming down upon him with all her weight, she forced his legs and arms, and finally his body, to sink gradually beneath the soft, yielding ooze. This done to her satisfaction, she stepped back on the log and, kneeling down, put her hands on his forehead and pressed gently until the back part of his head was also beneath the surface, leaving only mouth, nose, eyes, and ears exposed. Then she quickly smeared his face, forehead, and hair with black mud, after which, from the spot where Rosetta stood watching, speechless, nothing whatever could be seen but the slime and mire of the bog, although this was a little disturbed. To cover this disturbance of the surface, the crafty old woman, assisted by Rosetta, gathered fallen leaves and scattered them over the place where Mamie-Lou lay, especially over his head, about which she first placed, with apparent carelessness, some bits of rotten wood. She did not forget to scatter a few leaves over the whole surface of the bog, in order to give the impression that a gust of wind had been the moving cause of the whole.

"Now you des lay still, an' dey ain't never gwine

see you in de worl'," she said triumphantly; and
well she might, for the concealment of the negro
was complete.

And after rubbing her muddy hands on the
rough bark of a tree and wiping them on her
apron, the old woman felt secure in the thought
that all traces of her clever stratagem were removed.   The two men had abandoned their
guns, and it now occurred to Mammy Nanny that
the sight of these might excite suspicion; she
therefore hurriedly concealed them in the neighboring brush, after which the two women re-seated
themselves on the log under the tree, not daring to
leave the scene for the present, well knowing that
the sight of a black face moving in the bush would
likely draw the fire of the besiegers.

They had not long to wait.   More than ten minutes had elapsed since the signal was heard, the
whites having advanced slowly and cautiously; but
the circle was now contracting about the centre of
the pond.   As soon as they seated themselves, the
women heard sounds of approaching feet, — the
breaking of a twig here, the cracking of a dry leaf
there, and they wondered that they should be held
so long in suspense, forgetting that the whites
expected every movement to draw upon themselves the fire of a dozen rifles.

"Surrender!" cried a loud voice suddenly, and
a moment later the sheriff, McLeod, Simpson,
and young Gordon burst into the open space in

front of the two women. As if in obedience to the spoken demand, Mammy Nanny rose to her feet, but said nothing. Rosetta remained motionless.

"Where is they?" cried McLeod, staring vacantly about him.

"What!— just you two women?" cried the sheriff.

"What's gone with them?" ejaculated young Gordon.

"What a set of fools we was to let 'em slip through our fingers," said the disgusted Simpson.

"Thought you was goin' to make 'em surrender?" said the sheriff, angrily addressing Mammy Nanny. "'Stead o' that you come in h-yer and help 'em to git off, you —" he hesitated for want of an epithet sufficiently expressive of his wrath.

"Now you gwine jump on me 'caze you white mens went to sleep," argued Mammy Nanny, spiritedly.

"Who went to sleep? We didn't do no such a thing."

"Somebody sho' went to sleep," she asserted, positively, "for eve'y las' one o' dem niggers crawled out o' yuh dis mornin' fo' day,— crawled out o' yuh on dey belly thoo dat grass."

"Well, I'll be —!" cried McLeod and the sheriff in chorus.

Improving on the advantage gained, Mammy Nanny re-told the story with great variety of detail, and was, of course, corroborated by Rosetta as to every particular. The old woman had at first determined to tell the real truth regarding the escape of the other negroes while fighting was still going on and before the swamp was surrounded, intending to account for the disappearance of Bostwick and her grand-nephew by describing their pretended snake-like crawl through the grass past a sleeping sentinel. But, as these sentinels were present, the whole company of besiegers having now centred on the scene, and each would, of course, deny having slept, she decided to say that all the rioting negroes had thus escaped, shrewdly calculating that her story would compel belief, it being manifestly impossible for a dozen men to conceal themselves within the limits of the pond. Mammy Nanny had mastered the arts of deception in the practice of her profession.

" Seem like to me Bost'ick ought to be 'rested atter what he done," she calmly informed them. " But what could *I* do? I could n't holler to you mens. Dem niggers would 'a cut my t'roat dat quick ! " — snapping her fingers.

" Well," said the furious sheriff, "you two women can jes' leave here. That 's the best thing you can do. And you better behave yourselves, too."

Mammy Nanny cast a lingering look toward the bog, but neither she nor Rosetta was slow to obey.

"By George !" ejaculated McLeod, softly, a

minute or two later, as the baffled besiegers stood
discussing the situation,— " boys, there 's big game
up in that bay-tree. If it ain't a wild cat, it must
be a mighty big wild turkey." He stole forward a
few steps, and, suddenly bringing his rifle to his
shoulder, fired.

" I hit it," he then cried. " I seen it move."

He fired again, and then at once there appeared
to be unusual agitation near the top of the bay-
tree. The leaves and branches trembled, a heavy
body descended, rebounding from bough to bough,
and ·presently the lifeless form of Josh Bostwick,
the hunted desperado, fell almost at the feet of the
astonished McLeod, who started away from it with
a cry of horror.

The besiegers understood the situation at once
and forthwith the cry arose : " Spread out, boys !
Spread out ! There 's more niggers up these trees.
Don't let 'em slip down and run ! "

As the men leaped to obey, the sight of a black
face moving in the bush drew the fire of one of the
former sentinels. A moment later Mammy Nanny
ran into the open, followed by Rosetta, who directly
fell on her face and lay motionless. The former
looked anxiously toward the undisturbed bog, then
halted, with an air of relief, surveying her surroundings. The sight of Bostwick's body gave her the
key to the situation, and, without a word of inquiry, she turned to the fallen Rosetta, stooping
over her and investigating her wound. The young

woman was not dead, but seemed unable to speak.
The bullet had entered her breast. The sheriff
was deeply annoyed by these unexpected developments, when he returned to the open a few
moments later.

"What made you two women come back here?"
he demanded of Mammy Nanny, with anger.
"Now she's shot and she's to blame for it."

"We did n't know you white mens was out
shootin' women folks," retorted the old woman,
bitterly.

'We ain't, and you know we ain't. We told
you to leave, and why did n't you? I don't know
who shot her, but whoever did thought she was a
man. He saw her face in the bushes and thought
she was a man — runnin' away. Did you know
Bostwick was up that tree?"

"Who, me? I thought he crawled out o' yuh
'long wid the rest," she answered without the twitch
of a muscle. "Seem like to me he'd 'a' had better
sense 'n to climb a tree."

The besiegers were now returning to the open
at the centre of the pond, sorely perplexed. The
sun had risen and the light was too strong to permit of mistake; it was perfectly clear that there
were no more fugitives in the tops of trees or
hidden elsewhere in the little swamp. They were
forced to conclude that the old woman's story
must be true after all; as regarded Bostwick,
doubtless he was the last to crawl out and the sen-

tinel had awakened in time to prevent him, and thus he was compelled to conceal himself as best he could.

" Look at that moccasin !" suddenly cried young Gordon, who was strolling along the edge of the bog. " Watch me cut off its head."

Mammy Nanny started to her feet as she heard his exclamation and saw his rifle pointed toward the bog. She rushed forward, open-mouthed, in time to see a small moccasin curving across the mud within a yard of the spot where Mamie-Lou lay, but not in time to interfere. There was a flash, a report, and a moment later all recollection of the snake was lost at the sound of a smothered, inarticulate cry, and at sight of a violent irruption of the surface of the bog. A black, mud-coated creature took grotesque and sudden shape before the besiegers' astonished eyes. Leaping upward, with outstretched arms and hands which frantically clutched the air, it bounded to the shore and fell face forward on the ground, — a black human figure, lifeless and still. Young Gordon was the first to recover himself, run forward, and identify the murderer of his cousin Jack Sanford. As he bent over the prostrate figure, Mammy Nanny, who hovered near in speechless grief, suddenly leaped upon him like a cat, clawing his face with her long nails.

With some difficulty she was dragged from her victim, no violence being done to her the while.

After inciting the negroes to riot, the vicious and abandoned Rosetta's sex had not saved her from Simpson's whip, but Mammy Nanny's sex and gray hair protected her now. Cursing and reviling in the most frightful manner, she was led forcibly away from the spot.

The sheriff soon saw that there was nothing more to be done for the present except to have Rosetta removed and her wound attended to. The discovery of a second fugitive, this time concealed in so unlikely a place as a quagmire, had promptly led to a second and more careful search of the whole neighborhood. Every bit of soft earth was thrust through, every bush or tree was scrutinized, every rotten log was examined, but without further result. The posse concluded to disband. Young Gordon had already gone, wiping the flowing blood from his fair face.

"Boys," said the sheriff, finally, "let's go home. It's Sunday morning."

XXI.

CHURCH-BELLS were rung in the Neck as usual
a few hours later, and in the afternoon the population strolled about the streets in holiday attire or
sat and gossiped on the piazzas of the little houses,
although there was grief in upwards of a dozen
homes and anxiety on many a face. Here and
there the inevitable and apparently never-to-be-
ended conflict with the dominant race was discussed with passionate expressions from the women,
curses and threats from the youth, and sighs from
the old men; but for the most part the subject of
conversation was those who were dead, those who
would yet die or recover, interments already made
and such as were yet deferred, with much speculation as to the present whereabouts and ultimate
fate of those rioters who had escaped through the
pine woods beyond the pond and were still at
large.

All the houses of mourning were crowded with
sympathizing friends, even that of Zeno Hightower
where Rosetta lay near death's door. As Maum

Katie entered the yard at four o'clock in the after-noon, the piazza was full of gossiping women who informed her that the girl was not expected to live. Maum Katie was engaged in nursing Morton, but had asked an hour's leave of absence to visit Rosetta, Zeno Hightower being one of her friends. Being admitted to the room where the wounded young woman lay dying, as it was believed, she found another visitor in the person of Parson Smith, who had come to talk with Rosetta and comfort her weeping mother.

"You ain't got long to stay, and you must make your peace," he was saying to the prostrate figure on the couch, as Maum Katie entered. He had already prayed and exhorted at some length, but Rosetta, who appeared to be quite conscious, had made no response or in any way shown that she felt repentant.

"Ain't you got nothin' to say, my daughter?" the parson pointedly inquired at last.

"No," was the faint, but prompt and emphatic answer.

"Ain't you yet convicted of sin?"

"No."

He sighed, began to pray once more, and after a few minutes again addressed her.

"Don't you want to confess yo' sins, my daughter, while yet you got the time?"

"No."

"Ain't you never done nothin' you sorry for?"

" No."

" Sholy you want to ease yo' mind of its heavy
load befo' you die, po' sufferin' sinner? "

" No."

" Ain't you never done nothin' wrong to nobody? "

" No ! "

The parson looked nonplussed. " Don't you
want me to pray for you? " he asked helplessly.
" What you want me to do for you? "

" Go 'way and lem-me 'lone."

Maum Katie listened in amazement. Could this
stubborn and unrepentant soul be really on the
threshold of another world? It was hard for her
to believe, and, when a few days later she heard
that Rosetta's condition had improved and her
complete recovery was regarded as only a matter
of time, she was not surprised.

The embarrassed parson offered another prayer
and then retired, telling Zeno Hightower that he
would call again. As soon as he was out of the
room Rosetta faintly called Maum Katie to her
side.

" Now ole Smith is gone, I 'll tell you somethin',"
she half-whispered. " I holp to fool a young white
'oman once, and if you want to, you kin go tell her
all about it when she come back home. I goin'
tell you 'cause you been good to me and 'cause
she yo' friend. Me and Sam Thomas fooled her
'bout her sweetheart and it made trouble I reckon.

He's dead now and it don't matter if I tell on him. I swore I'd tell on him anyhow a Saturday, when I heard him tell ole Simpson to whip me good."

She began to swear, but became suddenly weak and was obliged to cease.

"What young white 'oman was it?" asked Maum Katie, after a few minutes.

"Reba Lawrence."

More questions were then asked and answers faintly given, and ere she departed Maum Katie heard the whole story of the forged letter which had so successfully substituted discord for peace and filled two trusting souls with harrowing doubt and grief.

The riot occurred on Saturday afternoon, the besiegers of the swamp dispersed early Sunday morning; Reba reached Barcelona Monday noon, in time to spend a few hours with her stricken aunt and cousin before the hearse came and Charlie Walton's funeral procession was formed. These two were absorbed in their own grief and did not mention Morton's name, and Reba waited, asking no questions. On their return from the cemetery she overheard some one riding past the carriage which she and Betty occupied remark that Jim Jones was said to be better, but that Robert Morton was not expected to live; his wound proved to be a very serious one and the doctors had discovered great difficulty in extracting the bullet, which was lodged somewhere in the abdomen.

The latter information came from Betty, who also overheard the remark of the passing horseman.

On their arrival at the desolate home of her aunt, Reba found her tried and true old friend Maum Katie impatiently awaiting her, and the race riot, with all the bitterness it involved, did not prevent these two from showing the pleasure it gave them to see each other again. Maum Katie had obtained leave and started for the mayor's house as soon as she heard of Reba's arrival, and she now lost no time in coming to the story of Rosetta's confession, observing with great satisfaction that her young friend, who leaned forward with expanded eyes and parted lips, seemed to grow radiantly beautiful as she listened.

Crossing the hallway of her house about an hour later — just at nightfall — Mrs. Morton, a soft-voiced, gentle, gray-haired woman, whose beautiful eyes were now full of sadness, looked through the open front door and was profoundly surprised to see Reba Lawrence mounting the steps.

"I hope you are quite well. I did not know you had returned," she said courteously but coldly, as she conducted her visitor to the parlor.

"How is he? Is there not hope?" demanded Reba, abruptly, her eyes glowing, a round red spot burning on each cheek.

"My son is very ill. There is little hope. We " — with a heavy sigh —"fear he will die."

"Let me go to him! Let me see him!" cried Reba.

"Oh, you cannot," said the elder lady after a moment, almost dumbfounded at sight of the anguish on the young girl's face. "You would excite him; the doctor would forbid it."

"Mrs. Morton — do — please — don't prevent me," the girl begged, drawing nearer.

"I fail to understand you," was the cold response. "How can you ask? Why should you wish to see him?"

"I love him. I shall die of remorse if — I *must* see him. No one can prevent me! We — we were engaged — "

"And you broke it off. If you loved him, why did you jilt him?" Mrs. Morton was now colder than ever, and her gentle voice had grown stern.

"How cruel — horrible — that sounds," muttered Reba, falling mechanically into a chair. "But — yes, I should have trusted him in spite of everything." She bowed her head upon the arm of the chair with a long-drawn sob. "There is no time to lose," she then cried suddenly, starting up and unfolding a crumpled bit of paper till now forgotten in the grasp of her hand.

"If you will not believe me, you will believe your own eyes."

"What does all this mean?" asked Mrs. Morton, bewildered, putting out her hand to take the proffered letter. "*We* thought you broke off your engagement on account of that Northerner."

" I was deceived by this letter. I have just learned that it was a forgery,— written by Sam Thomas," the girl rapidly explained.

" Why — why should he have done such a thing? " asked Mrs. Morton, after swiftly absorbing the letter which was to all appearances from the pen of her own son, and thus proof of a perfidious scheme.

" Because he hated *him,* — you remember the affair about Miss Black, — and because he — liked me."

" What an infamous — "

" Now, will you let me go to him? " interrupted Reba, urgently. " He loved me once, and it may help him to live — if I could — "

A minute later the two ladies entered the wounded man's room, and Mrs. Morton signed to her daughter, who sat watching, to withdraw. At sight of the pallid, swarthy face, the dark, strange eyes, now full of an abnormal glare, the girl uttered a low, indescribable cry, and, careless who might see or hear, she fell on her knees at the bedside, putting her hand upon his, and softly calling his name. The staring, glassy eyes fixed themselves upon her; gradually a soft, warm light suffused them, and an expression of intelligence and gladness stole over the whole face. But Morton was too weak to speak and his lips remained closed. The mother now softly withdrew, hope alive in her heart.

"I have come to ask you to forgive," whispered Reba, in response to his growing look of inquiry, her lips almost touching his ear, — "to beg you to live — to live for me; to tell you that I love you, love you, love you, and that unless you forgive me and live I shall die of remorse. I will only tell you now that they made me believe you did not love me, — and so I ran away; but now I know that they told me lies, and I have come back."

It was like the sound of a soft strain of music as she said finally: "If you will forgive me and take me back, my beloved, I am yours forever."

He made a convulsive movement of the arms as if to take her to him, and whispering, "Darling — darling — darling!" she bent over until their faces met and her lips rested upon his.

"I think he's going to pull through, after all," said the doctor, brightly, as he came out of Morton's room two hours later.

About six weeks after Reba's precipitate departure from Philadelphia, Mrs. Blossom received a letter from the South, which she opened and read eagerly, and over which she shook her head in solemn disapproval. The letter was dated at St. Augustine, was written by her nephew Paul Shepherd, and from it is quoted the following: —

"After leaving Barcelona I decided to come on here for a day or so, before returning home. . . .

"It is as you feared. She is going to marry that poor

devil of a Southerner, who has hardly a cent in the world, but who, according to report, is a very good sort of a fellow. I did not need to call on her and make a declaration in order to find that out. Everybody seems to know it, although it is said to be usual here for engagements to be kept secret until the cards are out. However, I called on her twice at her aunt's, and was very kindly received. Of course, I had common-sense and good taste enough to say nothing. We talked — well, of you and Philadelphia mostly. It is possible that you will be more disappointed than I was. Now that all is over, I am astonished to find myself suffering so little from anything like real regret. My wound, after all, must have been only skin deep. And yet she has haunted my mind ever since the night of the tournament ball here, when she seemed to me incomparably lovely with that tinsel crown on her head.

"You have said very little about her cousin, Miss Walton, who, it strikes me, is a young lady of a great deal of character. I met her for the first time the other day when calling on Miss Reba to say good-by, and I have been surprised to find myself thinking of her so often since. She is not beautiful, perhaps, but has a certain indefinable loveliness which leaves a lingering impression. And she has keen perceptions and a fine sense of the fitness of things. I had spoken guardedly of the riot, respecting their feelings, and expressing my sympathy in the best way I knew how, when she addressed me in a defiant, combative style which compelled my admiration.

"'I suppose you call this a "Southern outrage"?' she said, with fine scorn.

" ' I don't characterize it, I deplore it,' I said.

" 'The negro is the Pet of Politics, Colonel Sanford says,' she proceeded. ' You Northerners have adopted him as your pet. It is well for you,' she added, significantly, ' that you keep your pet at a safe distance.'

" Her brother was killed in the riot, you know, and only a few months ago she mourned the loss of a youthful lover, who was robbed and murdered by negroes. In spite of her combative attitude, I felt that it was possible for us to become the best of friends. If I had seen her first, — who knows? But I am writing nonsense.

" Your niece, Miss Black, whom I saw twice, talked more sharply still. The term ' red-hot ' may not be quite respectful, but it is the only one I can think of which is strong enough to describe her state of mind. She washes her hands of us and our criticism, and from all the indications I should judge that she expects to marry and make her permanent home here. I am informed that she is already in a position to make a choice between two very respectable men.

" I met Colonel Sanford, too, and with him talked more freely of the riot and the negro question in general. He is in failing health, but sent to ask me to call on him at his house. One is compelled to admire such a man. I am informed that he recently made a deed of gift of a farm to ' old Jerry Carter,' the negro whose innocent son, on the strength of strong circumstantial evidence, was lynched for the murder of Jack Sanford. The colonel is said to have endeavored to prevent this lynching, but none the less considered himself in honor bound to make some sort of reparation to the sufferers, and he presented the Carters with the farm which they had been occupying as tenants. This act is seen to be the more noble when it is known that Colonel Sanford is comparatively a poor man.

"The theories of this unusual man may not be practical, but he unquestionably has the good of his section and the whole country, the blacks as well as the whites, at heart. He is a genuine patriot, — a vastly different specimen from the creature who blatantly proclaims himself such at election times and concerns himself no more about it later on. He thinks there is little hope for the South, the whites or the blacks, apart from the gradual removal of the latter to Africa ; and certainly there is something radically wrong in the present situation.

"But the poor old Colonel is discouraged, seeing little or no hope at present for his colonization scheme, and for these reasons : The negro in the mass is poverty-stricken, helpless, living from hand to mouth, having as yet developed almost no capacity for organization or concerted action. The North is not inclined to sympathize with the scheme because it does not feel the pinch (some day it may), and because of sentiment, — a sentiment which would seem to accord the freed slave the right to remain in the South and acquire a supremacy over his former master ; in other words, to overturn the State and stand it on its head, in return for the wrongs of slavery. On the other hand, the South, from sad and hopeless experience, listens with apathy to the suggestion, regarding the negro as an immovable incubus, an old man of the sea which cannot be shaken off. Besides this, the planter selfishly fears that he will lose his crops while the negro is being exchanged for the white foreign immigrant.

"Such being the present situation, the thoughtful observer is oppressed with misgivings as he contemplates the future. What public and private disasters are to come through the negro's easily cajoled and venal vote, through his rapid increase and future numerical supremacy, through the fires of race hate, now carefully smothered on his — the weaker — side, and only now and then bursting forth to remind the world of what watches and waits behind the screen of servility and circumspection,— no human mind can estimate or foresee."

THE END.

THE WEDDING GARMENT.

𝔄 𝔗ale of the 𝔏ife to ℭome.

BY LOUIS PENDLETON.

16mo. Cloth, price, $1.00. White and gold, $1.25.

"The Wedding Garment" tells the story of the continued existence of a young man after his death or departure from the natural world. Awakening in the other world, — in an intermediate region between Heaven and Hell, where the good and the evil live together temporarily commingled, — he is astonished and delighted to find himself the same man in all respects as to every characteristic of his mind and ultimate of the body. So closely does everything about him resemble the world he has left behind, that he believes he is still in the latter until convinced of the error. The young man has good impulses, but is no saint, and he listens to the persuasions of certain persons who were his friends in the world, but who are now numbered among the evil, even to the extent of following them downward to the very confines of Hell. Resisting at last and saving himself, later on, and after many remarkable experiences, he gradually makes his way through the intermediate region to the gateways of Heaven, — which can be found only by those prepared to enter, — where he is left with the prospect before him of a blessed eternity in the company of the woman he loves.

The book is written in a reverential spirit, it is unique and quite unlike any story of the same type heretofore published, full of telling incidents and dramatic situations, and not merely a record of the doings of sexless "shades" but of *living* human beings.

The one grand practical lesson which this book teaches, and which is in accord with the divine Word and the New Church unfoldings of it everywhere teach, is the need of an interior, true purpose in life. The deepest ruling purpose which we cherish, what we constantly strive for and determine to pursue as the most real and precious thing of life, that rules us everywhere, that is our ego, our life, is what will have its way at last. It will at last break through all disguise; it will bring all external conduct into harmony with itself. If it be an evil and selfish end, all external and fair moralities will melt away, and the man will lose his common sense and exhibit his insanities of opinion and will and answering deed on the surface. But if that end be good and innocent, and there be humility within, the outward disorders and evils which result from one's heredity or surroundings will finally disappear. — *From Rev. John Goddard's discourse, July 1, 1894.*

Putting aside the question as to whether the scheme of the soul's development after death was or was not revealed to Swedenborg, whether or not the title of seer can be added to the claims of this learned student of science, all this need not interfere with the moral influence of this work, although the weight of its instruction must be greatly enforced on the minds of those who believe in a later inspiration than the gospels.

This story begins where others end; the title of the first chapter, "I Die," commands attention; the process of the soul's disenthralment is certainly in harmony with what we sometimes read in the dim eyes of friends we follow to the very gate of life. "By what power does a single spark hold to life so long . . . this lingering of the divine spark of life in a body growing cold?" It is the mission of the author to tear from Death its long-established thoughts of horror, and upon its entrance into a new life, the soul possesses such a power of adjustment that no shock is experienced. — *Boston Transcript.*

ROBERTS BROTHERS, Publishers,

BOSTON, MASS.

THE KEYNOTE SERIES.

KEYNOTES. A Volume of Stories. By GEORGE EGERTON. With titlepage by AUBREY BEARDSLEY. 16mo. Cloth. Price, $1.00.

THE DANCING FAUN. A Novel. By FLORENCE FARR. With titlepage by AUBREY BEARDSLEY. American copyright edition. 16mo. Cloth. Price, $1.00.

POOR FOLK. A Novel. Translated from the Russian of FEDOR DOSTOIEVSKY. By LENA MILMAN. With a decorative titlepage and a critical introduction by GEORGE MOORE. 16mo. Cloth. Price, $1.00.

A CHILD OF THE AGE. A Novel. By FRANCIS ADAMS. With titlepage by AUBREY BEARDSLEY. 16mo. Cloth. Price, $1.00.

THE GREAT GOD PAN AND THE INMOST LIGHT. By ARTHUR MACHEN. 16mo. Cloth. Price, $1.00.

DISCORDS. A Volume of Stories. By GEORGE EGERTON. 16mo. Cloth. Price, $1.00.

PRINCE ZALESKI. By M. P. SHIEL. 16mo. Cloth. Price, $1.00.

THE WOMAN WHO DID. By GRANT ALLEN. 16mo. Cloth. Price, $1.00.

Sold by all Booksellers. Mailed, postpaid, on receipt of price, by the Publishers,

ROBERTS BROTHERS, BOSTON.

A STRANGE CAREER.

LIFE AND ADVENTURES OF JOHN GLADWYN JEBB.

BY HIS WIDOW.

With an Introduction by H. RIDER HAGGARD, and a portrait of Mr. Jebb. 12mo, cloth. Price, $1.25.

A remarkable romance of modern life. — *Daily Chronicle.*

Exciting to a degree. — *Black and White.*

Full of breathless interest. — *Times.*

Reads like fiction. — *Daily Graphic.*

Pages which will hold their readers fast to the very end. — *Graphic.*

A better told and more marvellous narrative of a real life was never put into the covers of a small octavo volume. — *To-Day.*

As fascinating as any romance. . . . The book is of the most entrancing interest. — *St. James's Budget.*

Those who love stories of adventure will find a volume to their taste in the " Life and Adventures of John Gladwyn Jebb," just published, and to which an introduction is furnished by Rider Haggard. The latter says that rarely, if ever, in this nineteenth century, has a man lived so strange and varied an existence as did Mr. Jebb. From the time that he came to manhood he was a wanderer; and how he survived the many perils of his daily life is certainly a mystery. . . . The strange and remarkable adventures of which we have an account in this volume were in Guatemala, Brazil, in our own far West with the Indians on the plains, in mining camps in Colorado and California, in Texas, in Cuba and Mexico, where occurred the search for Montezuma's, or rather Guatemoc's treasure, to which Mr. Haggard believes that Mr. Jebb held the key, but which through his death is now forever lost. The story is one of thrilling interest from beginning to end, the story of a born adventurer, unselfish, sanguine, romantic, of a man too mystical and poetic in his nature for this prosaic nineteenth century, but who, as a crusader or a knight errant, would have won distinguished success. The volume is a notable addition to the literature of adventure. — *Boston Advertiser.*

Sold by all Booksellers. Mailed, postpaid, by the publishers,

ROBERTS BROTHERS, BOSTON.

POOR FOLK.

A Novel.

Translated from the Russian of FEDOR DOSTOIEVSKY, by
LENA MILMAN, with decorative titlepage and a criti-
cal introduction by GEORGE MOORE. American
Copyright edition.

16mo. Cloth. $1.00.

A capable critic writes : "One of the most beautiful, touching stories I have
read. The character of the old clerk is a masterpiece, a kind of Russian Charles
Lamb. He reminds me, too, of Anatole France's 'Sylvestre Bonnard,' but it
is a more poignant, moving figure. How wonderfully, too, the sad little strokes
of humor are blended into the pathos in his characterization, and how fascinating
all the naïve self-revelations of his poverty become, — all his many ups and downs
and hopes and fears. His unsuccessful visit to the money-lender, his despair at the
office, unexpectedly ending in a sudden burst of good fortune, the final despair-
ing cry of his love for Varvara, — these hold one breathless One can hardly
read them without tears. . . . But there is no need to say all that could be said
about the book. It is enough to say that it is over powerful and beautiful."

We are glad to welcome a good translation of the Russian Dostoievsky's
story "Poor Folk," Englished by Lena Milman. It is a tale of unrequited love,
conducted in the form of letters written between a poor clerk and his girl cousin
whom he devotedly loves, and who finally leaves him to marry a man not admirable in character who, the reader feels, will not make her happy. The pathos of
the book centres in the clerk, Makar's, unselfish affection and his heart-break at
being left lonesome by his charming kinswoman whose epistles have been his one
solace. In the conductment of the story, realistic sketches of middle class Russian life are given, heightening the effect of the denoument. George Moore writes
a sparkling introduction to the book. — *Hartford Courant.*

Dostoievsky is a great artist. "Poor Folk" is a great novel. — *Boston
Advertiser.*

It is a most beautiful and touching story, and will linger in the mind long
after the book is closed. The pathos is blended with touching bits of humor,
that are even pathetic in themselves. — *Boston Times.*

Notwithstanding that "Poor Folk" is told in that most exasperating and
entirely unreal style — by letters — it is complete in sequence, and the interest
does not flag as the various phases in the sordid life of the two characters are
developed. The theme is intensely pathetic and truly human, while its treatment is exceedingly artistic. The translator, Lena Milman, seems to have well
preserved the spirit of the original — *Cambridge Tribune.*

ROBERTS BROTHERS, PUBLISHERS,

BOSTON. MASS.

DISCORDS.

𝔄 𝔙𝔬𝔩𝔲𝔪𝔢 𝔬𝔣 𝔖𝔱𝔬𝔯𝔦𝔢𝔰.

By GEORGE EGERTON, author of " Keynotes."

AMERICAN COPYRIGHT EDITION.

16mo. Cloth. Price, $1.00.

———◆———

George Egerton's new volume entitled " Discords," a collection of short stories, is more talked about, just now, than any other fiction of the day. The collection is really stories for story-writers. They are precisely the quality which literary folk will wrangle over. Harold Frederic cables from London to the " New York Times " that the book is making a profound impression there. It is published on both sides, the Roberts House bringing it out in Boston. George Egerton, like George Eliot and George Sand, is a woman's *nom de plume*. The extraordinary frankness with which life in general is discussed in these stories not unnaturally arrests attention. — *Lilian Whiting*.

The English woman, known as yet only by the name of George Egerton, who made something of a stir in the world by a volume of strong stories called " Keynotes," has brought out a new book under the rather uncomfortable title of " Discords." These stories show us pessimism run wild : the gloomy things that can happen to a human being are so dwelt upon as to leave the impression that in the author's own world there is no light. The relations of the sexes are treated of in bitter irony, which develops into actual horror as the pages pass. But in all this there is a rugged grandeur of style, a keen analysis of motive, and a deepness of pathos that stamp George Egerton as one of the greatest women writers of the day. " Discords " has been called a volume of stories ; it is a misnomer, for the book contains merely varying episodes in lives of men and women, with no plot, no beginning nor ending. — *Boston Traveller.*

This is a new volume of psychological stories from the pen and brains of George Egerton, the author of " Keynotes." Evidently the titles of the author's books are selected according to musical principles. The first story in the book is " A Psychological Moment at Three Periods." It is all strength rather than sentiment. The story of the child, of the girl, and of the woman is told, and told by one to whom the mysteries of the life of each are familiarly known. In their very truth, as the writer has so subtly analyzed her triple characters, they sadden one to think that such things must be ; yet as they are real, they are bound to be disclosed by somebody and in due time. The author betrays remarkable penetrative skill and perception, and dissects the human heart with a power from whose demonstration the sensitive nature may instinctively shrink even while fascinated with the narration and hypnotized by the treatment exhibited. — *Courier.*

———

Sold by all Booksellers. Mailed by Publishers,

ROBERTS BROTHERS, Boston, Mass.

KEYNOTES.

A Volume of Stories.

By GEORGE EGERTON. With titlepage by AUBREY
BEARDSLEY. 16mo. Cloth. Price, $1.00.

Not since "The Story of an African Farm" was written has any woman delivered herself of so strong, so forcible a book. — *Queen.*

Knotty questions in sex problems are dealt with in these brief sketches. They are treated boldly, fearlessly, perhaps we may say forcefully, with a deep plunge into the realities of life. The colors are laid in masses on the canvas, while passions, temperaments, and sudden, subtle analyses take form under the quick, sharp stroke. Though they contain a vein of coarseness and touch slightly upon tabooed subjects, they evidence power and thought. — *Public Opinion.*

Indeed, we do not hesitate to say that "Keynotes" is the strongest volume of short stories that the year has produced. Further, we would wager a good deal, were it necessary, that George Egerton is a nom-de-plume, and of a woman, too. Why is it that so many women hide beneath a man's name when they enter the field of authorship? And in this case it seems doubly foolish, the work is so intensely strong. . . .

The chief characters of these stories are women, and women drawn as only a woman can draw word-pictures of her own sex. The subtlety of analysis is wonderful, direct in its effectiveness, unerring in its truth, and stirring in its revealing power. Truly, no one but a woman could thus throw the light of revelation upon her own sex. Man does not understand woman as does the author of "Keynotes."

The vitality of the stories, too, is remarkable. Life, very real life, is pictured; life full of joys and sorrows, happinesses and heartbreaks, courage and self-sacrifice; of self-abnegation, of struggle, of victory. The characters are intense, yet not overdrawn; the experiences are dramatic, in one sense or another, and yet are never hyper-emotional. And all is told with a power of concentration that is simply astonishing. A sentence does duty for a chapter, a paragraph for a picture of years of experience.

Indeed, for vigor, originality, forcefulness of expression, and completeness of character presentation, "Keynotes" surpasses any recent volume of short fiction that we can recall. — *Times*, Boston.

It brings a new quality and a striking new force into the literature of the hour. — *The Speaker.*

The mind that conceived "Keynotes" is so strong and original that one will look with deep interest for the successors of this first book, at once powerful and appealingly feminine. — *Irish Independent.*

Sold by all booksellers. Mailed, post-paid, on receipt of price by the Publishers,

ROBERTS BROTHERS, BOSTON, MASS.

A CHILD OF THE AGE.

𝔄 Novel.

BY FRANCIS ADAMS

(KEYNOTES SERIES.)

With titlepage by Aubrey Beardsley. 16mo. Cloth. Price, $1.00.

This story by Francis Adams was originally published under the title of "Leicester, an Autobiography," in 1884, when the author was only twenty-two years of age. That would make him thirty-two years old now, if he were still living. He was but eighteen years old when it was first drafted by him. Sometime after publication, he revised the work, and in its present form it is now published again, practically a posthumous production. We can with truthfulness characterize it as a tale of fresh originality, deep spiritual meaning, and exceptional power. It fairly buds, blossoms, and fruits with suggestions that search the human spirit through. No similar production has come from the hand of any author in our time. That Francis Adams would have carved out a remarkable career for himself had he continued to live, this little volume, all compact with significant suggestion, attests on many a page. It exalts, inspires, comforts, and strengthens all together. It instructs by suggestion, spiritualizes the thought by its elevating and purifying narrative, and feeds the hungering spirit with food it is only too ready to accept and assimilate. Those who read its pages with an eager curiosity the first time will be pretty sure to return to them for a second slower and more meditative perusal. The book is assuredly the promise and potency of great things unattained in the too brief lifetime of its gifted author. We heartily commend it as a book not only of remarkable power, but as the product of a human spirit whose merely intellectual gifts were but a fractional part of his inclusive spiritual endowments. — *Boston Courier.*

But it is a remarkable work — as a pathological study almost unsurpassed. It produces the impression of a photograph from life, so vividly realistic is the treatment. To this result the author's style, with its fidelity of microscopic detail, doubtless contributes. — *Evening Traveller.*

This story by Francis Adams is one to read slowly, and then to read a second time. It is powerfully written, full of strong suggestion, unlike, in fact, anything we have recently read. What he would have done in the way of literary creation, had he lived, is, of course, only a matter of conjecture. What he did we have before us in this remarkable book. — *Boston Advertiser.*

Sold by all Booksellers. Mailed by the Publishers.

ROBERTS BROTHERS, Boston, Mass.

PIERRETTE

AND

THE VICAR OF TOURS.

BY HONORÉ DE BALZAC.

Translated by Katharine Prescott Wormeley.

In *Pierrette*, which Miss Wormeley has added to her series of felicitous translations from the French master-fictionists, Balzac has made within brief compass a marvellously sympathetic study of the martyrdom of a young girl. Pierrette, a flower of Brittany, beautiful, pale, and fair and sweet, is taken as an undesired charge by sordid-minded cousins in Provins, and like an exotic transplanted into a harsh and sour soil she withers and fades under the cruel conditions of her new environment. Incidentally Balzac depicts in vivid colors the struggles of two shop-keepers — a brother and sister, who have amassed a little fortune in Paris — to gain a foothold among the bourgeoisie of their native town. These two become the prey of conspirators for political advancement, and the rivalries thus engendered shake the small provincial society to its centre. But the charm of the tale is in the portrayal of the character of Pierrette, who understands only how to love, and who cannot live in an atmosphere of suspicion and ill-treatment. The story is of course sad, but its fidelity to life and the pathos of it are elements of unfailing interest. Balzac brings a score or more of people upon the stage, shows each one as he or she really is both in outward appearance and inward nature, and then allows motives and circumstances to work out an inevitable result. To watch this process is like being present at some wonderful chemical experiment where the ingredients are mixed with a deft and careful hand, and combine to produce effects of astonishing significance. The social genesis of the old maid in her most abhorrent form occupies much of Balzac's attention in *Pierrette*, and this theme also has a place in the story of *The Vicar of Tours*, bound up in this same volume. The vicar is a simple-minded priest who is happy enough till he takes up his quarters with an old maid landlady, who pesters and annoys him in many ways, and finally sends him forth despoiled of his worldly goods and a laughing-stock for the country-side. There is a great deal of humor in the tale, but one must confess that the humor is of a rather heavy sort, it being weighed down by a dominant satirical purpose. — *The Beacon.*

One handsome 12mo volume, uniform with "Père Goriot," "The Duchesse de Langeais," "César Birotteau," "Eugenie Grandet," "Cousin Pons," "The Country Doctor," "The Two Brothers," and "The Alkahest." Half morocco, French style. Price, $1.50.

ROBERTS BROTHERS, Publishers, Boston.

BALZAC IN ENGLISH.

Lost Illusions: The Two Poets, and Eve and David.

By HONORÉ DE BALZAC.

Being the twenty-third volume of Miss Wormeley's translation of Balzac's novels. 12mo. Half Russia. Price, $1.50.

For her latest translation of the Balzac fiction cycle, Miss Wormeley gives us the first and third parts of "Illusion Perdue," under the caption of "Lost Illusions," namely, "The Two Poets" and "Eve and David." This arrangement is no doubt a good one, for the readers are thus enabled to follow the consecutive fortunes of the Angouleme folk, while the adventures of Eve's poet-brother, Lucien, which occur in Paris and make a tale by themselves, are thus left for a separate publication. The novel, as we have it, then, belongs to the category of those scenes from provincial life which Balzac found so stimulating to his genius. This story, certainly, in some respects takes high rank among them. The character-drawing is fine: Lucien, the ambitious, handsome, weak-willed, selfish, and easily-sinning young bourgeois, is contrasted with David, — a touching picture of the struggling inventor, born of the people and sublimely one-purposed and pure in his life. Eve, the type of a faithful large-brained and larger-hearted wife, who supports her husband through all his hardships with unfaltering courage and kindness, is another noble creation. David inherits a poorish printing business from his skin-flint of a father, neglects it while devoting all his time and energy to his discovery of an improved method of making paper; and through the evil machinations of the rival printing firm of the Cointets, as well as the debts foisted on him by Lucien in Paris, he is brought into money difficulties and even into prison. But his invention, although sold at a sacrifice to the cunning Cointets, gets him out of the hole at last, and he and his good wife retire on a comfortable competency, which is augmented at the death of his father into a good-sized fortune. The seamy side of law in the provinces is shown up in Balzac's keen, inimitable way in the description of the winding of the coils around the unsuspecting David and the depiction of such men as the brothers Cointets and the shrewd little pettifogging rascal, Petit Claud. The pictures of Angouleme aristocratic circles, too, with Lucien as high priest, are vivacious, and show the novelist's wonderful observation in all ranks of life. The bit of wild romance by which Lucien becomes the secretary of a Spanish grandee lends a fairy-tale flavor to the main episodes. Balzac, in whom is united the most lynx-eyed realism and the most extravagant romanticism, is ever and always one of the great masters in fiction of our century.

Sold by all booksellers. Mailed, post-paid, on receipt of the price by the Publishers,

ROBERTS BROTHERS, Boston

BALZAC IN ENGLISH.

A GREAT MAN OF THE PROVINCES IN PARIS.

By HONORÉ DE BALZAC.

Being the second part of "Lost Illusions." Translated by Katharine Prescott Wormeley. 12mo. Half Russia. Price, $1.50.

"A Great Man of the Provinces in Paris" (Part Second of " Lost Illusions ") is a formidable revelation of journalistic "enterprise" under the Restoration, such as only an eye-witness or a real sufferer could give. The thread of the story of "Lost Illusions" is again taken up, with the weak and brilliant figure of Lucien Chardon, and carried through all the complications and entanglements of Parisian newspaper life. He elopes with a "married flirt," and is speedily disillusioned when he arrives in the metropolis, by finding his goddess old, ugly, and ridiculous in comparison with the style and charm of the Parisian *elegante*. He himself, handsome as an angel, gifted, poetic, but shifty, is a true type of the provincial Apollo Belvedere marching forth to conquer the worlds of fashion and literature, without any resources but his beauty and his wit. Balzac, the matchless delineator of the Empire and the Restoration, introduces this curled darling (wonderfully like Alfred de Musset !) into the arcana of journalism, makes him the pivot of suppers and scenes characteristic of the time of Louis XVIII., shows him every variety of the genus publisher then flourishing, gives us fascinating glimpses of the great world of the Bourbons, and sets Lucien in an entrancing environment of gorgeous vice in which one illusion after another is mercilessly dispelled. Noble and beautiful chapters and faces occur by the way to redeem the ugliness and unrighteousness of the rest. Balzac has never painted a more pathetic face than poor fallen Coralie's, or a more striking and noble-minded group than the Brotherhood. Such features redeem a book charged with the foulness of a life inconceivable to Anglo-Saxon minds, and unfit for any pure soul to become familiar with, even through the brilliant, mirage-producing medium of a genius like Balzac's. — *The Critic.*

The art of Balzac, the wonderful power of his contrast, the depth of his knowledge of life and men and things, this tremendous story illustrates. How admirably the rise of the poet is traced; the *crescendo* is perfect in gradation, yet as inexorable as fate. As for the fall, the effect is more depressing than a personal catastrophe. This is a book to read over and over, an epic of life in prose, more tremendous than the blank verse of " Paradise Lost" or the " Divine Comedy." Miss Wormeley and the publishers deserve not congratulations alone, but thanks for adding this book and its predecessor, " Lost Illusions," to the literature of English. — *San Francisco Wave.*

Sold by all booksellers. Mailed, post-paid, by the Publishers,

ROBERTS BROTHERS, Boston.

BALZAC IN ENGLISH.

THE BROTHERHOOD OF CONSOLATION.

(L'ENVERS DE L'HISTOIRE CONTEMPORAINE.)

By HONORÉ DE BALZAC.

1. Madame de la Chanterie. 2. The Initiate. Translated by Katharine Prescott Wormeley. 12mo. Half Russia. Price, $1.50.

There is no book of Balzac which is informed by a loftier spirit than "L'Envers de l'Histoire Contemporaine," which has just been added by Miss Wormeley to her admirable series of translations under the title, "The Brotherhood of Consolation." The title which is given to the translation is, to our thinking, a happier one than that which the work bears in the original, since, after all, the political and historical portions of the book are only the background of the other and more absorbing theme, — the development of the brotherhood over which Madame de la Chanterie presided. It is true that there is about it all something theatrical, something which shows the French taste for making godliness itself histrionically effective, that quality of mind which would lead a Parisian to criticise the coming of the judgment angels if their entrance were not happily arranged and properly executed; but in spite of this there is an elevation such as it is rare to meet with in literature, and especially in the literature of Balzac's age and land. The story is admirably told, and the figure of the Baron Bourlac is really noble in its martyrdom of self-denial and heroic patience. The picture of the Jewish doctor is a most characteristic piece of work, and shows Balzac's intimate touch in every line. Balzac was always attracted by the mystical side of the physical nature; and it might almost be said that everything that savored of mystery, even though it ran obviously into quackery, had a strong attraction for him. He pictures Halpersohn with a few strokes, but his picture of him has a striking vitality and reality. The volume is a valuable and attractive addition to the series to which it belongs; and the series comes as near to fulfilling the ideal o' what translations should be as is often granted to earthly things. — *Boston Courier.*

The book, which is one of rare charm, is one of the most refined, while at the same time tragic, of all his works. — *Public Opinion.*

His present work is a fiction beautiful in its conception, just one of those practical ideals which Balzac nourished and believed in. There never was greater homage than he pays to the book of books, "The Imitation of Jesus Christ." Miss Wormeley has here accomplished her work just as cleverly as in her other volumes of Balzac. — *N. Y. Times.*

Sold by all booksellers. Mailed, post-paid, by the Publishers,

ROBERTS BROTHERS, BOSTON.

An Historical Mystery.

Translated by KATHARINE PRESCOTT WORMELEY.

12mo. Half Russia. Uniform with Balzac's Works. Price, $1.50.

An Historical Mystery is the title given to "Une Ténébreuse Affaire," which has just appeared in the series of translations of Honoré de Balzac's novels, by Katharine Prescott Wormeley This exciting romance is full of stirring interest, and is distinguished by that minute analysis of character in which its eminent author excelled The characters stand boldly out from the surrounding incidents, and with a fidelity as wonderful as it is truthful. Plot and counterplot follow each other with marvellous rapidity; and around the exciting days when Napoleon was First Consul, and afterward when he was Emperor, a mystery is woven in which some royalists are concerned that is concealed with masterly ingenuity until the novelist sees fit to take his reader into his confidence. The heroine, Laurence, is a remarkably strong character ; and the love-story in which she figures is refreshing in its departure from the beaten path of the ordinary writer of fiction. Michu, her devoted servant, has also a marked individuality, which leaves a lasting impression. Napoleon, Talleyrand, Fouché, and other historical personages, appear in the tale in a manner that is at once natural and impressive. As an addition to a remarkable series, the book is one that no admirer of Balzac can afford to neglect. Miss Wormeley's translation reproduces the peculiarities of the author's style with the faithfulness for which she has hitherto been celebrated. — *Saturday Evening Gazette.*

It makes very interesting reading at this distance of time, however; and Balzac has given to the legendary account much of the solidity of history by his adroit manipulation. For the main story it must be said that the action is swifter and more varied than in many of the author's books, and that there are not wanting many of those cameo-like portraits necessary to warn the reader against slovenly perusal of this carefully written story; for the complications are such, and the relations between the several plots involved so intricate, that the thread might easily be lost and much of the interest be thus destroyed The usual Balzac compactness is of course present throughout, to give body and significance to the work, and the stage is crowded with impressive figures. It would be impossible to find a book which gives a better or more faithful illustration of one of the strangest periods in French history, in short ; and its attraction as a story is at least equalled by its value as a true picture of the time it is concerned with. The translation is as spirited and close as Miss Wormeley has taught us to expect in this admirable series. — *New York Tribune.*

One of the most intensely interesting novels that Balzac ever wrote is *An Historical Mystery*, whose translation has just been added to the preceding novels that compose the "Comédie Humaine" so admirably translated by Miss Katharine Prescott Wormeley. The story opens in the autumn of 1803, in the time of the Empire, and the motive is in deep-laid political plots, which are revealed with the subtle and ingenious skill that marks the art of Balzac. . . The story is a deep-laid political conspiracy of the secret service of the ministry of the police. Talleyrand, M'lle de Cinq-Cygne, the Princess de Cadigan, Louis XVIII., as well as Napoleon, figure as characters of this thrilling historic romance. An absorbing love-story is also told, in which State intrigue plays an important part. The character-drawing is faithful to history, and the story illuminates French life in the early years of the century as if a calcium light were thrown on the scene.

It is a romance of remarkable power and one of the most deeply fascinating of all the novels of the "Comédie Humaine."

Sold by all booksellers. Mailed, post-paid, on receipt of price by the Publishers,

ROBERTS BROTHERS, BOSTON.

A MEMOIR OF HONORÉ DE BALZAC.

Compiled and written by KATHARINE PRESCOTT WORMELEY, translator of Balzac's works. With portrait of Balzac, taken one hour after death, by Eugène Giraud, and a Sketch of the Prison of the Collège de Vendôme. One volume, 12mo. Half Russia, uniform with our edition of Balzac's works. Price, $1.50.

A complete life of Balzac can probably never be written. The sole object of the present volume is to present Balzac to American readers. This memoir is meant to be a presentation of the man, — and not of his work, except as it was a part of himself, — derived from authentic sources of information, and presented in their own words, with such simple elucidations as a close intercourse with Balzac's mind, necessitated by conscientious translation, naturally gives. The portrait in this volume was considered by Madame de Balzac the best likeness of her husband.

Miss Wormeley's discussion of the subject is of value in many ways, and it has long been needed as a help to comprehension of his life and character. Personally, he lived up to his theory. His life was in fact austere. Any detailed account of the conditions under which he worked, such as are given in this volume, will show that this must have been the case; and the fact strongly reinforces the doctrine. Miss Wormeley, in arranging her account of his career, has, almost of necessity, made free use of the letters and memoir published by Balzac's sister, Madame Surville. She has also, whenever it would serve the purpose of illustration better, quoted from the sketches of him by his contemporaries, wisely rejecting the trivialities and frivolities by the exaggeration of which many of his first chroniclers seemed bent upon giving the great author a kind of opera-bouffe aspect. To judge from some of these accounts, he was flighty, irresponsible, possibly a little mad, prone to lose touch of actualities by the dominance of his imagination, fond of wild and impracticable schemes, and altogether an eccentric and unstable person. But it is not difficult to prove that Balzac was quite a different character; that he possessed a marvellous power of intellectual organization; that he was the most methodical and indefatigable of workers; that he was a man of a most delicate sense of honor; that his life was not simply devoted to literary ambition, but was a martyrdom to obligations which were his misfortune, but not his fault.

All this Miss Wormeley has well set forth; and in doing so she has certainly relieved Balzac of much unmerited odium, and has enabled those who have not made a study of his character and work to understand how high the place is in any estimate of the helpers of modern progress and enlightenment to which his genius and the loftiness of his aims entitle him. This memoir is a very modest biography, though a very good one. The author has effaced herself as much as possible, and has relied upon "documents" whenever they were trustworthy. — *N. Y. Tribune.*

Sold by all booksellers. Mailed, postpaid, on receipt of price, by the publishers,

ROBERTS BROTHERS, BOSTON.

𝕭𝖆𝖑𝖟𝖆𝖈 𝖎𝖓 𝕰𝖓𝖌𝖑𝖎𝖘𝖍.

THE VILLAGE RECTOR.

By Honoré de Balzac.

Translated by Katharine Prescott Wormeley.   12mo.
Half Russia.   Price, $1.50.

Once more that wonderful acquaintance which Balzac had with all callings appears manifest in this work. Would you get to the bottom of the engineer's occupation in France? Balzac presents it in the whole system, with its aspects, disadvantages, and the excellence of the work accomplished. We write to-day of irrigation and of arboriculture as if they were novelties ; yet in the waste lands of Montagnac, Balzac found these topics ; and what he wrote is the clearest exposition of the subjects.

But, above all, in "The Village Rector" is found the most potent of religious ideas, — the one that God grants pardon to sinners. Balzac had studied and appreciated the intensely human side of Catholicism and its adaptiveness to the wants of mankind. It is religion, with Balzac, "that opens to us an inexhaustible treasure of indulgence." It is true repentance that saves.

The drama which is unrolled in "The Village Rector" is a terrible one, and perhaps repugnant to our sensitive minds. The selection of such a plot, pitiless as it is, Balzac made so as to present the darkest side of human nature, and to show how, through God's pity, a soul might be saved. The instrument of mercy is the Rector Bonnet, and in the chapter entitled "The Rector at Work" he shows how religion "extends a man's life beyond the world." It is not sufficient to weep and moan. "That is but the beginning ; the end is action." The rector urges the woman whose sins are great to devote what remains of her life to work for the benefit of her brothers and sisters, and so she sets about reclaiming the waste lands which surround her chateau. With a talent of a superlative order, which gives grace to Veronique, she is like the Madonna of some old panel of Van Eyck's. Doing penance, she wears close to her tender skin a haircloth vestment. For love of her, a man has committed murder and died and kept his secret. In her youth, Veronique's face had been pitted, but her saintly life had obliterated that spotted mantle of smallpox. Tears had washed out every blemish. If through true repentance a soul was ever saved, it was Veronique's. This work, too, has afforded consolation to many miserable sinners, and showed them the way to grace.

The present translation is to be cited for its wonderful accuracy and its literary distinction. We can hardly think of a more difficult task than the Englishing of Balzac, and a general reading public should be grateful for the admirable manner in which Miss Wormeley has performed her task. — *New York Times.*

Sold by all booksellers. Mailed, post-paid, on receipt of price by the Publishers,

ROBERTS BROTHERS. Boston, Mass.

Balzac in English.

MEMOIRS OF TWO YOUNG MARRIED WOMEN.

BY HONORÉ DE BALZAC.

Translated by KATHARINE PRESCOTT WORMELEY. 12mo.
Half Russia. Price, $1.50.

"THERE are," says Henry James in one of his essays, "two writers in Balzac, — the spontaneous one and the reflective one, the former of which is much the more delightful, while the latter is the more extraordinary." It is the reflective Balzac, the Balzac with a theory, whom we get in the "Deux Jeunes Mariées," now translated by Miss Wormeley under the title of "Memoirs of Two Young Married Women." The theory of Balzac is that the marriage of convenience, properly regarded, is far preferable to the marriage simply from love, and he undertakes to prove this proposition by contrasting the careers of two young girls who have been fellow-students at a convent. One of them, the ardent and passionate Louise de Chaulieu, has an intrigue with a Spanish refugee, finally marries him, kills him, as she herself confesses, by her perpetual jealousy and exaction, mourns his loss bitterly, then marries a golden-haired youth, lives with him in a dream of ecstasy for a year or so, and this time kills herself through jealousy wrongfully inspired. As for her friend, Renée de Maucombe, she dutifully makes a marriage to please her parents, calculates coolly beforehand how many children she will have and how they shall be trained; insists, however, that the marriage shall be merely a civil contract till she and her husband find that their hearts are indeed one; and sees all her brightest visions realized, — her Louis an ambitious man for her sake and her children truly adorable creatures. The story, which is told in the form of letters, fairly scintillates with brilliant sayings, and is filled with eloquent discourses concerning the nature of love, conjugal and otherwise. Louise and Renée are both extremely sophisticated young women, even in their teens; and those who expect to find in their letters the demure innocence of the Anglo-Saxon type will be somewhat astonished. The translation, under the circumstances, was rather a daring attempt, but it has been most felicitously done. — *The Beacon.*

Sold by all booksellers. Mailed, postpaid, on receipt of price by the Publishers,

ROBERTS BROTHERS, BOSTON. MASS.

www.ingramcontent.com/pod-product-compliance
Lightning Source LLC
Chambersburg PA
CBHW021754110726
47902CB00006B/1517